STAR AXE

DUNCAN McGEARY

First Edition - 2024

CHAPTER I

Kenlahar sat in the corner of the Archives fidgeting, while his master browsed the pages of an old and dusty manuscript. The idleness, the unending wait, irked the young apprentice healer. He felt doomed to watch the dust swirl endlessly under the eaves of the stuffy room. Someday the dust might be swept away, he reflected. Someday it might escape out the narrow doorway. Someday an industrious sister might, by chance, venture into the ancient library and sweep the place. More likely, he thought, most of the dust would fly from under her broom and still be hovering long after she left.

Soon darkness would fall over the island. Kenlahar would be forced to leave the stifling but comfortable tomb of the Archives and walk down the long and drafty corridors to the Courtyard of Moons. There he would be called forward by the solemn Elders to face the Star Axe. And yet, he still did not know what his answer to the inescapable summons of the Axedelve would be. It was not proving easy for someone who was already a pariah to choose between joining the strong and glorious Axe-Kith—or remaining forever alone and outcast.

Already the smaller, more reassuring sounds of everyday life had abandoned the House of Lahar. A portentous hush filled its many rooms and hallways instead. Downstairs, Kenlahar knew, the other young men were even now preparing for the fateful ceremony. The walls were shaking with the bustle of armed and excited warriors. The floors groaned under the weight of their march.

1

But within the Archives the only sounds were the soft rustle of paper on paper as the Healer Coron turned the pages of his book, and the low drumming of rain on the roof. Kenlahar imagined he could even hear the still and continuous settling of the dust. He thought of the Archives as crowded with his friends, for its floors were cluttered with loose piles of familiar parchment, and it was crammed to the roof with shelves of mankind's histories and fables.

He watched the old man slowly droop his head in an attempt to read the archaic script in the dying light. He wanted to talk with the Healer Coron, but he had learned to never interrupt the old man while he was reading.

Instead, Kenlahar stared gloomily out the narrow library window. Ancient and majestic in the dusk, the House of Lahar towered over a forested island set in the middle of the vast, muddy River Danjar. The rambling mass of stone of wood served as the home of an entire people—the descendants of the Starborn God, Lahar; multiplied by a hundred generations. Standing alone in a wilderness of swamps, it glistened and sparkled in the rain-filled sunset. Kenlahar could see almost all of the huge building sprawled over the island.

The gold on the dome of the Great Hall shone brightly, though the day was dark and overcast. Behind it lay the Courtyard of Moons— usually empty, but now crowded with people waiting for the Axedelve to begin. Around the Great Hall and the Courtyard of Moons, the rest of the structure had been added, decade by decade and room by room. Now, almost the entire island was under one roof.

The roofs stretched haphazardly downward, and Kenlahar's eyes followed their twisting contours. Water streamed down a tortuous route of drains. Some of the ramshackle lower roofs, extending, in places, all the way to the river, were hidden entirely by the heavy mists. The river was rising, Kenlahar saw—soon it would be flooding the lower levels of the House of Lahar.

Suddenly, the Healer Coron stirred himself and lit a dim lamp. As the light slowly changed, Kenlahar caught an image of himself in the dust-coated, rain-splattered window. His dark features and hollowed cheeks were intensified by the troubled frown of his black eyebrows. He winced at this reminder of his swarthy appearance, for it was a constant mark of his difference. He sometimes felt as if he were a small dark shadow among the hulking blond brothers and sisters of the House of Lahar.

"Healer Coron?" he ventured.

The Healer Coron cleared his throat and frowned, but continued to read. The old man acted deeply hurt by Kenlahar's rejection of his teachings. He seemed to be resolutely ignoring his apprentice.

Exasperated by his master's refusal to answer him, Kenlahar sidestepped the strewn books and marched to the window. He forced it open, waving his arms at the cloud of dust and coughing. "Coron!" he shouted.

Moist air wafted in, lifting scrolls from the Healer Coron's desk. The old man grabbed ineffectually at the flying paper and stared at his apprentice. "Well?" he demanded. "What is it? This treatise must be examined thoroughly, for it describes a potion I have never before encountered. If I am allowed to discover its contents, I may save someone from great pain. So, out with your question, so I may be done with it!"

Kenlahar blushed, feeling uncomfortable under the glaring eyes of his master. The Healer Coron's eyes were dark behind a pair of thick glasses. Magnified and piercing, they stood out in a face the color of faded parchment and laced with wrinkles. Their strangeness had always made it difficult for Kenlahar to judge what the old man was really thinking.

"I am sorry, Healer Coron," he said. "It is just that I cannot stand to watch the dust gather any longer. I think you have been here so long you no longer even notice it."

The Healer Coron slammed his book shut with a dull thud. "What is really bothering you, Kenlahar?" Despite his forbidding tone, the old man had finally given Kenlahar a chance to say goodbye. He turned confused eyes to his teacher. "Healer Coron, why is it that a healer may not also join the Axe-Kith?"

"You know the laws of Lahar, Kenlahar," the old man growled. "A healer of the House of Lahar must have a past free of all bloodshed. Otherwise he weakens—or even loses—his Atima, his Starborn power to heal. You must make a choice, Kenlahar. Only Lahar was both warrior and healer. And remember this, Kenlahar, Lahar valued his Starborn attribute of Atima, far more than his ability to take life. A healer can be worth many, many warriors."

"But, Healer Coron, it is the duty of every brother to defend the House of Lahar!" Kenlahar knew that he was only echoing the views of the Elders, and what he heard from the other boys everyday in the Great Hall, every night in the dormitories. But he could not stop himself now. "To feel a good weapon in your handcar is living!"

"Living—and dying!" the Healer Coron retorted, not bothering to hide his disgust. "Young men tend to forget that the other happens in war, as well. We have fought the Warlord and his minions, the Qreq, for a hundred years, Kenlahar. In all that time we have never been defeated. One more young man in the Axe-Kith will not make much of a difference, but one less healer will."

The old man came haltingly from around his desk to place a gnarled hand on the slumped shoulders of his apprentice. "*Here* is where you belong, Kenlahar. You are not a warrior. You are a healer and a scholar. It is what you have been trained for and what you know best. You would never survive a battle, you know."

A blaring of horns, announcing the commencement of the Axedelve, startled them both into silence. Kenlahar was relieved to be saved from further argument, sorry now that he had started the conversation at all. He rose to leave, avoiding the hurt eyes of his master.

At the door of the Archives the Healer Coron grabbed his apprentice's arm, pleading one last time. "It is not too late to change your mind, Kenlahar. Please—do not abandon my teachings."

Kenlahar did not answer, though he had not yet made up his mind to go through with the Axedelve. In this gloomy silence, the apprentice and his master proceeded into the hollow, deserted corridors. Their shadows loomed between each of the flickering torches ensconced in stonewalls, only to melt again as they passed. Everyone else appeared to be already below in the Courtyard of Moons, in anticipation of the ceremony.

As they neared the more populated and familiar lower hallways, Kenlahar wondered, as he often had before, just how many people lived in the huge building. Perhaps the Elders knew, but the Elders never told. If someone should be fool enough to try and count the family of Lahar, room by room, he would soon become hopelessly lost in the labyrinth. The tangled maze of halls and rooms had been built with no perceivable order, when and where they were needed. At times of the Axedelve the family might gather in the Courtyard of Moons, but on such occasions no one thought of counting. Kenlahar only knew that, while many of the faces he encountered were familiar, he had never met all the family. Yet—somehow—they had all seemed to know who he was.

They heard the crowd long before they emerged into the moonlit square. But what Kenlahar saw, appeared at first glance to be frozen tableau of statues. His eyes were drawn to the columns of the Axe-Kith, who blocked the light of the twin white moons called the Sistern. They cast long, even rows of silhouettes upon the walls. Where the blades of their tall spears crested the walls, the harsh glare of Bantling, the red moon, sent jagged shadows stretching across the cobblestones.

Kenlahar joined the hushed throng of women, children, and old men. But when he looked around for the Healer Coron, the old man appeared to have vanished, swallowed by the crowd. He had apparently decided to let Kenlahar ponder his choice alone. The skies above the island looked as though they would keep the Courtyard of Moons well lit, even after the fall of night. A rainstorm had threatened to draw a curtain of dark clouds over the island, but as the Axedelve began, the skies remained filled with the soft glow of partially eclipsed moons. Only on the northern horizon was there a void—pierced by a single, bright star.

At the ritual command of the High Elder, the name of the first youth to be initiated into the Axe-Kith was announced. Kenlahar held his breath—but someone else's name rang through the yard instead. With a mixture of fear and pride, he watched the other youth kneel and bow his head before the Star Axe of Lahar, courting the virgin force of the war charm. The young man stayed unmoving in this cramped posture for long minutes without response. In mounting anxiety, Kenlahar watched him straighten and march back across the Courtyard of

Moons. The warrior passed before Kenlahar, looking neither right nor left, and took a position among the phalanxed warriors.

"Kenlahar!" The grave intonation of his name by the High Elder startled him. Reluctantly, Kenlahar stepped from the security of the crowd and advanced to the dais. His salute to the triumvirate of Elders was quickly affirmed by short nods. He dutifully started to pray to the single star in the northern sky, his dark eyes cast carefully skyward, as if transfixed by the flickering specter of his god's home. He stood apart and alone, his arms rose high over his head in supplication.

He cried out as he had seen the others do, as if from deep within a trance. "Hear me! Hear me, Lahar!" His low voice echoed through the giant courtyard and it seemed that at that evocation the Sistern reached their zeniths, creating briefly in the night skies the richness of a noon's light. Kenlahar knelt as though in reverence before the ancient talisman of the Star Axe where it was embedded at the hilt into the dais.

Though he kept his face averted, according to custom, he could not prevent his eyes from flashing toward the seeming apparition of the eldritch-hued Alcress. The blade of the ancient battleaxe appeared to be gathering and heightening the radiance in the alcove, and its pocked meteoritic ore glowed with the eerie blue of starlight.

Kenlahar felt strongly attracted and drawn to Alcress.

Soon, he was conscious of only the Star Axe's silver glow, which seemed to be bursting out from the dark red background of the Elder's robes. Kenlahar experienced a sudden, strange conviction of his right, his privilege—even, his legacy—to possess and wield Alcress. He needed only to kiss the Star Axe of Lahar where it was bound by a crude leather thong to the hardwood haft—and he would be Commander of the Axe- Kith; Master of the House of Lahar!

Then he shook his head, feeling very foolish for believing that he could succeed where so many generations of warriors had failed. The training of the Healer Coron once again asserted its power over his thoughts. From somewhere deep inside of himself, the young apprentice summoned the courage to reject the Star Axe.

As the Elders leaned forward in their thrones expectantly, Kenlahar stepped back from the dais, and turned from the Star Axe. "I have made a mistake," he said quietly, though words of refusal had never been heard before. "I must decline the Axedelve."

He looked around for the Healer Coron's approval, but the old man was still nowhere to be seen. When Kenlahar tried to rejoin the anonymity of the crowd, they started to draw away from him in contempt, and as the meaning of his words began to be fully understood, there was a hostile grumbling. It was at that moment that the dark rainclouds over the island chose to finally envelop the twin Sistern. In their stead, the red light of Bantling, their detested brother moon, seemed to spread its hex through the square. The apprentice healer thought he could hear the words, "Wraith-taint!"

The accusation was not new to Kenlahar, nor was the ostracism. But never before had the hostility that had always underlain the tolerance of the family, threatened to burst into violence. As the first cold gusts of rain blew into his face, he felt a dull thud in his side where someone had thrown something or had awkwardly struck him. The quarantine of space around him began to close dangerously. Soon others would join in the buffeting of the heretic, he thought numbly.

"You dare to deny the Axedelve!" Above the noise of this sudden fury came a shrill, querulous voice. Lightning revealed the tall crooked figure of the Lashitu, shaman of the House of Lahar, pointing an oaken staff from the steps of the Great Hall.

Kenlahar was unable to summon an answer, and appeared to be standing alone and defiant. The anger in the Lashitu's craggy visage grew as the seconds passed without an explanation, and he began to open his mouth to stir the still waiting and wrathful crowd.

"High Elder!" The Healer Coron's frail shout barely managed to pierce the outcry. "May I address the Council of Elders?"

The High Elder, who had been as stunned as everyone else of Kenlahar's refusal, nevertheless quickly gave the old man a chance to rescue his apprentice from the mob, if he could.

"High Elder," the Healer Coron said hurriedly in the ensuing grudging silence, "I have often told you of my need for an apprentice. It is past time I made my choice of a successor. In accordance with the laws of Lahar, a healer's past must be free of bloodshed. I have observed the young man, Kenlahar, for many years and I know him to be the best possible choice. It was *I* who encouraged my apprentice to decline the Axedelve—not out of disloyalty, but for the benefit of the House of Lahar."

The High Elder could not keep his relief from showing. He nodded briefly. "The healer is indeed free to choose his own successor," he acknowledged, and swiftly turned his attention to the next on the list. As the High Elder called out the name of another candidate, Kenlahar found himself letting out the breath he had been holding. A few people sent angry or pitying last glances at Kenlahar, but when the rest of the ceremony of the Axedelve passed without incident they seemed to forget his presence.

Finally, the last of the young men rose and turned from Alcress in defeat. The Elders slumped back again in their thrones and a ritual wail of despair emerged from the women and children. Kenlahar shivered at the weird keening. As usual, the family had been certain that the presaged and immanent potency of the Star Axe would be aroused. Surely this time, they had thought, one of them would consummate the tryst and lead them into battle against the Warlord. But they had failed, just as every other generation in Lahar's long lineage had failed.

Thus did Kenlahar attempt in vain to deny the power of the Star Axe, and defy the plans of the Raggorak—the Five Starborn who guided the fates of all the peoples.

CHAPTER II

A few hours later Kenlahar stumbled through a changed world. The crowded Courtyard of Moons was no longer quiet, no longer solemn. Far above, brightly colored rain canopies had been raised, flapping noisily in the wind. Bonfires burned on the bare stones of the square, and the smoke found exits where rain was somehow frustrated. The people danced in a jumble—alone, paired or in groups, it didn't seem to matter.

Only Kenlahar was still unhappy. He was borne by the ebb and flow of this mass toward the central spit. First, a young girl greeted him with garlands in her hair, but wearing little else. She handed him a goblet of wine, spilling half and laughing and vanishing into the crowd. Then another girl, also with garlands in her hair but dressed more modestly, whirled by him, kissing him briefly before she too disappeared. Sensing his sobriety, the people seemed intent on making him as befuddled with drink as they were themselves. They seemed to have forgotten, or no longer to care, that he had refused to Axedelve. Tossing back goblet after goblet of wine, Kenlahar soon forgot to aspire to the central spit, or to his original goal of feasting on the tantalizing roast pig.

Without much surprise he found himself dancing with Sanra. He had always been struck by her sculptured face, slender frame, and calm manner. There had always seemed to Kenlahar to be an ethereal quality to this girl.

Now that image of Sanra was broken forever as he danced with her in the pandemonium. Her ivory skin was flushed and her blue eyes glittered. With a careless grin and a blood red flower in her blond hair, she didn't at all resemble the sedate girl he remembered. "Sanra!" he found himself shouting with pleased, gladdened tones and in his drunken state he felt he said much more, though actually he only repeated her name, and then again.

Neither of them made any attempt to stop, or move on, or change dancing partners. But finally—reluctantly—they both had to submit to their exhaustion. They wandered idly toward a gate almost overgrown with vines, set in the east wall. The night was now dark and murky as they slipped out of the Courtyard of Moons and ventured into the forest. The brilliant skies were hidden by rainclouds. The two lovers wended their way through the woods, talking and laughing nervously in the dim light. The undergrowth glowed ghostlike from the little sliver of moonlight. The trees seemed to be spaced by some god's design, yet they kept stumbling into branches hidden in the gloom.

The small forest was more a nursery and farm than a natural wild, for every inch of the valuable land was utilized. Concentrated plots of garden straggled along one narrow edge of the island, and grew anyplace else where a few feet of land was left unoccupied by the spreading structure of the House of Lahar. Downriver, there was one small patch of grassland, reserved for the few, precious head of livestock. The Needle of Lahar, a pinnacle of granite, was visible from every vantage point, towering over the northern end of the island, and separated by a narrow moat formed from the encroaching river. One end of the island was entirely taken up by an elaborate series of docks, and on most mornings a fleet of fishing boats would venture forth from there.

Kenlahar was only a little surprised when he felt his hand taken in Sanra's soft firm grip. He said nothing, but returned the clasp, tenderly counting the fingers of her hand. After a while, he dared to gently break her hold, and instead he hesitantly wrapped his arm around her waist. He did not look down as they continued on in silence, but he hoped that when he did her face would not be calm, emotionless. They passed a patrol of the Watch, who smiled knowingly at them both.

Finally, he found a private turn in the well-worn path, hidden from all onlookers. Now silent and unwilling to break the spell, they waded into the deep underbrush at the side of the narrow trail. Soon they heard the sound of a swift creek, buried beneath the heavy undergrowth. A huge, decaying log, a last remnant of the old forest, created a bridge over the brush-choked stream. On the other side they found a grotto, cut into the bank of the stream, silent and carpeted by a soft moss.

Gratefully, Sanra sank onto the thick and surprisingly dry carpet of growth. "It's beautiful," she breathed, and Kenlahar realized that he had been wrong—her words did not destroy the spell, but enhanced it.

"I discovered this grove while exploring, when I was a child," he said. "I have always come here when I wished to be alone. Of course, I have no hope it is truly secret—but I have never seen anyone else here. I pledged to myself that I would never show it to another." "Why have you shown it to me?" she said teasingly. "When I vowed that, I was too young to realize that someone like you could even exist. I *still* find it hard to believe."

"What would convince you?"

He turned to her, pulling her against him, and found her waiting for his kiss. Later, as they lingered dreamily in the cove, he asked, "Why did you stop coming to the Archives, Sanra?"

Few of Kenlahar's brothers and sisters ever deigned to visit the cavernous Archives, but for a little while Sanra had come to the old room almost every day to read.

But then, only months before, she had abruptly stopped coming. It was only after she had left that Kenlahar and realized how little he really knew about her. He had not been able to find her again.

For the first time that night, an unhappy expression passed over her face. "I have not visited the upper levels since my husband..." She couldn't finish, and began to cry softly. Kenlahar coaxed her head onto his shoulder, feeling the dreamlike spell slipping away from them.

"Husband?" he said, dismayed. "Why did you not tell me?"

"It would not have mattered. I could only see you by coming to the Archives. I was afraid that if I told you, you would avoid me, or follow me to the tunnels. My husband would have killed you if he had found out."

So that is why she had never told him anything of herself, he thought. That is why she had not allowed him to get close; why she had quit coming to the Archives. He had not even known.

"When my father found out I was seeing you," she continued unhappily, "he forbade me to see you anymore. He threatened to tell Jakkem. My husband is a cruel man. If he ever believes that I have betrayed him—he might do anything." Suddenly, she pulled away from him, noticeably putting on a bland, masklike expression—that calm look that Kenlahar had always noticed first, but had never known the reason for.

"Now—" she said. "I don't care. My father was a Quarrier. Last month he died in one of the flooded mines."

Kenlahar said nothing, but suddenly felt very wet and miserable from their stroll through the damp brush. Even the land under the House of Lahar is not wasted, he thought. The Quarriers risked drowning in the constant floods to tunnel for precious metal ore deep beneath the island—sometimes even under the river itself.

It was left for Sanra to say what he also was thinking. "I feel somehow that we should not be in love. Not so soon after…" Her voice trailed away again. "We shouldn't be here alone."

"Very well. We'll go back."

Above the leaden skies were passing into another dark day. The muted light seemed to intensify the dull colors of the forest. Above the tops of the trees they could see the shimmering lights of the Courtyard's fires beckoning them back. They once more entered the yard's boisterous confines, and saw that the revelers would not soon relinquish the area.

When Sanra's eyes widened in fear he looked involuntarily over his shoulder. He sensed instantly that the huge man approaching them meant harm. The man's eyes bulged in a round, florid face, and his lips were curled in a malevolent smile. His bulk required aggressive elbowing for him to make any progress in the crowded jumble.

Kenlahar heard Sanra scream, "No, Jakkem—" and felt himself become sober as the blood rushed to his head. The people surrounding them fell silent, though most of the crowd continued celebrating, uncaring or unaware of the impending fight.

Jakkem stopped only inches away from her. "How can you dance with this man, Sanra?" he demanded. "Your father died as a Quarrier, strongest and bravest of the Axe-Kith, and yet now you dance with this coward! Come along, Sanra." He grabbed her arm.

"Let her do what she wants," Kenlahar said.

Jakkem turned to address the nearest revelers belligerently, "Are we going to let the spawn of an Outsider celebrate with us? We fight the Qreq, but what about the enemies within our House? Have you forgotten that he declined the Axedelve? This traitor's mother was exiled because of her loose ways, and now he is trying to steal my wife, as well!" He threw his wine goblet viciously against Kenlahar's chest.

Kenlahar was stunned by the mention of his mother. As his face flushed with anger and shame, he knew that he must react or be thought a coward.

Before he could bring himself to move, Balor was there. With blinding swiftness the warrior entered the circle of watchers and threw Jakkem onto the stones of the square. Kenlahar was ashamed of the sudden sense of relief that coursed through his body at the sight of his friend.

As children, Balor and he had been chosen by the Healer Coron to be his apprentices. But where Kenlahar had come to the worlds of the Archives and the Hospice and had fallen in love with their secrets, the old man had had to let the combative Balor free after merely teaching him to read and write. Balor had joined the Axe-Kith at the last Axedelve.

Yet the two boys had remained strong friends. Kenlahar knew that he had always been protected, to some extent, by the respect in which Balor was held. From those first days, the friendship had shielded him from the countless blows and cruel jokes of the other boys.

Tall and muscular in his light armor, Balor loomed over the other men. At his side a huge sword was sheathed in battered leather, and his dark blue cloak was torn and stained from many battles. His hair was long and blond, as was characteristic of the family, and tied in a knot behind his neck. He was clean-shaven as was the custom, but instead of the usual blue eyes, he had clear brown eyes of the same tint as Kenlahar's.

When Balor allowed Jakkem to get to his feet, Kenlahar saw that though Balor was as tall as the other man, his friend now seemed dwarfed by the size of Jakkem. The leer was gone from Jakkem's face, but the two men had not yet given in. The two men began to circle each other warily. Then the bigger man lunged at Balor, his arms spread wide to crush the fight out of his opponent.

Balor backed away and then struck out. A cut opened over Jakkem's eyes. Blinded, he lunged again and again at Balor, trying vainly to close with the quicker warrior. Finally, Balor stepped aside and clenched his hands, bringing them down hard on Jakkem's back. The big man flopped to the ground and did not move again, but lay there weakly cursing them.

"Why did you have to get in the way?" he shouted. "I didn't want to fight you, Balor! It's the Outsider I want to teach a lesson to." He pointed at Sanra. "That is my woman!"

"She is free to do what she wants," Balor said. "But when you attack Kenlahar, you had better be prepared to fight me. Do not go near my friend again, or I will kill you!" he added in a menacing and ugly tone.

Kenlahar was still standing as though rooted to the spot, stunned by the fight. Sanra pulled urgently at his arm, but he would not move. He listened to Jakkem's flow of curses with a withdrawn, haunted look. Only when Balor pulled at his other arm, were his friends able to lead him from the still raving Jakkem.

Kenlahar was humiliated. He doubted that he would have ever responded to Jakkem's challenge. Once again his friend had saved him. But it would not always be so! Again and again he glanced sideways at Sanra, trying to somehow gauge her reaction.

Sanra revealed only her anger. "I have refused Jakkem my love, but now it seems he has followed me. I owe him nothing, Kenlahar. There are no bonds between us. He is jealous and spiteful and he was trying to hurt you. Don't let him succeed."

"You could not risk violence, Kenlahar," Balor added. "You are a healer. To strike back would have debased your Atima."

"I was not thinking of my Atima," Kenlahar said miserably. "I was simply frightened. I had thought that once I chose the life of a healer I would never be faced with violence again."

"I fear it is a dilemma you will always face, Kenlahar," Balor said. "As long as you live in the House of Lahar, there will be people who will want to fight you. But there is no need to dirty your hands on scoundrels. You come to me if anyone threatens you again."

Kenlahar turned his face away. Nearby, the Elders still sat on their thrones, now watching the festivities with paternal smiles on their faces—they no longer appeared stern and forbidding. The Star Axe was also on harmless display, now appearing as nothing more than an ordinary battleaxe. Awe kept most of the dancers at a distance from Alcress, and in this space people clustered, watching the revelers or talking softly. Once again Kenlahar stared at the battleaxe in fascination.

With wine still running through his veins, Kenlahar could almost believe that by simply reaching out and touching the Star Axe, it would perform magic in his hands. He found himself daydreaming again of adventures beyond the swamp—a battle with each of the Five Raggorak hidden among the Five Peoples—and a triumphant return to the House of Lahar. Again, he shook his head at his foolish fantasies.

As if Balor could read his thoughts, the blond warrior smiled and said, "The family would never insult you, never harm you again, if you would just leave the House of Lahar with me."

"Leave?" Sanra said, feeling the first pangs of fear. "Where are you going, Kenlahar?"

"Don't worry, Sanra," Kenlahar said. "It is just an old dream—an old argument." As children, he and Balor had explored the island, looking for secret passages and hideaways, hatching their childish plans to explore the Outside.

Only Balor had not yet given up on his dream, he thought. He looked down at Sanra's pale worried face and smiled. "I am not going anywhere, Sanra. Not now."

"Why not, my friend?" Balor's eyes were gleaming in the dim light of early morning. "Kingdoms are waiting for us—the two of us. Think

15

on what you could learn, Kenlahar! Herbs and medicines. New magic and old science!"

Kenlahar felt himself being caught up in Balor's dream despite himself. Outside. To most members of the family the "Outside" was beyond the swamp, at legendary Swamp's End—both a beacon of hope and a symbol of danger. The family both feared and scorned the Outside; feared it because few ventured Outside and returned, and because it was from there that the Qreq had come; scorned it, because they felt themselves to be the last bastion of civilization. Still, legends of its fabulous treasures drew some young men away. On the other hand, tales of its terror kept most young men at home. Kenlahar himself had always suffered from this fear and scorn because of the rumors about his mother.

"We don't really know anything about Outside," he said. "All we have is old hearsay and older legends."

But Balor dismissed this objection with a wave of his hand. "Don't you want to see Swamp's End, Kenlahar?" He went on in a different tone, and it seemed to Sanra as if he was trying to assuage all of Kenlahar's doubts.

"You will never know what the family is really thinking about you if you stay, Kenlahar. Jakkem may have been voicing what they are all feeling. Do you want to spend the rest of your life healing people who will feel no gratitude, who will hate you instead? I intend to leave, Kenlahar—with you or without you. But after what the Elders did to you mother, you should be convincing *me* to leave instead!"

Kenlahar felt the wave of pain he always suffered at the mention of his mother's fate. But he had learned long ago to ignore the hurt—or it would end by overwhelming him. "No, Balor," he said firmly. "I will not leave."

Yet, for some reason, Sanra did not believe him. She suddenly knew that she was going to somehow lose the man she loved, so soon after she had found him. It was at that moment that she vowed not to let Kenlahar leave without her—a decision that was to lead her far beyond the swamp.

Suddenly, they realized with surprise that the Courtyard of Moons was almost empty. They began to drift back to their rooms and their

16

beds—there would be no work done that day. Kenlahar said goodbye to Balor at the door of the Great Hall, not acknowledging the question in his friend's eyes. At the junction of the women's rooms Sanra did not turn aside, but continued on—trembling at having so boldly invaded the men's quarters. With Sanra sleeping in his arms, Kenlahar thought no more of leaving the House of Lahar.

CHAPTER III

Signal fires—beacons of danger—flared on the Needle of Lahar, and horns trumpeted alarm from the watch- towers. From around the sharp turn upriver of the House of Lahar, Qreq warships swung ponderously into view. Kenlahar watched the mustering of the Axe-Kith from a small balcony on the roof of the docks. The flimsy structure was perched on thick piles set in the river, and concealed beneath it a labyrinth of canals and piers. The boats of the House of Lahar disembarked below him, struggling against the rising tide of the River Danjar.

The muddy and sluggish river continually overflowed its banks and covered the surrounding land with a thick, grasping mud. During the rainy season, which was most of the year, the mud turned the countryside into an impassable swamp. Very little grew in the land called the Tream, and all life was eventually buried beneath a thick layer of bog. Only an intricate system of canals had tamed the River Danjar enough to save the island from the fate suffering by the rest of the Tream. Once the river had been the highway of the House of Lahar. Lahar and his followers had even adopted the swamp- men's name for the river—for "danjar" meant north, in their language. But now that path led nowhere. Now, the Qreq dominated the river, and few of Kenlahar's generation had ventured far from the Island Laharhann. Now, the House of Lahar was the single valuable prize of a war for survival.

The opposing forces maneuvered for position all morning long, with constant probing and testing, feint within feint within feint. Kenlahar, who had never seen war, thought these first brief skirmishes to be the battle itself, and started to relax at the ease with which the Qreq invaders were being repulsed. He knew that soon he would be needed in the Hospice, but he lingered a while longer on the docks. The gigantic fortress warships of the Qreq continued to tack back and forth across the wide river, searching for an opening. The smaller fighting boats of Lahar stretched in front of them and darted downriver to fire volleys from longbows whenever one of the Qreq ships came close.

Suddenly, a shift in the wind filled the giant black sails of the raider ships. As one, the thirteen huge vessels turned toward the line of defense drawn by the fleet of Lahar. They drove downriver, sweeping aside everything before them. Sails flapped in the wind. The beat of the Qreq war-drums quickened and became louder with each passing second, and the hundreds of oars dipped in accord, bending under the force of thousands of galley slaves. The black warships, already larger than anything Kenlahar had ever seen afloat, loomed as even more awesome. As the wave of ships approached where he was standing, it seemed to Kenlahar that nothing could stop them, and for the first time he could hear the inhuman war chants of "Qreq! Qreq!" from which the fearsome warriors derived their name.

But the closer the Qreq came, the stronger the resistance grew. The cresting wave began to dissolve into violent spurts, and the more numerous boats of Lahar regrouped, their yellow sails swarming beneath the larger ships. In desperation, the warriors of Lahar boarded the enemy ships and as they did the wind died.

Yet one of the Qreq ships kept plunging forward toward the pier where Kenlahar watched, as if propelled by some invisible force. It did not turn aside to assail the more populous, vulnerable parts of the island—but drove onward to Kenlahar's lonely spot.

The huge vessel skirted the low balcony and its bulwarks loomed over him, grinding into the wood structure of the docks. A Qreq warrior jumped down onto the balcony and confronted Kenlahar, moving with manic speed. "Kenlahar!" he heard, and he threw himself onto the floor of the platform.

Though the naked, emaciated Qreq arm looked incapable of wielding the curved sword held in long fingers, the weapon sliced only inches over Kenlahar's head. But Kenlahar would not have escaped a second time. He felt a surge of relief as he caught a swirl of blue, which he recognized as Balor's cape. Then Balor was moving between the ill-matched opponents, stabbing upward and forward. The balcony's railing stopped the Qreq's desperate retreat abruptly and the blade pierced his chest. The abnormally large, hairless head of the Qreq jerked to emit his death cry.

Though it was his enemy who had died—an enemy who had tried to kill him—Kenlahar had to turn his face from the bloodshed. The scream of the dying man still pounded into his mind. For a moment, he imagined that the scream was directed at him; it was as though it formed words, imploring him for help, demanding help—accusing him!

"Are you all right, Kenlahar?" Balor was shaking him. "Get inside, you don't belong here!" By the time he forced himself to once more look on the battle, Balor had already disappeared from view, lost in the melee of war.

It was raining hard. But Kenlahar could not dislodge himself from the balcony, despite Balor's warning. Hands grasping the railing and turning white under the pressure, he was only vaguely aware of the rain that ran down his stringy black hair and turned his dark brown cloak an even darker shade. Below him the docks were in flames, where flung torches had reached their target.

Already men were clambering up and down the ramshackle lower roof, throwing buckets of water from the river onto the fires. The dusk grew even darker as the last of the blue sky was surrounded and conquered by gray skies, and his shadow—cast by the jagged light of the burning ships—danced against the wall at his back.

Suddenly, the giant bell within the dome of the Great Hall shook the balcony with peals of victory, and the cheers of many warriors reached him from the river below. The nearest warship was in flames, and drifting slowly downriver past the balcony. Other giant fortress ships were turning and retreating ponderously upriver, triple banks of oars dipping to the beat of the pace- drums, still dignified, even in defeat. The smaller, faster boats of the House of Lahar continued to harass them, darting in and out of their wakes. Between, dismembered bodies bobbed in the current, staining the river red in circles around them.

Three of the huge raider ships had been left behind- burning quickly, sinking slowly. Mingled with the smoke drifting across the river was the smell of burning wood and canvas, a stench of roasted flesh. Kenlahar gagged—the smell almost seemed good to him.

With a shock, Kenlahar realized that the wounded were already being unloaded onto the docks, and had been unloading for some time. He released his grip on the railing of the balcony and rubbed the flow of blood back into his hands. With a guilty haste, he left the balcony and hurried toward the Hospice.

He had to concentrate on finding his way, for he had seldom visited the docks. But at last he stood before the wide Hospice doors. As Coron's only apprentice, Kenlahar had already learned much of what the old man could teach. But his real talent would be the next few hours—soon he would discover if he truly possessed the Atima. With a deep sigh, he heaved open the heavy doors.

A flood of light revealed pandemonium. The cots and tables and even the floor were quickly being filled by the writhing, moaning wounded. Kenlahar gave the room a quick survey, was satisfied that Balor was not among the wounded. With a swift urgency, young women moved among them, bringing some order to the chaos. The air in the Hospice was filled with the overpowering odor of herbs covering the smells of sickness. In the middle of the room was a low table piled high with clean rags. The women surrounded the table, tearing the cloth into neat strips of bandages. Sanra approached him, and blushed under his stare, "The Healer Coron said that I could help you, Kenlahar."

Coron barely acknowledged Kenlahar's arrival, simply throwing him a helpless look, and shouting, "Hurry, we have need of healers!" The old man had already begun to supervise the tending of the wounded. "Shield the barbs before you pull out that arrow!" he roared at one of the hapless women. The old man's major problem though, Kenlahar quickly observed, seemed to be holding back the Lashitu,

21

who was chanting his incantations over the healer's shoulder as he worked. The Healer Coron did not approve of the Lashitu and was trying his best to ignore the shaman's presence. But the Lashitu had not yet been finished chanting his powers, his greatness, or the invocation of his protectors' names—which appeared to include all the High Gods and most of the minor spirits. They made an impressive list, Kenlahar thought, and only wished that the spells had some healing effect.

The family still believed in the two worlds of the real and the supernatural, and this was reflected in the Hospice. The healer dealt with the undeniable need for the binding of wounds, while the Lashitu called upon the spirits to help, and claimed responsibility for all recoveries. Each thought the other was unnecessary.

The Lashitu contemptuously drew a sign in the air before Kenlahar and muttered, "Wraith-taint..." The young apprentice found it hard to turn from the shaman. Yet, he had heard it before, and the wounded were still waiting to be cared for. He shrugged and stooped over a bleeding warrior, grasping his hands almost violently over the wound, his fingers pinching the artery. Behind him, the Lashitu began to chant with hypnotic repetition: "The River flows / Flowing free/Bind the flow!/Bind the flow! The River flows/ Red river flowing free/ Bind the flow!/ Bind the flow!..."

Kenlahar was swiftly immersed in trying to heal the battle wounds and soon forgot his irritation with the Lashitu. Even the endless chanting began to fade into the background. Eventually, the Hospice settled into a purposeful quiet, disturbed only by the moans of the wounded. Throughout that day, Kenlahar was aware that Sanra did not leave his side as he moved among the wounded. Her smock was caked with blood, yet she still seemed to remain somehow unruffled by it all. None of her blond hair managed to escape the confines of a bun. Her face stayed placid and unmoving, with a single streak of blood across her forehead. Kenlahar found himself admiring her more and more as the nightmarish night wore on.

Much of the next day had passed before the wounded ceased coming and the Hospice began to empty out. Late in the afternoon, as Kenlahar worked bent over in the dim light of the torches, what

Kenlahar had feared, happened. Balor was brought into the room, dazed by a wound to his forehead.

Lashitu, his face now bloodied, swooped down on him, howling his spells in a hoarse voice. Balor quailed and shouted, "Qreq!" Moving quickly to the uproar, Kenlahar found himself with a fist raised over the scrawny back of the Lashitu. The Healer Coron cried out his name in horror, but he had already stopped himself from striking. Instead, he jerked the shaman from Balor harshly. A dangerous gleam in the Lashitu's eyes changed his angry words into a wary question. "What are you doing to him?"

"He is possessed!" the Lashitu screeched, moving away from the young healer. "The wraith-taint must not be allowed to fester and grow!" The beaked nose of the shaman pointed in the air like a finger. Kenlahar noted the accusation with weary anger.

"There is no demon in him," the apprentice retorted, "but the infection of poison. Balor needs rest—not the fearful pesterings of a sorcerer. If I possessed the authority I would banish you from this room. But authority or not, if you come near this man again you will regret it!"

But the Lashitu was enraged, and the crooked figure descended again on Balor. Kenlahar tried to hold him back, realizing that the Lashitu looked like a Qreq with his tall, skinny frame and sparse wispy hair. But the weary apprentice was unable to keep the wiry shaman back, and they stumbled struggling against Balor. "What is happening here!" The shout reverberated through the Hospice and the Lashitu fell silent at last. They turned to see a Captain of the Watch glaring at them from the doorway. The Watch were the elite warriors of the Axe-Kith and their commander was an old grizzled veteran. The green uniform of the Watch could not quite conceal his disfigured body. The legendary Captain Jonla had been wounded many times in his battles with the Qreq, but as long as he still walked and could still carry a weapon, he would continue to lead his men. The Elders had learned to rely on his knowledge and craftiness—and his loyalty. For the Watch also served as the police of the House of Lahar.

Now it appeared that Captain Jonla had been wounded once more. One arm crossed his chest to clutch the ripped muscles of his other arm.

His face was drawn and Kenlahar saw that his armor was chipped and encrusted with dried blood. "What is your name?" he roared.

With a start, Kenlahar realized that he was speaking to him. "Forgive me, Captain Jonla. My name is Kenlahar."

Captain Jonla started at this name, and stared at Kenlahar strangely. Then Healer Coron had reached the door, greeting the wounded warrior, and casting a warning look at his apprentice. But Captain Jonla would not be put off. "Why are you not tending that man?" he demanded, angrily shaking off the Healer Coron and pointing into the corner where Balor laid shaking and sweating. "Must a man be mortally wounded before you tend to him?"

Kenlahar felt his face flush at the unfair accusation but said nothing in defense, instead turned to calm his friend. The Lashitu, he noticed bitterly, seemed to have faded inconspicuously into the background. Balor was slowly regaining his senses.

"Kenlahar? Where am I?"

"It is all right, Balor. You are in the Hospice. You are safe now." There were a few minutes of quiet as Balor laid back, with his eyes closed. Soon he was sleeping soundly, while Kenlahar cleaned the festering wound. By morning, Balor would be completely recovered, he thought.

Into this hush the Healer Coron spoke softly to Kenlahar and Sanra, without using their names. "Go! Rest. I can take care of any emergencies. You must sleep before there is another battle." The old man also dropped his eyes significantly to the reclining Captain of the Watch, who was dozing while the healer worked on his arm. It seemed that Kenlahar had made yet another enemy.

With one last warning glance at the Lashitu, and a wary look at Captain Jonla, they left the Hospice for the first time in over a day. They did not know it, but they were to never see the Hospice again.

CHAPTER IV

The sounds of splintering wood woke them. Kenlahar sat up with the light in his eyes. Beyond the light he glimpsed two figures through the smashed shards of the door. He glanced quickly at Sanra, who stared back, and he realized foolishly that both of their mouths had dropped wide open.

"What!" he gasped. "Who—?"

"Stand up, Kenlahar!" one of the intruders demanded, stepping into the room. The green uniforms of the Watch, now that he could see them, the insolent tone of voice, but most of all, the timing of the encroachment, sparked the smoldering resentment and rebellion within Kenlahar.

"You have no right to break into my room!" he shouted and lunged for the nearest warrior. Too late, he recognized the bent shape of Captain Jonla, with his arm now in a sling. The old warrior easily grabbed Kenlahar with his good arm. The apprentice was pinned helplessly against the wall, and his cheek flattened against the wood. His breath was forced from his body by the impact.

When Kenlahar said nothing more, and ceased struggling, Captain Jonla relented and released him. Kenlahar sat heavily onto the bed next to Sanra. She was staring at him with frightened and pleading eyes. Touching his face softly, she said, "Please, Kenlahar. You mustn't fight him."

Captain Jonla was standing threateningly over them. He waved his free hand at Sanra. "You should listen to her," he said harshly. "At least *she* seems to have some sense!"

Once again Kenlahar felt the shame of not being able to defend her. "What do you want," he managed to whisper.

"The Elders wish to see you. I was warned that you might be a spy for Warlord." He said this last with more than a touch of scorn, obviously not believing that Kenlahar could be dangerous. "All I want now is your word that you will not try to escape me. It shouldn't be necessary to bind or carry you."

There was no choice, Kenlahar saw. "I will do as you ask," he said wearily.

Captain Jonla relaxed slightly and motioned for him to follow. The party set off for the Great Hall at a brisk pace. Sanra was left behind without another word, and with only a last bitter glance from Kenlahar. She stood at the shattered doorway, wondering and uncertain whether she should follow. As she watched them recede, Kenlahar appearing as a small, helpless, dark shape bounded by the giant warriors of the Watch, Sanra remembered her vow to abide by Kenlahar no matter what happened. She set off inconspicuously after the small party.

———

The Chambre of the Great Hall was the center of life in the House of Lahar, the largest of its many enclosures. It was crudely, but magnificently built. Its huge logs were said to have been hewn by the Star Axe itself, and the beams crisscrossed high above, their shadows casting intricate patterns on the dome. Kenlahar had never seen it so empty. His steps and those of his guards echoed in the vast hall as he approached through semi-darkness on a smooth stone floor. Only the raised podium at the end of the hall was lit.

On the dais sat the Council of Elders in their dark ceremonial robes. The long dais served as a barrier between the Elders and the rest of the Chambre. Legend said that it too was carved from a single tree of the old forest and not from the many low swamp trees whose wood was used throughout most of the House of Lahar. As always, the Star Axe was set in display before the Elders, with its blade buried in the flattened log.

At first, there did not seem to be anyone else in the hall, except the two warriors who had brought him. Sanra melted unnoticed into the shadows at the rear of the hall. But when Kenlahar was finally ordered to stop, he saw Coron and Balor off to one side, surrounded by soldiers. Balor looked at Kenlahar with a defiantly supportive expression. His head was heavily bandaged but otherwise he looked well. The Healer Coron, on the other hand, looked away from his questioning glance. The Lashitu was there as well, glaring at him, having apparently claimed his lawful place on the Council.

One of the Elders called Kenlahar's name once, though he stood in full view of the tribunal. Kenlahar was pushed forward another step by Captain Jonla, and discovered that his rage had been replaced by resignation. "You wish to leave the House of Lahar?" the Elder asked officiously, without once looking up from the papers before him.

Kenlahar refused to answer, confused and angry by the injustice of the charge. The Elder finally looked up. "Come boy, we have been told by the Healer Coron that you and Balor wish to leave the island."

The Lashitu, who sat on the Elder's right, turned and said plaintively, "I knew it was a mistake, letting those two be taught by Coron."

"Remember, it was Coron who reported this transgression."

"Yes, and lucky for him that he did!" the Lashitu answered in the same peeved tone.

Kenlahar was stunned by what he had just learned. Now he remembered how close the Healer Coron was to the Elders. The old man would do anything to keep him from leaving. But who had told him such a lie—and why?

He realized that the High Elder was speaking to him. "Tell me, son. Why would anyone wish to leave the House of Lahar and venture into the Tream? The worst thing we could do would be to grant your wish. Such a fate is so dire that we have hesitated to use it as a punishment!"

"Only one person has left the island in my lifetime," the Lashitu added in spite. "And *she* did not leave of her own free will."

"Ah, yes," the High Elder said in a low voice. "The mother—I had forgotten that." He cleared his throat. "Nonetheless, we cannot knowingly allow our young men to risk their lives in such foolish ventures."

The kindly tone of the High Elder made Kenlahar look closely at him for the first time. He saw with surprise that the High Elder was actually a fairly young man. Though the gray hair at his temples made him look dignified, an amused glint in his eyes belied the severity.

When Kenlahar still did not speak up the High Elder continued in a bemused tone, "We have heard very little of you since your...ah, remarkable birth, Kenlahar. And now, in a period of just two days, your name is *all* I have heard. Initially there was your rather surprising refusal of the Axedelve. Then, last night, the Healer Coron came to me with the news that you were planning to leave the island.

"There is something strange about the Healer Coron, but there is no denying he knows a great deal." The High Elder stared into Kenlahar's eyes. "This time I listened very carefully to what the old man had to say, for it came following some surprising information from the Watch. I would like the Council of Elders to hear what I have already been told. Captain Jonla?"

All heads turned to regard the legendary leader as he hobbled forward. The old warrior cleared his throat and said stiffly, "During the Axedelve, a small party of Qreq managed to sneak onto the island. We were able to slay all the Qreq but one, who we captured and questioned. It appears that the only purpose of the Qreq patrol was to find and ensnare one person—someone named...Kenlahar!" Captain Jonla glared at Kenlahar with undisguised suspicion.

"Soon after," the High Elder continued the story with puzzlement written in his face, "one of Captain Jonla's own men *also* came to me and suggested that you were intending to leave our island—hinting as well that you were a spy for the Warlord."

Captain Jonla interrupted, angrily demanding to know who had gone to the High Elder without notifying him first. The High Elder supplied the name, with a note of contempt. "He said his name was Jakkem. I have never seen or heard of him before."

This brought a hiss of anger from Balor. "Jakkem! He is nothing more than a bully and a liar. If there are any traitors in the House of Lahar, it is he!" Balor suddenly wrenched away from his guards and stepped forward to confront the Elders. "This has gone far enough. I have already told you. It was not Kenlahar who wanted to leave, but I. I do not understand why Coron turned us in!"

"Ah, yes," the High Elder continued, as if he had not heard the outburst, in a mystified manner. "Then there is Balor. One of our finest young warriors I am told—and fiercely loyal to you, Kenlahar." Once more, the High Elder turned his bemused eyes to the apprentice healer. "Do you have an answer for all these riddles and charges, young man?"

"I think I can give you the answers you want." It was the Healer Coron who stepped before the dais, instead—leaving his guards balking behind him at his sudden shift. The room quieted and everyone turned their eyes on the old man. The High Elder shifted uncomfortably on his throne, and the Lashitu eyed the old man uneasily. The Healer Coron seemed to have suddenly taken on an invisible mantle of authority. Neither of his students had ever seen him like this before. Nor, apparently, had the Elders.

"Fifty years ago," the old man said in a surprisingly strong voice, and his manner compelled all of them to heed his words, "when we were stronger, and the Qreq weaker, we could have gone to the Warlord's Haven and rooted them out. But we have bided our time too long. Now all it will take to destroy us will be one well-placed torch! Without help, that day is nearer than any of you realize. The Warlord is marshaling his Qreq for the final assault. Our only hope is to find allies…" Kenlahar stared at the old man, astounded by the outpouring of words. The Healer Coron had always discouraged just such talk. Now he was setting forth a convincing case for breaking the isolation of the House of Lahar—one that Balor and he had presented to the old man many times, to no avail.

"But you betrayed us," Balor objected from the side of the room. "You turned us in to keep us from getting help!"

"No!" the Healer Coron answered vehemently. "I knew that you could never survive without an escort through the swamp. Only the Elders could give authorization for that." At these words, the old man turned once more to the dais. "We must move quickly, for Toraq, the Sorcerer King, has discovered that there is someone dwelling within the House of Lahar who is heir to the Star Axe."

"But the Sorcerer King was defeated by Lahar, with the Star Axe!" the High Elder objected.

"Defeated?" the old man mused. "Yes, he was defeated, but he was not destroyed, as we had thought. For he had risen again from whatever limbo he lay for so long. The Warlord of the Qreq is...Toraq, the Sorcerer King!"

Kenlahar was astonished by the fear in the old man's voice, until he remembered the terrifying legends of the Sorcerer King. He saw the same fear spread through the Chambre. The Warlord had been a deadly enemy, he thought. The Sorcerer King was doom itself!

The Healer Coron nodded, satisfied by the reaction. "Now you may understand why I ask for such a desperate quest—to send Kenlahar into the Tream for help. *Any* risk must be taken, if we are to survive." The Healer Coron seemed about to go on with his dire predictions, but he stopped, realizing perhaps that he had already frightened them enough.

None of the others moved or spoke. They stared at the Healer Coron, stunned by the succession of revelations. "There is one more thing Kenlahar must know before he leaves the House of Lahar and fulfills his destiny." The old man looked at his student with an apology written in his eyes. "You have become a man, Kenlahar. It is right that you should become one in form as well as substance."

Kenlahar looked questioningly into the Healer Coron's face. At last I shall be told the truth about my mother, he thought. At last I shall be told my lineage!

"You have always known that there was something tainted in your birth," the old man said. "I tell you the full story now only by risking exile. The Elders decreed that no one would ever be allowed to tell you the truth." He looked in the direction of the dais, but the Elders made no effort to stop him from speaking. "Your mother was exiled, Kenlahar, as you have always suspected. But the reason—*that* you have never known." He rubbed his eyes wearily, "How can I tell you?"

"Tell me!" Kenlahar demanded. He tried to catch the Healer Coron's eyes, but the old man was avoiding his gaze.

"Many years ago, an Outsider came to the House of Lahar. That stranger was arrested, but your mother took him as her swain, and helped him escape. For this sacrilege, she was sentenced to the certain death of exile. Since that time, this story has not been told. The family has always felt that there is something different about you, Kenlahar. And they are more right than they know. Only I, among the living, know the truth. Only I know the identity of that stranger—your father. I have waited until this moment to tell you, for the truth would not have helped you. Now …" the Healer Coron paused, seeming to search for a way to tell him. "The best way to reveal the truth is to show you. Touch the blade of the Star Axe, Kenlahar!" he commanded. Kenlahar was startled. "Touch it?"

"Yes, quickly!" the old man ordered, guiding Kenlahar the last few feet to Alcress.

Kenlahar extended his hand gingerly, and one finger brushed the-blade. The blinding flash that emerged from Alcress was that of a falling meteor. He jumped back and threw his arm over his eyes. Then it seemed to grow dark in the hall. When his eyes had once again adjusted to the dim light of the torches, he saw the Watch on their knees before him. It was the Lashitu, who had taunted him for as long as he could remember, who now said reverently, "You are the one for whom we have waited so long!"

The Healer Coron pulled the Star Axe from its hold in the dais and started to remove the blade of the battleaxe from its ancient and brittle haft, which he threw to the floor. He carefully sheathed the Star Axe in a battered scabbard, which he proferred to Kenlahar.

Kenlahar hesitated before taking weapon. To his relief, it remained quiescent in his hands. The Healer Coron helped him tie the scabbard around his neck, securely bound to a cord. Bewildered, he said, "But I felt nothing! What must I do with it?"

"That, Kenlahar," the Healer Coron said, "is what you must discover for yourself! You must learn to use it. You must go Outside and learn." The old man seemed to be trying to will the resolve- into Kenlahar's mind—-student and teacher locked in a steady gaze.

Captain Jonla protested. "But if Kenlahar can wield the Star Axe, there is no need for him to leave! Is this now what we have waited for? Kenlahar can lead us into the next battle against the Warlord!"

With a cry, one of the guards—who always lined the walls of the Chambre, inconspicuous and unnoticed—sprang forward with his blade drawn. Though Kenlahar had time to raise the Star Axe in protection, it moved sluggishly upward, displaying no special power. Only the quick action of Captain Jonla saved Kenlahar. To his relief, the old warrior stepped swiftly in front of him and easily skewered the charging guard.

"*There* is our spy!" the High Elder exclaimed.

"Or one of them," the Healer Coron contradicted.

"We must assume that the Warlord knows that someone with the power of the Starborn is here. Unless and until Kenlahar learns to use Alcress, he will be easy prey for Toraq. He must flee—now!

"Kenlahar alone will not be able to save us. The Star Axe is only an empty vessel, which must be imbued with the power of the Starborn. But *if* he has a chance to learn its secrets, and *if* he can bring help, and *if* the Warlord remains unaware that it has been aroused at last—then we shall have a chance."

The High Elder spoke finally. "Kenlahar must not go alone. We must choose Companions to the Star Axe—our own Raggorak. Balor will go as he wanted, and Captain Jonla will lead a company of the Watch. Be sure that you take along the man named Jakkem. The Lashitu also, I think, would not be left behind."

Indeed, the Lashitu was looking at Kenlahar with very different eyes, with almost worship in his gaze. "You must go tonight," the High Elder continued, "at the darkest, most secret hour. If the Warlord finds out that the Star Axe is active he will redouble his efforts to destroy us. I want you to leave with as little fanfare as possible—the Warlord must not know you have left. Not yet. Later, it may take some of the burden off us if he knows you are Outside. Until then, no one outside this room is to know what happened here tonight."

Sanra saw that the audience was about to end, and slipped quietly out of the Chambre. She had watched the proceedings from the back of the room with dismay. The hope that Lahar, or his descendant, would return in the time of the House of Lahar's greatest need and bear Alcress to victory as the prophecy presaged, had truly been their only hope. But she would never have guessed that it would be Kenlahar. She did not want it to be Kenlahar!

She had seen that Kenlahar was very different from the others. Not just because of his small stature and dark colorings. He had a quality of strangeness, of almost alien demeanor. She had never been able to discover what that aura of strangeness portended. It was only then that she remembered what everyone else had avoided saying. In the old tongue, Ken-Lahar meant "Son of Lahar!"

CHAPTER V

The troops were not in their battle armor, but were dressed instead in the green of the Watch. Many wore the rain resistant cloaks that the scouts bought at great expense from the Swamp People. No amount of experimenting could discover the secret of the materials in the cloaks. The Swamp People seemed to have a different art of weaving, Kenlahar reflected. Perhaps even of thought.

The ordeal of the last few days had left Kenlahar exhausted. They had remained in the Chambre until this early hour. In that time the Lashitu had refused to leave Kenlahar's side. The apprentice noticed the change in the shaman's attitude with sour humor. Balor was busily helping command the warriors. His dream of becoming a member of the Watch had been unexpectedly fulfilled at a young age, Kenlahar thought.

Captain Jonla strode across the docks with the assurance of command. The old warrior was renown for his knowledge of the Tream. Most of the family preferred to know little of the swamp, but Captain Jonla spent much of his life exploring its endless wastes. His hair and eyes were light, as was most of the family, but he appeared dark, for he had been browned by long days in the sun. His arm was still in a sling, seeming to add to his crooked hunch. He approached Kenlahar and shoved a bundle of rain gear in his hands, asking brusquely if there was anything he wished to do before they left.

Kenlahar suddenly remembered that with all the activity and excitement he had not yet said farewell to Sanra. But Captain Jonla was waiting impatiently for an answer, so he reluctantly shook his head. The warriors were already beginning to load into the boats. The first mingling of sunlight into the dark was only a few hours away. Kenlahar thought tiredly that it was just as well that he did not have to explain to Sanra.

One of the warriors near him was staring at Kenlahar, and he recognized with a start, Jakkem's scowling face. Kenlahar had hoped he could avoid Jakkem, but now he supposed wearily that he would have to face him. He would stay out of the big man's way if he could, but he was afraid that next time he might lose his Atima forever. But Jakkem did not speak. He obviously was not going to challenge the bearer of the Star Axe. At least not yet.

Kenlahar was about to step into a riverboat when he caught sight of the Healer Coron and Sanra in the shadows of the dock. The old man waved uneasily. Kenlahar hesitated and then, daring Captain Jonla's scowls, he walked back quickly to clasp his teacher.

"Old man," he said. "Being chosen to study under you, even for a little while, is the best thing that has ever happened to me. If it had not been for you, I would have thought the House of Lahar was the only civilized place on earth! The rest would have been the Tream, a hellish blank, or Outside—legends and myths as it is for any ignorant dolt. If only…"

The old man smiled and relaxed. "I am sorry, Kenlahar. I only wish I could come with you, but as you have reminded me many times, I am not a young man." Kenlahar was astonished to see that the old man had tears in his eyes. Now, for the first time, Kenlahar began to wonder who the Healer Coron really was. He remembered how the old man always seemed careful to avoid any questions about his past. No one could remember when the Healer Coron had first appeared behind his desk in the Archives. Nor did anyone really know how old he was. Only now did it strike Kenlahar as strange.

Now Sanra timidly emerged from behind the Healer Coron, and Kenlahar went to her, taking her hand. "I'll be back, Sanra."

Her fingers tightened on his. "I know you will, Kenlahar. But I am afraid you will not be the same." "People don't ever really change, Sanra. They just become more of what they are." He lifted her chin and kissed her. Turning, and resolutely not looking back, he did not see Jakkem approach her as well.

"I'll be back, Sanra," Jakkem mimicked, grinning. "And I assure you, I *will* be the same person."

She stared back at him coldly. "Oh, I am sure of that, Jakkem. But I will not change either! If I were you, I would not expect me to be waiting here for you!" Jakkem's smile widened and he patted her cheek. She pulled away sharply, and re-entered the shadows of the dock's shelter. She did not see his smile turn to a look of rage.

Captain Jonla's command to board was passed along, and the last of the party untied the boats and embarked. None of the Companions noticed a small figure, disguised in the bulky green cloak of the scouts, emerge from the shelter, glide across the docks, and slip into one of the lead boats.

———

The Healer Coron watched his two students leave with a pride he tried not to show. He turned away from the fleet of boats as they slipped away from the pier, and walked through the empty, early morning hallways of the House of Lahar.

He smiled to himself. It had been part of the role the old man had played to discourage the boys yearnings to leave, until it was the proper time. He had to be certain neither boy would leave without his knowledge. But now the time had come at last.

Sanra was an element he had not counted on, he thought with a frown. He had seen her jump into the third boat, but had not tried to stop her. Sanra could not change what was about to happen—what had been ordained would happen a thousand years before.

Entering the Archives and sitting behind his desk with a sigh, the old man lifted a pitted and scoured lump of metal, of the same texture as the Star Axe, from a concealed drawer. Then he leaned back in his chair and closed his eyes. For the next few minutes the Healer Coron did not move, but he was not inactive, not asleep. One by one, other thoughts entered his consciousness. Thoughts that, like their voice, reflected the diverse personalities of the visitants. Eventually, five different thought patterns were greeted by and shared the mind of the old man.

"He has left the House of Lahar," the old man announced to the visitants. "He is on his way at last!" "Good!" the first of the thoughts boomed. "I should like to test this boy to see if he is truly the one." Another thought, brash and confident, reprimanded the other. "The Star Axe has chosen. Why do you insist on questioning it?"

"I for one, am still surprised that Balor was not the one," a fourth presence added. This visitant seemed thoughtful and concerned. It contrasted with the louder, arguing voices.

"I have always known it would be Kenlahar," the Healer Coron said. "He suffered the more. Fortunately or unfortunately, only Kenlahar had to pay the price of his mother's actions. Balor did not inherit his father's features and therefore never learned the truth."

The fifth thought finally chimed in, timidly—but with logic. "Alcress has chosen and there is nothing we can do to change that. We need the Axe-bearer to defeat the Warlord—we are all agreed on that. It is our duty to help him on his path, to help him find the answer to the Star Axe."

Thoughtful entity had the last word. "I still think it ironic that we of the Raggorak should help the descendant of Lahar gain his rightful throne—the throne we denied his father. I just hope we do not regret it!"

———

The boats were flat-bottomed, with high sides that slanted slightly outward. They had sails, but they were built unmistakably for one purpose and one purpose only—to weather the rapids. Even though an experienced riverman was at each of the helms, the trip was still violently hazardous. Kenlahar knew that only a long, meandering detour through the treacherous Tream was more dangerous.

It was the very length of the rapids that was the major problem, every yard of the way a potential sinkhole, capable of capsizing any craft. Though the rivermen constantly updated the maps of the river channels with every report of the scouts, the changing nature of the river often confronted them with sudden danger, and a deep channel could disappear overnight, to be replaced by caved-in bank of the river.

Thus Kenlahar, as the most valuable member of the party, found himself in the last of the Five boats, unaware that in a preceding boat Sanra pretended to sleep, covered from the rain and the eyes of the soldiers. The oars were silent and muffled as the boats were guided into the slower currents.

They passed three campfires of Qreq sentries, moving at what seemed to Kenlahar to be a maddening crawl. The fires winked through the swamp reeds; malevolent eyes searching in the shadows. The boats drifted by the camps silently; none of the party daring to breathe. But no cries arose from the banks and they drifted on, eventually dipping the oars in deep, but muffled strokes.

By morning, it was safe enough to make some noise and Kenlahar could hear Balor's low and increasingly hoarse throat calling out the hazards from the leading boat. When it became light enough to see the shapes of the other boats, Captain Jonla ordered them ashore and by full light the boats lay camouflaged under piles of decaying, rotting swamp grass. Eventually, Kenlahar was even able to sleep through the pesterings of the millions of flying, crawling insects that filled the deep swamp.

The next night's journey brought them to the Statue of Kings. Bigger than the Great Hall, and made of stones bigger than a room, the ancient statue straddled the river the way boys try to straddle creeks. Even after all the time he must have been standing there, Kenlahar could still see the nobility, the royalty, in his face. For years the rivermen had been telling tales of the great statue. But to Kenlahar, seeing it was final proof of the existence of a great civilization — somewhere on the other side of the Tream. The civilization that had built the Statue of Kings could not have disappeared!

Between the massive legs of the statue, Kenlahar could see the swirling white water of the rapids—a terrace of falls, studded by huge boulders. The pilots cried out for the anchors. Only the lead boat continued on, to land on the gravel ramp set below the eastern foot of the statue. Balor sprang ashore, and Kenlahar heard Captain Jonla in the boat at his side mutter, "This is where the Qreq will be waiting for us, if they intend to ambush us. We must carry the boats on the portage around these rapids, and we have to do it in the light of the day. Our only chance is that the Qreq do not know of us—or cannot believe we would attempt a long journey on the river."

After disappearing from view for several anxious minutes, Balor reappeared and waved them in, not very confidently. He met them at the causeway, shrugging his shoulders expressively. "I could detect nothing, but there are many places they could still be hiding among the ruins. Too many places to be examined."

Captain Jonla nodded and ordered sentinels around the perimeter. The other men he set to removing the gear in preparation for carrying the boats on their long portage. Then Balor and Captain Jonla moved off to one side and studied an ancient map, filled to the edge with unfamiliar landmarks and strange names.

Left to his own devices and finding that he only got in the way of the closely structured unloading drill, Kenlahar began to forage about the rubble of one of the statue's legs. He noticed a small hole in the side of the huge stone foot and, half curious and half in an attempt to escape the Lashitu, he crawled into the crevice. The Lashitu had taken to following him, and was becoming somewhat of a pest. He saw with relief that the shaman had evidently decided not to follow after him this time.

Once inside, Kenlahar was surprised to see how large the hollow really was. There was a narrow, circular staircase hugging the inside of the statue's inner walls, and he began to climb it idly. Reaching out, he lifted a brick from its precarious hold in the crumbled mortar of the wall, and skipped the stone down the steep steps. Suddenly, he noticed that someone had recently disturbed the dust of the deserted tunnel. He wondered who else might have visited the ruin, and looked about him uncertainly.

More of the crumbled mortar, bouncing down the steps over him, and an echoing rumble, alerted him to the danger at last. Looking up he saw the vivid sight of Qreq warriors, pale, hairless and brandishing crude spears—and equally surprised, apparently. All stayed frozen for a moment, then Kenlahar turned and flew down the steps five, six at a bound, miraculously gauging his jumps accurately. He dived out the small hole at the bottom, sure that at any moment his legs would feel the bite of a sword. He cried out at the top of his lungs.

The Lashitu joined him, shrieking for help, and pulled him out of the hole. Already, Captain Jonla and Balor had reacted to the shouts and the sight of him. They reached the exit at about the same moment the first of the Qreq warriors dared to poke his head out. Balor's sword flashed, and the Qreq fell back, screaming and leaving his weapon in a pool of blood on the ground outside. Balor laughed triumphantly. "We can keep them in there all day!"

But Captain Jonla's dark face grimly surveyed the terrain, sure that there were other Qreq hiding among the ruins. Suddenly he pointed. Qreq appeared on the other side of the causeway, milling at the edge. "Back to the boats!" he shouted to his men. "Don't wait for us. Cast off!"

The men of Lahar saw at once that the river was their only escape route, though they retreated in a proud, disciplined column and were able to scoop up most of what they had already unloaded. The four Companions at the foot of the statue however, were farthest from the water, and cut off from the main body of warriors. It was quickly evident that the Qreq had been waiting for them, and only because Kenlahar had stumbled on them prematurely did they escape from being completely isolated from the river.

It became a disordered race—a rout—to reach the river's edge before the Qreq caught up with them. They didn't make it. Just a few dozen feet away from the river, Jonla and Balor were forced to turn and face the Qreq at last. At first Kenlahar did not notice the fighting behind him, then he stopped, feeling inexplicably paralyzed. The Lashitu grabbed at his arm, urging him intensely to flee, but Kenlahar did not seem to hear him.

A wedge of Qreq rushed toward Kenlahar, almost overwhelmingly Jonla and Balor who hastened to confront them. "Run, you fool!" he heard Balor shout, as if from a distance. After a brief, violent flurry the surprised Qreq fell back. Balor dropped to one knee, clutching his shoulder, and the sight of his friend falling finally stirred Kenlahar to action. He rushed forward with an alarmed shout, and with the help of the Lashitu, dragged Balor the last few feet to the bank. They dumped him into the boat unceremoniously. Captain Jonla charged the Qreq one last time, showing no sign of his many wounds, and brandishing his sword menacingly with his one good arm. The Qreq hesitated long enough for Jonla to also jump into the boat, casting off just before the Qreq rushed them.

The swift, churning water rapidly carried them away from the spears of the enemy; a spurt of motion so violent that it took Kenlahar by surprise, throwing him backwards into the boat. Four of the boats had made it away, and the other three were already vanishing down the rushing main channel. Captain Jonla somehow managed to pilot their riverboat to one side of the torrent, into slightly calmer water. The crew rowed and steered at the maelstroms edge, straining precariously to hold off the suction of the rapids. Kenlahar held onto the side of the boat in shock. He did not believe that the other boats would survive the rushing white water.

Then he saw bundles of cargo and human arms flailing in the river. The shapes vanished underwater. Some reappeared moments later, desperately attempting to remain afloat; others did not re-emerge until minutes later, far down the river. Most of the objects and bodies did not come back up at all. For a moment Kenlahar thought he saw Sanra's face among the lost men, and he cursed his mind for playing tricks on him. But when the head bobbed up again, he was oddly sure that it was her. He tried shouting at Jonla, but the roaring water drowned out his voice.

When Sanra's head again went under, Kenlahar knew that it was for the last time. Captain Jonla had still made no motions to indicate that he was going to attempt a rescue. Without thinking, Kenlahar dived into the river. His body stiffened as he felt the heavy shock of frigid water. He gasped for breath. The tail end of Captain Jonla's angry shout reached him, but he ignored it. Looking about him desperately, he saw blond hair a few yards away, and a yard underwater. He kicked his legs under the body and locked them, reaching for the head of hair.

Then he was fighting simply to keep both his and Sanra's heads above the swirling water. They were fast approaching another set of plunging falls when he felt something trying to lift him up by the back of his tunic. But he desperately held onto Sanra, and did not let go until he saw her lifted safely into the riverboat. Then he let go. He felt himself going under just before strong arms caught him under his armpits.

Once inside the boat he pressed his face thankfully to* its rough wood sides, wishing to never move again. "The Star Axe!" someone was shouting into his ears over the thunder of the falls. "Do you still have the Star Axe?"

His stab of fear turned to an equally strong lift of relief as he searched under his cloak and his fingers encountered the blade. He told himself to wonder later why the metal head had not dragged him under. Then he passed out.

When he awoke, he was still in the same cramped position, but the boat was at last motionless. His cheek was half-stuck to the side of the boat where it had pressed, apparently for many hours. Surveying his surroundings, he saw that the boat was tied precariously to the root of a tree, uncovered by the crumbling bank. Below, a finger peninsula of pitted gray jutted out into the river's flow, catching what little flotsam survived the rapids. The river looked deceptively calm now, the roaring of the rapids a dull throb in the background. Kenlahar cursed the dark water, the life and death dealing River Danjar.

Sanra lay beside him, evidently well, breathing deeply. But the Lashitu was nowhere in sight, and Kenlahar wondered briefly if he had also been lost in the river. Maybe a dozen others were in view—half of who lay sprawled asleep or injured. The others were setting camp, building a fire, or standing guard.

Captain Jonla and Balor stood balancing on a large rock between the boat and the steep bank. They were arguing again, and had not noticed yet that he was awake. Balor, he saw, had a crude bandage on his shoulder.

"I say we go on by river," he was shouting. "We still have a boat, and a map that shows us a clear route—and some of the men are too wounded to go on by foot." "No," Captain Jonla answered, as if he had been repeating himself for some time. "The Qreq know we are on the river now. All they need to do is wait for us—there is no way we could avoid another ambush. But if we melt into the Tream, they will never find us." "Yes, and *we* would be lost as well. The best way to avoid the Qreq is to be swift, and the quickest route is by the River Danjar.'"

"It is my decision to make," Captain Jonla said with finality. "We will abandon the river and strike east. We will stay here for one day, to wait for any survivors, and to rest up. It will take the Qreq at least that long to arrive here by foot."

Kenlahar tried to get up, and moaned at the sudden pain in his cramped muscles. The two men fell silent, looking at him questioningly. But they made no comment, or any movement to help him as he climbed up the bank and hobbled to the fire. Kenlahar saw the accusing looks of the men of the Watch and he wondered what had happened to change their attitudes. Warming himself from the flames of the fire, he said through chattering teeth, "Bring the wounded to the fire. If possible everyone else should wear dry clothing; if not, stay near the fire. I will also need a sharp knife and boiling water."

"Do as he says," Captain Jonla commanded, and then said to Kenlahar in an undertone, "Heal Balor's shoulder first, if you can. I am going to need someone who has sense and will *fight*."

Kenlahar winced at the barb, for it was obviously directed at him alone. It was only then, as Captain Jonla walked contemptuously away, that Kenlahar remembered the Star Axe. Why had he not thought to use it in the fight? he thought. That was the question in the eyes of the warriors! The accusation had even been in the look that Balor had given him. He reflected on how little the Star Axe seemed to weigh—he had almost forgotten he carried it. But he could not use that as an excuse. Though there seemed little point in concealing the Star Axe now, his instinct still told him not to use it in violence if he could possibly delay that day. Besides, he thought, rebelliously, he wanted to cling to his Atima for as long as he could.

Balor's wound turned out to be shallow, and Kenlahar decided that the chief risk was of infection. He pulled the precious leaves of the herb Coron had called Earthsmoke from his pouch, and applied it generously to every wound. It will spoil soon anyway, he thought, after having become so sodden in the rain and the river. Only one of the warriors would have had to be carried, and though the wound to his leg should not have been fatal, he died in a short time. As a precaution, Kenlahar compelled them all to quaff yet another herb, that which Coron had called Sweetbark, which he boiled in the remaining hot water. If the Qreq had begun poisoning their weapons, as the Swamp People were wont to do, they would be readied. Balor refused to say anything to him as Kenlahar worked on his wounded shoulder, and walked away after the bandage had been applied. For the first time the friendship between Balor and Kenlahar was strained.

When Kenlahar had at last finished he went to Sanra's side. She had still not woken. He bathed her face with the Sweetbark, and she stirred but did not waken. Kenlahar could see no injuries on her frame and concluded that she had withdrawn into sleep.

He turned from the fire worriedly just as the Lashitu appeared to greet him with news of an auspicious communion with the god Lahar. The shaman had apparently gone off alone to pray to his god, Kenlahar thought. He nodded grimly—it seemed ironic that the Lashitu should be the only one of them cheerful on this day.

"Kenlahar?" he heard behind him, and turned to see Sanra finally sitting up. She was searching the darkness for him with blurry eyes. He hurried into the light of the fire. "I'm sorry, Kenlahar," she said. "I had to follow you. I was afraid I would lose you."

"Yes, Sanra," he said gently. "It's all right."

"I didn't mean to cause trouble by following you," she said again, dazed. "It's just that I was sure that I would lose you forever if I let you go off without me." "I know, Sanra. Go to sleep now. We can talk later." Kenlahar stayed by her awhile longer, cupping her head in his arms, until she began to breathe evenly. He laid her head down carefully on his blanket, and left the fire. He searched for Captain Jonla in the dark, finding him at last sitting alone by the boat, staring out onto the surface of the river.

44

"What are you going to do about Sanra?" he asked abruptly.

"Do?" Captain Jonla answered, startled. But he refused to pull his eyes from the River Danjar. "What else can I do? The girl will have to come with us." Kenlahar started to object, but Jonla suddenly grabbed his arm and pointed out into the darkness! "There!" he hissed. "Do you see it?"

Kenlahar winced and strained his eyes in an effort to see something in the flashing reflections of moonlight in the dark flow. He was just about the turn and say that he could see nothing when he caught sight of what looked like the shadow of a twisted log pass over one of the patterns of light. "Come with me!" Captain Jonla shouted, jumping into the boat and slicing the rope with his sword.

"What is it?" Kenlahar asked, barely making it aboard the craft before it pulled away from the bank. "Can you see what it is?"

"I'm hoping…1 pray it is one of my men." Kenlahar was unaccustomed to rowing and soon Captain Jonla was cursing at his ineptitude. But they managed to make some lopsided progress toward the object. Soon Kenlahar saw that it was one of their own boats, turned over, with the body of a large man draped over its hull. Jonla grabbed at the body and struggled to lift it. When Kenlahar added his strength, the body flopped into the boat. After more ineffective rowing by Kenlahar, and more cursing more Jonla, they reached shore. They barely avoided capsizing their own craft pulling it onto the bank.

It took four healthy men to carry the man the few yards from the bank to the fire. Kenlahar rolled him over with some effort and caught his breath. It was Jakkem! Kenlahar bathed the face of the half drowned and half frozen man with the last of the Sweetbark. The herb and the warm fire seemed to revive the unconscious man after some time, and Jakkem's eyes opened. They showed fear. But the furtive glances he sent about the camp seemed to reassure him, and Kenlahar thought he caught a kind of veiled slyness come over the man's features, to disappear just as quickly.

"Did you see any others?" Captain Jonla demanded. "Did anyone else escape?"

Kenlahar judged that the look of terror that crossed Jakkem's face was real. "The Qreq were waiting for us on the banks," he said. "They dragged us off into the Tream if we came ashore and…" he shuddered, and grabbed Captain Jonla's arm. "I heard them screaming."

"All of them? Were they all killed?"

"Most of us stayed in the river, to drown rather than face that!" Jakkem coughed weakly and shut his eyes. "I was the last. Then I saw the overturned boat drifting by. That is all I remember clearly."

Captain Jonla continued to question him, until Kenlahar reluctantly saved him from further interrogation. "This man must mend if he is to travel with us," he announced.

The Healer Coron would have been truly proud of his conscientiousness, he thought, for there was one question he very much wanted to ask the man as well. Indeed, Kenlahar found it puzzling that the question had not already been asked by Captain Jonla, and just as difficult to believe that the old warrior had not seen what Kenlahar had seen. He had been certain that he had recognized the overturned boat they had pulled Jakkem from. It had been the one craft the Companions had abandoned in their escape—left securely tied and surrounded by Qreq at the portage!

CHAPTER VI

No other survivors appeared on the river over the next two days, though Captain Jonla never left his vigil on the shore—all of which seemed to bear out the story Jakkem had given. But the fact that no other bodies or flotsam drifted down, Kenlahar thought, justified his own suspicions as well. How had Jakkem managed to stay afloat when nothing else had? he wanted to ask.

Most of the wounded made rapid recoveries, especially Jakkem. After just a few hours, Jakkem did not look anything like a man who had spent a half a day in the freezing water. Indeed, to Kenlahar he looked healthier than almost anyone else. This miracle also did nothing to allay Kenlahar's fears. But he said nothing, for Jakkem had inexplicably become a favorite of Captain Jonla. Jonla was keeping the big man beside him, and over the next few days Jakkem grew bolder in his taunts. While Captain Jonla did not encourage Jakkem's jeers, he did nothing to stop him either.

Balor had become uncharacteristically withdrawn and sullen. Kenlahar feared that like the other warriors, Balor held him responsible for the disaster that had befallen them. Every stage of the trek seemed to be wearing down the esteem the warriors had originally held for Kenlahar as Axe-bearer. When no marvels had ensued, and Kenlahar had not even used the Star Axe to save the other Companions, the warriors of the Watch had begun to regard him almost with scorn.

Balor did not join in the hostility, but he too seemed hurt by Kenlahar's failure.

Kenlahar was .too preoccupied with Sanra's recovery to be sensitive to the glares. She had slept almost to the time of departure, waking occasionally to the disconcerting questions from Kenlahar. But she reassured him that she was well. With the Lashitu hovering solicitously nearby, these three stayed isolated from the others.

Finally, the two days of the deathwatch ended and they scuttled the boat, removing all signs of their camp. For the first few days into the swamp, Captain Jonla led the troop quickly and expertly through the traps and snares of the Tream. The swamp was a mire of shifting pools and treacherous earth, death to any but the Swamp People. Even the primitive clans of the Tream rarely ventured far from the more hospitable climate of that part of the swamp that bordered the River Danjar.

It was still early in the rainy season, and they were able to wade through most of the pools, being careful to avoid the quicksand. They quickly disregarded any attempt to keep clean or dry. They would jump from rock to rock; or from the base of one tree to the base of another; or to any spot that offered a chance of firm footing. Kenlahar and the Lashitu, who were unused to any heavy exercise, and especially Sanra, who was still very weak, were barely able to maintain the fast pace. They became a small group of stragglers. The true Companions of the Star Axe, he thought bitterly—an apprentice healer, a younger woman, and a madman!

The blisters came first, then the aches. Kenlahar did what he could with his herbs, but the toll on their bodies seemed to accumulate much faster than his remedies. After a while, as the unceasing rain continued to pour down on them, each Companion wrapped his cloak a little tighter around himself, and withdrew into his own world, peering miserable out into the drizzle. Each Companion seemed to clutch one object, one garment, which he tried to keep dry, to remind him of what it was like to be warm and comfortable. They soon became immured to the rain, resigned that they would never escape it. Fires were all but impossible to light, and it seemed that half of the warriors load consisted of dry wood.

Everywhere the patrol saw the giant snails that played such an important part of the Swamp People's lives—as food, and as religious symbols. Kenlahar looked at the slow moving creatures distastefully. They smelled from yards away and were impossible to avoid.

Captain Jonla ordered them not to harm the animals, but to set them gently aside. "The People of the Cormat may be watching us even now," he warned, and his men looked at the barren landscape doubtfully, nervously.

Kenlahar was feeling more and more alone and miserable as the time passed and the landscape stayed - the same. The rain was beginning to freeze, chilling them if they quit moving for even a moment. But soon, the three of them would gladly have suffered the cold if they could have stopped. Balor volunteered to be the lead scout and was ahead of the other Companions most of the time. The other warriors of the Watch made no attempt to help Kenlahar, or his two fellow stragglers. They found themselves slipping and falling constantly behind the sure-footed scouts. By mid-afternoon of the third day, Kenlahar sensed that Sanra would soon be unable to keep up with the others. Reluctantly, he approached Captain Jonla and asked for a few minutes of rest. Jonla looked at him with disdain, but his eyes carefully examined Sanra. Then he turned away and said, "We shall stop at the next island."

Kenlahar looked to where Jonla had indicated, and shook his head tiredly. He knew that, even at the speed with which they were moving, it would be a good hour before they reached their destination. But he would not protest again. Instead he satisfied himself by helping Sanra toward the distant island.

They were wading through one last patch of the fen that could not be avoided—as happened more and more frequently the farther they traveled from the river—when Kenlahar felt one of his legs kicked out from under him. He fell with an astonished shout, and his arms sunk into the muck up to his elbows. He struggled to rise from the grasping mud. When he at last freed himself, with Sanra's help, he heard a mocking laughter behind him. He turned angrily and saw Jakkem leering at him. His body filled with rage.

With a speed that surprised them all, he tackled Jakkem, bringing the big man down hard. Kenlahar found himself in the unexpected position of crouching over the stunned warrior with his fist raised, but he was unable to rid himself of the training of a healer and could not strike the man. After warding off a few wild punches from below, he got off his enemy.

The two men faced each other, and warriors drew in a circle around them. His opponent dwarfed Kenlahar, and Jakkem smiled with satisfaction. "You fight like a child," he sneered. "I will show you what happens when you attack a Quarrier."

Despite himself, Kenlahar looked desperately around him for help. But this time Balor was nowhere to be seen, and Captain Jonla remained off to one side, appearing to study the path before them. Suddenly, the silence was broken as the warriors began exhorting and cheering. Kenlahar was surprised to hear more than a few encouragements for himself. Apparently Jakkem was not at all popular among his comrades. But Kenlahar realized that the man he was fighting was twice his size and trained to fight. The battle would be over quickly, and Kenlahar did not believe he could be the winner.

So far, Jakkem had not drawn a weapon, and Kenlahar was ashamed of himself for surreptitiously feeling the blade of the Star Axe. But now Jakkem was on his feet and Kenlahar no longer felt constrained from hitting him with his fists. He remembered how Balor had fought Jakkem and he struck out with his clenched hands, but his blows were ineffectual. At the last moment he pulled back from the full force of his thrusts, for he could not relinquish the training of a lifetime. Jakkem merely grunted as the blows glanced off him and, crouching, slid under Kenlahar's arms. He started to squeeze.

As Kenlahar began to lose consciousness, he realized dimly that Jakkem meant to kill him. He was aware that both Sanra and the Lashitu had fallen on Jakkem's broad back, striking the warrior wildly, to no avail. Finally, Captain Jonla stepped in, sharply ordering Jakkem to release Kenlahar. Even so, Jonla was forced to order two other warriors to help him pry Jakkem's arms from his deadly grip around Kenlahar.

"I will have no more fights," he said harshly, as if he had not allowed it to happen in the first place. "It is my duty to see this man to Swamp's End, and intend to see him there alive. I will not have him hurt!"

———————

Kenlahar laughed bitterly as he remembered Captain Jonla's words. His laugh turned abruptly into a groan as Balor tied a truss around his sore chest, with the concerned advice of Sanra. Balor had returned just in time to find Kenlahar being carried unconscious the last few yards to the island, and he had hurriedly built a campfire a small distance from the fires of the Watch. "They tell me that you had him down, Kenlahar. Why did you not strike him while you had the chance?"

"I don't know," Kenlahar moaned. "Next time you can be sure that I will." Except for his first brief, surprising burst of fury, his opponent had obviously had the best of the fight. Kenlahar doubted that he had even drawn Jakkem's blood—thus, perhaps, keeping his Atima despite his best efforts. At least Balor had decided to forgive him, it seemed, so Jakkem may have done him that much of a favor.

"He is good in a brawl," Balor said of Jakkem as he laid out their bedrolls. "It is probably the only thing he is good for." He paused, and then said hurriedly, as if he were unaccustomed to apologizing, "I am sorry for not speaking to you these last few days. If I had been around, this would not have happened. I warned him to leave you alone! I will make sure that Jakkem never has a chance to come near you again."

"No, Balor," Kenlahar said. "He won't come after me again. Captain Jonla will see to that. Besides, it was I who attacked him. Let it rest." Still, Kenlahar wondered if he should have told Balor of his suspicions about Jakkem. There was nothing substantial to tell his friend, just a few unguarded glances from Jakkem, full of hate and malice, and the boat, which could not have come free unless the Qreq had wanted it free. That these suspicions had no support in evidence would not keep the mercurial Balor from killing Jakkem if he thought the big man was a traitor. Kenlahar decided it was up to him to keep

51

the matter from reaching that point. Later he was to realize that if he had told someone, he could have perhaps saved many other lives.

"Sing the Song of Lahar," he urged suddenly.

Balor did not seem surprised at the request, for the ancient music had often sustained the two friends before. He pulled a small stringed instrument from his pack and began tuning the wet strings. Soon the first few chords of the Song of Lahar were filling the small island. He began chanting the many stanzas of the Song of Lahar in its dateless, forgotten language: Though unintelligible it did not matter—every child knew the tale.

Then Balor began to interpret the story in his own flowery prose of the common tongue, strumming his instrument with strong, clean chords of accompaniment. His clear voice rang out with fervor, as he set forth his own prelude to the ancient tale.

"Behold! The god Lahar!

"On the night of his coming, the celestial sphere orchestrated even the mood of its heavenly light. The nine-score constellations of the Starborn, arrayed in splendid gallery, hearkened to his arrival. The adored Sistern joined as one to greet him. Even Bantling bowed to his coming.

"Behold! The evil Toraq, Sorcerer King of Kernback!

"Long did he brood in his hate. Deep did he delve the primeval depths, where foul creatures did dwell. So Toraq assailed the Starborn, with all manner of fell beasts, and hosts of men corrupted.

"Behold! The wondrous Alcress!

"Wrought in the hallowed armory of the Starborn, and possessed of divers shapes and powers. With his mighty Star Axe, Lahar did sunder the scepter of Toraq, and in his wrath smote the winged helm of Kernback, casting down the Sorcerer King.

"Behold! The treacherous Raggorak!

"Five-headed Council of Starborn, Lieutenants of Lahar—and betrayers of the Troth! They banished Lahar to the Tream to die.

"Behold! The Song of Lahar!"

As Balor began to sing the full song, Kenlahar realized that it had been a mistake to request the recitation. Before, the Sorcerer King had been a mythical evil, and the Warlord's true nature had been a mercifully kept secret. Now the Star Axe hung from his neck, and the Qreq pursued him.

Balor's full, rich voice rose and fell with the rhythmic flow of the Song of Lahar. Buoyant and lifting in the beginning, as it told of Lahar's coming to his world; the song grew harsh as it told of war with the tyrant Toraq; then peaceful and harmonious as it related the wise monarchy of Lahar—and finally, it became a sad, dirge-like chant as it described Lahar's fall from power and exile to the Tream.

The fire was dying down, and Kenlahar wished they were all asleep if only to escape the cold night air. The misting rain never seemed to stop, and by now every bit of clothing he had brought with him was soaked either by the rain or the river. Above, one of the Sistern moved imperceptibly between the outlines of two dark trees. They settled back in wet, musky blankets.

Just as he was sure that everyone else was asleep, Kenlahar heard the low voice of Balor.

"Let me give you some counsel, Kenlahar," his friend said sleepily. "Don't push Sanra and yourself so hard. Don't let Captain Jonla wear you down. Make him go at your pace. After all, remember who you are!"

He was surprised to hear Sanra, at his other side, also speak, "What does Captain Jonla have against Kenlahar?"

"You don't know?" Balor seemed surprised. "No, I guess you wouldn't. Captain Jonla believes that Kenlahar let his men die at the Statue of Kings by not using the Star Axe. He also thinks that Kenlahar is running away, that he should have stayed at the House of Lahar and faced the Warlord."

There was a few seconds of stunned silence, and Kenlahar reflected with some resentment that he had not asked to attempt this quest. He had not wanted to possess the Star Axe. And now he had fallen short in the eyes of Jonla and the disillusioned warriors.

Balor then continued in a thoughtful tone, "What I think really bothers Captain Jonla is that you are finally doing what he has always wanted to do himself. Captain Jonla is a valuable man and the Elders have held him tightly to keep him from going Outside. Still, they say that he has seen more of the Tream than any other man of the House of

Lahar. Do not misjudge him, Kenlahar. You are the bearer of the Star Axe and he will do what is right for you in the end."

It was the Lashitu's turn to speak up and he irritably told them to shut up.

After a while, when their breathing told him that they were all asleep, Kenlahar gently woke Balor again. "If anything happens, take care of Sanra first. Protect her, Balor! If the Star Axe cannot protect me, the quest is senseless anyway. Promise me this, Balor."

Balor could not think, in his groggy stage, of any situation where he would not be able to protect them both. He promised readily, "All right, Kenlahar. Get some sleep."

As the young healer tried once more to sleep, his thoughts began to turn back to the fight. He tried to block the thoughts out, but they kept filtering through. Finally, he quit resisting, and let his thoughts flow where they would. At last, his deep weariness proved stronger than his fear.

The next day, Captain Jonla once again set a brisk pace. Now that Kenlahar was aware of what Jonla was trying to do to them, he resolved not to complain again. He found unexpected comfort by secretly fondling the Star Axe beneath his cloak. The blade seemed to restore some strength to his legs, enough even to enable him to help Sanra as well. Balor had chosen to stay with them for a while. He saw the effort Kenlahar was making and shook his head in exasperation. But he said nothing, merely helping them when the terrain was rough.

Over the next few days the terrain remained difficult and the rain unrelenting. Captain Jonla was still leading the company quickly and surely, and Kenlahar and Sanra kept up as much as their sore muscles would allow. The Lashitu had proved to be tougher and wirier than Kenlahar had thought possible, but even so, it was the shaman who complained the most about the cruel pace.

The Lashitu was as small as Kenlahar, and almost as dark—the effects of age. Kenlahar did not know how old the shaman was, but he seemed dried up with years. Sanra's clothes were caked with mud and her face was streaked with dirt. Yet she remained willing and uncomplaining. Each night the Companions would sit apart from the others, as though they were an unneeded addition, Kenlahar thought, rather than the very reason for the mission.

Yet, finally even Captain Jonla began to slow his pace noticeably. Several times Jonla was forced to stop and survey the trail. Balor was sent forward once again to explore. Late one afternoon, Captain Jonla called Kenlahar to him. "This is as far as I've ever come," he said. "We are entering the lands of the Swamp People now. I do not know how they will receive us. It is my hope that they will ignore our trespass. Still, it will be much rougher going from now on."

"We will keep up," Kenlahar said proudly, defiantly.

Captain Jonla turned and looked him over carefully before locking gazes with him. "Yes, I think maybe you will. I have been watching you, and you have done better than I expected. And now I will apologize and explain my hurry. We have been traveling steadily northward and this winter will bring a cold such as you have never felt. I hope to spare us the worst of it by reaching Swamp's End before the first snows." He started to walk away, but then hesitated. He turned for one last word. "It is time that you helped stand guard."

Kenlahar's duty turned out to be simply staying awake at the edge of the camp, beside their fire, something that was not very difficult for him to do. The other sentries were obviously expected to be the real shields. Still, he was happy that Captain Jonla at last trusted him enough to include him in the company.

He had not long been on watch when he heard a new sound between the croaking and squeaking that everyone else in the patrol seemed to take for granted. At first he wasn't sure that this new din was not just another strange animal, one he had not heard yet. It would have to be a very strange creature, he thought, to let off such a booming roaring sound!

He was saved from having to make more of a judgment when—or so it seemed in the dim light—Balor jumped vertically from his prone position beside the fire. The warrior just as abruptly threw himself back down again, this time with Kenlahar crushed beneath him. The healer cried out in alarm, but was certain that Balor could not hear his shout through the racket. At least Balor did nothing to answer him, but instead seemed intent on attempting the impossible task of pulling on his armor without once letting go of his grip on his sword.

Captain Jonla strode through the camp, yelling commands that no one could hear. But by motioning he was able to create some order among the soldiers. Then, just as unexpectedly as it had started, the roaring ceased. Captain Jonla's voice could now be clearly heard. "In a circle!" he was shouting. "No—stay away from the fires, you fools! Notch your arrows."

Then there was a surprising silence. Even the persistent droning of the animals and insects had stopped. Kenlahar and Sanra had been put in the middle of the circle of men. He fingered the blade of Alcress, realizing foolishly that it still did not have a handle, and wondering of what possible use it would be if he were captured. It was the last time he would have a weapon that was useless! he vowed. Away from the fire they began to get cold, but they did not dare move. The men crouched without stirring, facing outward into a long, dark night.

As light slowly crept over the horizon, Kenlahar saw a strange sight. Surrounding the protective circle of men was a circle of arrows, with one for each man, driven into the soft ground only inches away from their feet. Still, the men of Lahar crouched without moving. Nothing stirred in the swamp and little by little the Tream resumed its former noisy existence. But just as Kenlahar began to relax in the warm light of morning, the roaring started again.

Out of the low reeds stepped a young girl. She was small and dark, with long black braids that fell to her shoulders. A ragged, splotched brown dress reached her knees. She wore nothing on her feet. When one of the men in front of Kenlahar drew back an arrow threateningly, he was immediately speared by a score of arrows that seemed to come from nowhere. "Do not move!" Captain Jonla shouted urgently.

As the swampgirl approached Kenlahar saw that, despite her size, she was at least as old as he and, despite the heavy layer of dirt on her face, she was also very pretty. When she stopped in front of the circle of men, the roaring ceased. She spoke with a strange, slurred accent. "Why have you invaded our lands?"

Captain Jonla stepped forward with his arms stretched harmlessly in front of him. "Peace to you, sister. We wish the Swamp People no harm."

The girl simply repeated her question. "Why have you invaded our lands?"

"We wish to reach Swamp's End." Captain Jonla waved his arms to the north. "Beyond the swamp..." The swampgirl frowned briefly, "Swamp's End?" Then she nodded and said, "Follow me." As she turned to lead the way, Captain Jonla ordered his men to follow her in single file. Balor took up the point again, just behind the girl, and tried to talk with her. Kenlahar and Sanra, with their shadow, the Lashitu, followed him. The rest of the company and Captain Jonla brought up the rear.

Kenlahar could not see the other Swamp People at first, but when he looked back he saw two small dark men stripping the dead soldier. As they neared a large and comparatively dry wooded island, Kenlahar saw other men on either side of them, stepping in and out of the shadows of the swamp. The loud booming sounded again and Kenlahar noticed one of the swampmen blowing into a large shell. The cries of children and the barking of dogs answered it. Naked children came out of the trees and danced around the troop as it wound its ways into the village. Dogs snapped at their heels.

They abruptly entered a large clearing in the center of the island. Small mud huts dotted the clearing, and women were sitting in the entrances of the huts cleaning out the large shells that decorated all the buildings. Old men sat talking around a large bonfire in the middle of the clearing. At the other end of the village, a party of men entered carrying baskets of shells on their back.

All talking and working ceased when the troop approached the village. They were marched up to the largest hut and stopped at its low entrance. Kenlahar thought that it must look incongruous to see the tall blond warriors of Lahar helpless and surrounded by their grimy escort of swampmen. No wonder the people of the House of Lahar had always viewed him suspiciously! He looked more appropriate among the dark swampmen than he did among his own kind. The villagers surrounding them were silent, the parents looking dirty and grim, and the children wide eyed.

The swampgirl ducked into the doorway and reappeared a second later with a large man, wearing a magnificent white beard that reached his chest. Under the beard was a large paunch and a voice that boomed, "They call me the Cormatine."

Jonla stepped forward. "I am Captain Jonla and these are free men of the House of Labor. Why have you stopped us? We mean you no harm. We wish only to reach Swamp's End."

The voice of the man was loud and powerful, seemingly without effort. "We know who you are, Captain Jonla. We have seen you many times as you have wandered our lands. We did not stop you, for you did no harm. But now you have entered the Tream—with a large party of armed men—on the Day of the Cormat.

This cannot be allowed." The Cormatine's voice echoed in the clearing.

One of the swampmen cried out, "The Tryst!" and others took up the cry in the clearing. The Cormatine allowed the shouts to go on for some time, and then raised his arms in silence. "The People of the Cormat have demanded the Tryst. One of you must submit. If he lives you will all go free. If he fails you—you will all be sacrificed to the Cormat."

The leader of the swampmen let his eyes wander over the men of the House of Lahar. Kenlahar felt the eyes pass over him once and then come back to him. He wondered if he imagined the speculative look the Cormatine gave him.

"Who will dare the Tryst?" Kenlahar was now sure that the Cormatine was looking at him alone, and he felt a compulsion to make himself known. Balor and Kenlahar stepped forward at the same moment. "Get back, Kenlahar!" his friend said harshly.

The Cormatine smiled and motioned toward Kenlahar. Two of the swampmen took his arms and led him away from the troop. Behind him, he could hear the protests of Balor, which were cut off abruptly as Kenlahar was pushed into the hut and the door slammed behind him.

"Take me!" Balor demanded. "Let me be the one." When the Cormatine continued to ignore him, he broke away from his guards and lunged for the swamp leader.

The Cormatine motioned again. Balor was stopped far from his goal, and dragged to another of the huts on the opposite side of the village. The door slammed shut behind him as well, and he heard and saw no more.

CHAPTER VII

There were no windows in his prison, and it was dark, except for the few shafts of light through the cracks of the door. Kenlahar did not know how long he spent in the darkness of his prison. But the time passed slowly, and he had enough time to fully regret his hasty decision. Balor or Jonla would have been more qualified to take any test, he thought ruefully.

When the door finally opened, the new day's light blinded him. The Cormatine stepped into the hovel, closing the door behind him, and carrying a small torch that he set in the wall. In his other hand was one of the large snail shells, which he pushed towards Kenlahar. "Drink this," he commanded.

"What is it?"

"It is the blood of the Cormat. Drink it!"

Kenlahar put the shell to his lips and tasted a small amount. It was bitter, and had a strong fishy flavor, but it was not unpleasant. He drank the rest of it slowly. Is this the Tryst? he wondered. He sat on the floor and waited for something to happen. His eyes fastened on the torch and he watched the flames dance. The flames slowed down so that it seemed he could watch each flame as it reached its peak and then settle again.

Then his mind exploded. From far off he heard the Cormatine's voice. Without thinking, his head turned and he stared into pale eyes. He felt himself sinking into them, their life attracting his emptiness as a piece of wood is sucked under by an undertow. The descent was stopped by a loud voice. "Kenlahar!" The ceiling was blurring through watering eyes. It was exertion to blink. The eyes slipped slowly over the surface of the ceiling, unable to stay in one place without effort.

The pestering voice paused seductively, and Kenlahar felt the first faint urge to answer. The loud voice continued on in a conversational level. Kenlahar felt himself drawn to it. "Kenlahar!" He found himself answering and immediately felt betrayed. He had not intended to talk. The sound of his name had jerked him around, and before he knew it he wanted to answer more than he' had ever wanted anything. He felt euphoric.

"Kenlahar...you will answer each question truthfully and completely. You cannot lie to me. I can make you do or say anything— and make you forget everything afterward. Do you understand?"

"Yes." Kenlahar felt happy to forget.

"Now...what do you know of the Nameless Ones—the Raggorak?"

Kenlahar began to gladly tell all he knew, but he was cut off.

"That is enough. You do not know much and yet too much." The Cormatine paused. "Do you believe they really exist?"

"I was not sure." Kenlahar laughed. "Now I am. You are one. The Healer Coron was one!"

"You are very clever, Kenlahar. You got that with amazingly few clues. That's good. But you will forget this. Now for the most important question...what would you do to the Raggorak?"

Kenlahar felt a cloud on his delirious happiness. "I would destroy them," he answered.

The Cormatine seemed taken aback. "Why?"

"Because I do not wish for my people to be controlled when they are not aware of it. I will not allow you do to me what you did to my father."

"I see. If it were up to me you would die right now, even if it did mean a victory for Toraq. Nevertheless, you did pass the Tryst, and the Star Axe has decided. I will wait."

Kenlahar's awareness had splintered and with one part of his mind he continued to answer the Cormatine's questions; another part of him bore down on a sense of wrongness. He concentrated on his feeling of evil, slowly eliminating everything from his awareness but the cause of his discomfort. At the same time, he continued to mindlessly answer the Cormatine's insistent questions.

He found and identified the evil, and his awareness rejoined to find himself saying many things of danger to the Companions—while being unable to tell the swamp leader of the danger to his own people. His muscles would not respond to his urgings and the Cormatine would not ask the one question that would save them. At last, the Cormatine seemed satisfied. He rose and called for a guard to open the door. "Now, you will sleep, Kenlahar. You will forget all that we have talked about today."

───────

It was dark in Balor's prison and he felt the door again, but it was still locked tight. He was sitting back down on the bare floor when he heard a noise at the back of the hut. A square of not quite blackness opened near the floor and then was blocked off as someone scuffled through. Balor backed into the corner and stayed silent, catching his breath as the intruder walked directly toward him. A hand brushed across his face, and he grabbed at it violently. "Who are you?" he hissed.

"Quiet!" he heard the intruder whisper, and he recognized the slurred accent of the young swampgirl. "I wish to help you!" She took his hand and started to lead him to the back of the hut. "I can lead you to Swamp's End."

"Wait!" Balor held back. "Why do you do this? What of the others?"

"I cannot do anything for them!" When Balor still did not move she said, "I do not have time to answer questions. Save yourself!"

"No! We have to try to set Kenlahar free. He who is to take the Tryst!"

"It is impossible!" But she hesitated as she saw that he meant what he said. "I will try." She ducked out of the opening.

After a few seconds, still suspecting a trap, Balor scrambled after her. Outside, both moons of the Sistern were full and the sky was glittering, full of stars. Balor could see clearly from their light. They crept around the hut until he could see the guards at his door. Beyond, the central village fire still burned and he could see that there was some kind of celebration going on around it. Figures danced in the light of the bonfire, and the sound of singing drifted over to him.

The swampgirl caught his attention and pointed to the small hut where Kenlahar had been taken, at the edge of the village. He nodded. They ran to the shadows of the next hut, and he breathed a little easier now that they were out of sight of his guards. They worked their way to the small hut, running from building to building.

As they neared their goal, Balor saw that there was only one guard. He sighed in relief. Apparently they did not fear Kenlahar very much. One guard he could disable, with surprise on his side. He motioned for the girl to wait and then went to the darkness at the edge of the village and groped on the ground until he found a stout piece of wood. He worked his way around the hut and came up behind the guard, inching forward and hefting the club in his hand. He wondered how hard to strike, and then the guard turned his back to him.

Balor took two steps forward and brought the branch down hard on the guard's head. The branch broke and the guard slumped, unconscious. Balor dragged the guard to the side while the girl ran up and cut the fastenings of the door. She threw it open.

The interior was silent and pitch black. Looking questioningly at the swampgirl, Balor cautiously entered, his hand extended blindly. He slowly ventured his right foot along the ground until he stumbled over something. Now that his eyes were adjusting to the deeper darkness, he could distinguish the shape of Kenlahar on the floor.

"He has taken the blood of the Cormat," the swampgirl whispered. Her tone grew urgent and insistent. "Hurry, he is drugged!"

Balor knelt beside his friend and shook him gently, and then with force. Kenlahar woke groggily. He could remember nothing of what had happened during the Tryst.

"Hurry, we must go!" the swampgirl said again, and pulled Balor to the door.

"I will not leave without the others," Kenlahar said, still sweating and shaking from the effects of the drug.

Balor stood in the doorway, hesitating. The swamp- girl's insistent tug on his arm stopped suddenly. "I cannot save you now!" she said and disappeared into the darkness.

Seconds later, guards marched up to the large hut. But they did not even see Balor and Kenlahar in their fury until they were within just a few feet. Then Balor stepped into the light of their torches, showing his hands, and they jumped back in alarm. But when he made no threatening motions they angrily rushed the two men of Lahar.

The guards, deadly silent, marched the Axe-bearer and Companion up to the ceremonial hut. One pounded on the door. Inside, they expected to find another dank and dark hovel, but instead boisterous voices, somehow deadened by thin reed walls, greeted their entrance. The Cormatine turned from the head of a long woven table and, grinning broadly, raised a tankard in welcome. "So—you have returned to us!" he boomed.

Dismayed, they let themselves he led the rest of the way into the room. The celebration was nearing its conclusion and the hut was overcrowded with the important members of the swamp village— identifiable by the fact that they had more meat on their bones and were not quite as filthy as the rest. They had been dismissed from notice— apparently they had been satisfied the two would not try to leave without their Companions.

The Cormatine was spooning out cupfuls of some liquid, and as the aroma reached Kenlahar he suddenly felt that there was something about the fluid he should remember. As the Cormatine neared the end of his ceremonial chant and began to raise the cup to his lips, with the others following his example, Kenlahar remembered. With a cry, he sprang forward and dashed the cup from the Cormatine's lips.

In astonishment, the others did not drink from their mugs—except for one man who had evidently had too much of another kind of drink already. The guards had already begun to raise their daggers, outraged by the sacrilege, when the man shrieked and fell from his chair. He saved Kenlahar's life by losing—horribly—his own.

Within a few minutes he was dead.

The Cormatine stared at him, while the others reacted by hastily dumping the contents of their cups. Their leader also poured the deadly poison onto the ground before him, and then did a strange thing. He grabbed the bag containing the potion and handed it to Kenlahar.

"Pour it from your hand to my cup," he commanded. When Kenlahar had done as he was told, the Cormatine took a long draught of the liquid. The others gasped in surprise, but when he did not fall over stunned, they began to look on Kenlahar with a new, almost worshipping respect. Then the Cormatine dropped reverently to his knee.

"You are now our Cormatine," he said. "The Cormat has chosen you. He speaks through you now." In an undertone he quickly explained to Kenlahar the customs of his people. "In the right hands, the blood of the Cormat is a healing agent. In all others it becomes a deadly poison. No one knows before the change whether he is still the Cormatine—or how long he will hold the power before he passes on to someone else. But if it was poison when you tasted it," he concluded, puzzled, "why did you not die? If it was not poison, how did you know?"

"I just knew..." Kenlahar said. How could he explain how he had detected the small mote of evil in the potion—much as one could taste the first souring of milk. And how he had sensed that it would change and grow with time.

The Cormatine seemed to understand Kenlahar's silence. The ways of all Cormatine's were mysterious., "We owe you our lives," he said. "What would you have us do?"

"Free the others of the company and help us to Swamp's End. This is all I ask."

"It will be done," the Cormatine answered, and barked out orders. The People of the Cormat swept aside as Kenlahar passed, and he briefly had a heady but uncomfortable feeling that he could have commanded anything of them, and they would have followed.

He himself had to wake the others by pouring some of the converted blood of the Cormat over the heads of the drugged warriors. The Cormatine bequeathed him a leather bag full of the Cormat's blood, which he tucked under his cloak, alongside the Star Axe.

It was only as they were leaving that Kenlahar realized that Jakkem had not been among the sleeping prisoners. He had thought that Jakkem had entered the village with them, but now he was gone. When had Jakkem slipped away? Now that he thought about it, Kenlahar could not remember seeing the big man for several days. He had not thought anything of it, for surely Captain Jonla knew of the disappearance, perhaps had even ordered him off somewhere before they had been captured.

Later, he was to regret that he had not raided an outcry then, when all the Companions could've heard him.

The next morning, the swampmen led the reunited Companions on trails through the mire that none of the men of the Watch, not even Captain Jonla, would have ever seen. The Cormatine had stressed to the guides the importance of their charge, and the swampgirl—who was again leading the escort—seemed to lake her duty very seriously.

The People of the Cormat-had shown they were in command in their own lands, and Kenlahar began feeling that they were free from danger at last. He was stunned therefore when a scout materialized from the heavy fog and urgently whispered to the swampgirl. The girl approached the men of Lahar with puzzlement lining her dark face.

"Qreq," she said, her accent grating on the word. "They are many and are coming fast. They do not seem to care that they are about to die! We shall have to split into more than one company. Some of us may escape. The new Cormatine must above all survive." She nodded at Kenlahar.

She spoke rapidly to the swampman who had brought the news in their own language, and he grasped Kenlahar tightly by the arm and led him away from the troop. He caught only a glimpse of Sanra and Balor, their worried faces not yet reacting to the sight of him leaving, and then they were behind him. If it had been up to Kenlahar, at that moment, he would have stood his ground and dared the Qreq to find him. It was time, he told himself, that he tested the power of the Star Axe.

Still he followed the grim, silent swampman. They made good progress and Kenlahar was beginning to wonder if, perhaps, everyone had been able to evade the Qreq—when a dying scream somewhere behind him quickly changed his mind. Soon he was running with an endurance he could only have imagined a few weeks earlier. It seemed to him that they ran throughout the night. Soon he was no longer paying attention on what lay behind, and concentrated on making that next staggering step. So it would have ended, but for the young unknown swampman.

He pushed Kenlahar in the back, warning him of the danger. "Run on!" he cried. "Do not stop, Cormatine!" Soon the faceless man—for Kenlahar could not now even remember what the swampman looked like—was lost in the fog. Kenlahar strained to hear the guide's last cry over his own gasping breath, but all he could hear was a diminishing number of Qreq war cries.

He ran on, cursing his cowardice and the necessity for it. The pain in his side grew almost intolerable, and he set each new landmark to arise on the horizon as his goal. Finally, even the pain in his side seemed to fade in the struggle for breath. He did not know if he was escaping—or running right at his enemies.

———

The Cormatine watched the Companions leave the village and turned back into the ceremonial hut. It was empty now. Spilled flasks and unfinished meals were strewn across the table and onto the floor. From his bag of holy instruments, which hung near the door, he pulled forth a gray lump of metal.

"I am sending him to you," he announced into the empty air. "I suggest that you keep a watch for him on the borders. If anything should happen to the others, he would not survive long."

"I will be waiting," a quiet thought answered. "Are you satisfied now that he is the one?"

The Cormatine grunted and said, almost reluctantly, "He passed the Tryst. Yet he does not seem willing to carry his burden. I have sent one of my daughters along with him. She will see to his safety."

The quiet visitant did not answer verbally, but the Cormatine felt his sense of fulfillment. He had long planned for this moment. Soon he would be meeting the Axe-bearer at last!

The next morning found Kenlahar hopelessly lost. The fog had finally lifted, revealing a hilly terrain covered by vegetation similar to that of the Island Laharhann. Tall evergreens and low-lying brush had replaced the swamp reeds. But this forest did not end abruptly at the edge of the River Danjar, or at the walls of the House of Lahar, but continued on in an uneven and seemingly endless expanse of green. It struck him hard that, for the first time in his life, he was beyond the Tream—Outside! The idea of a land where he would never again need to worry about such simple, but constant concerns as his next footing, was exciting—yet frightening. The green of the hills, dark evergreen and blue-green poplars, had hints of autumnal color throughout. To a man who had lived among the decaying fen trees it was as if he had never before seen color in nature. The rustling of the breeze through the branches made him feel as if he had never truly heard the clean sounds of the wilderness.

His back was propped up to a large pine, where he had dragged himself after he had finally collapsed. The fear of the Qreq had finally faded enough for his tired legs to assert their dominance over his will. He sat quietly, unheeding of the small insects that climbed over him, exploring this new obstruction in their world. He was becoming thirsty and hungry—and increasingly cold. For the first time, the effects of his steady northward journey were being felt. Rarely in his life had Kenlahar felt such cold! Now the chill seemed to be striking into his very bones, and his sweat turning to ice.

Common sense told him to either keep moving, or find shelter. But his willpower would not respond to his intellect. As the morning wore on, the chill actually seemed to be leaving him. He began to feel a warm, comfortable drowsiness; to dream of a dry, comfortable room, somewhere high in the House of Lahar. A stuffy room perhaps, with a fire crackling. He would sit un- moving with a book spread over his face, able to rest at last. There would be time to move on later.

The hands shaking him awake were not, therefore, welcome. "Go away," he mumbled. "Leave me alone!" He did not understand the irritating words of the voice that responded, but they were urgent, glaring. Then, just as suddenly, he *wanted* to wake. The urgent words had struck a chord within him, and an unwelcome, but strong need to open his eyes again possessed him. But the sticky fluid in his eyes seemed to have crusted and no amount of panic would open them. He felt and heard a fire close to him and its heat, rather than warming him, seemed to be sending icicles into his legs. His eyes snapped open.

The man over the fire did not acknowledge him, but simply continued tending the roaring fire. Kenlahar looked at him warily, too weak to move. The man was clad in a long robe, which appeared to be woven in many colors, but a closer examination showed an overlapping collection of stains. The man's hair was pure white, flowing to his shoulders, and his hands were gnarled and stained to an almost permanent dark brown shade.

After a while the man rose and approached Kenlahar, carrying a large spoonful of the potion. The warmth that coursed down Kenlahar's throat was harsh, but left him alert. Now the long-haired man took the iron pot off the fire and set it for a few minutes in the broken shards of a frozen puddle. Still, the man remained silent, and Kenlahar was unwilling to break the silence first. Nodding to himself, the man lifted the pot from the ice and brought it to Kenlahar's side.

Kenlahar prepared himself for another harsh dose of the fluid, but was instead surprised when his hand was forced into the pot up to his wrist. The excruciating pain of that made him cry out involuntarily. The mixture was boiling hot! Later, after the painful tingling had at last left his hands and legs, he realized that the water could have only been lukewarm.

The stranger calmly thrust his other hand into the pot before Kenlahar had time to recover from the first shock, or fully appreciate what was happening. Again he cried out in pain. Throughout the whole painful process, the man did not speak, or reveal any emotion in his face or manner. But he had a calm, forceful timing to his ministrations.

Whenever Kenlahar was relieved of one painful treatment, he was subjected to another. The man pulled the pot from his side, and Kenlahar leaned back with a relieved sigh. But then the stranger poured the warm liquid onto his feet instead. He forced himself not to scream.

Later, as he discovered the Hermit's gentle nature, Kenlahar realized that the emotionless facade was an effort to suppress his own anguish. The Hermit disliked inflicting any pain—even when that pain healed the sick.

The Hermit never did speak that day, or the next, but seemed to know the exact moment that Kenlahar was capable of a difficult conversation. For he knew something that Kenlahar had not realized yet—that the two men spoke different languages. When he was finally able to move on, the Hermit—as Kenlahar had begun to think of him— patiently started to teach him a new language. He began by pointing out the names of herbs and foliage. Kenlahar was soon to learn of the Hermit's seemingly endless knowledge of plant life.

The Hermit's home was two days distance from where he had found Kenlahar, the old man explained. But the two days passed, and then another two days. The Hermit went slowly, both to allow Kenlahar to regain his strength, and to pursue the real purpose of his exploration—the collection of medicinal herbs. As Kenlahar listened carefully to the Hermit's tongue, and became accustomed to the accent, he began to understand more and more of what the man was saying. The new language, he soon realized, was simply an ancient variation of his own, and he was soon able to decipher almost every sentence. The long and painful days he had spent interpreting the ancient books of the Archives now helped him phrase questions to the old Hermit.

To begin with, Kenlahar asked the stranger over and over again for news of the Companions. But the Hermit did not seem to have any knowledge of any other travelers, and only shook his head in sorrow as Kenlahar described his long journey. The Hermit seemed a learned man, and Kenlahar produced the Star Axe for him to inspect. The old man did not seem impressed with the talisman, and told him that undoubtedly the secret of the Star Axe could be found in the voluminous libraries of Kernback.

The Hermit's unerring instinct showed itself again and again. As Kenlahar began to understand more, the Hermit began to give more and more detailed explanations of his beloved herbs.

By the end of the second day, for instance, Kenlahar had learned that the seed that looked so much like the head of a snake was the godly gift for the cure of the serpent's bite; he learned to mix the seeds of another herb in wine to "comfort the heart and drive away all sorrows" and so on. Kenlahar was surprised to find himself retaining much of this encyclopedic knowledge, which only encouraged the Hermit to expound more. It was the beginning of a doubling of the apprentice's knowledge as a healer. He only wished that the Healer Coron could have had a chance to trade wisdom with the Hermit.

There was almost no ailment that did not have a corresponding cure in what was, until now, an insignificant appearing plant; and the Hermit was not shy in using them—constantly mixing potions for the cure of the slightest itch or sore. And in a land where Kenlahar would have starved a few days before, they ate an exotic yet filling diet.

On the morning of the second day, the cold, dark clouds lifted to reveal mountains. Like a line of ancient warriors, the peaks marched across the horizon, tall and white from the first snows of the season. Kenlahar counted eight summits in his eight, each seeming larger and grander than his neighbor.

As tall as the mountains appeared, the blue sky dwarfed them. Kenlahar's horizons—the horizons of the Tream—had always been low, weighed down by heavy clouds. But this sky just kept going upward to a dark blue roof, where the stars could almost be seen in the daylight. The low mists lying halfway between the foothills and the mountains, only added to the mystery of the peaks. The foothills were matted with specks of autumnal color. The reds and yellows dotted the green evergreens. The bright colors were luminous in the early dusk.

It made Kenlahar sad that the self-absorbed, self- important people of the House of Lahar, caught in the drabness of the Tream, could not see this, and would not believe him when he returned to tell them.

The Borderland, as the Hermit's land was called, lay between the Tream and the mountains. Forested and hilly, it was the domain of the both the Hermit and a breed of farmers who scratched a living on the rocky soil of the small valleys and dales.

The Hermit insisted on harvesting one more herb before returning home, in the valley called Dunhollow.

"It is a rare, wondrous fruit," the Hermit said. "And grows on one small plant in all the Borderland. I stumbled upon it many, many years ago—and have tended it with care and patience, for it is fertile just once every hundred years." The old Hermit was caught up in, excitement as he told of the possible nearness of the next fertile seeding. The Hermit's shambling gait picked up in its pace.

"Does this herb have great virtues?" Kenlahar asked, wishing that they could just get on with their trek to the Hermit's home, which he was now beginning to think of as Swamp's End.

The Hermit paused and seemed to hesitate before answering. "It has the greatest of all virtues—prescience. The power to see into the future. I have need of its powers this day. And yet, I must warn you, there is danger—for it may embrace deep evil. I never know before taking the herb how it will affect me." He did explain how the evil would manifest itself, and Kenlahar shook his head, puzzled and somehow reluctant to ask. A shadow seemed to have drawn across the peaceful face of the Hermit.

The glen of Dunhollow was a small clearing, overshadowed by trees, till keeping the frost of the last night hard in its cold shade. At the very edge of the hollow was a small, scraggly bush, dull green, with small bright berries at the end of each thick stock. The plant did not appear in any way remarkable to Kenlahar, but the old Hermit handled the berries delicately, and with obvious relish. The smell was overpowering; an acrid sour smell. The Hermit gave out a handful of the berries to Kenlahar, and himself messily swallowed another handful. Kenlahar's faith in the Hermit was all that enabled him to overcome the sudden revulsion he felt towards the odor.

Even so, he swallowed—just one—and waited for it to take effect. The Hermit already seemed in the throes of some trance, and a streak of green juice escaped out of the corner of the Hermit's mouth. Kenlahar however, felt nothing. The frost slowly melted in the late afternoon's light.

Melted in the intense heat—a heat such that no man could endure! The landscape changed from the forest to a thick humid jungle, and Kenlahar turned to remark on the heat to—Sanra? But Sanra was not there! Of course, Sanra was not there. The environment shifted again; both the forest and jungle were disappearing, all growth was disappearing. And desert sands burned his feet. "Sanra," he heard someone...himself?...crying. "Sanra!".

When he woke, a day had passed. The old Hermit had fallen and lay sprawled in such a painful position that Kenlahar feared he was injured. As he rearranged the Hermit's limbs into a less tangled posture, the old man awoke to stare at him with weak, but frightened eyes. Only by leaning down could Kenlahar hear the Hermit. He picked up the old man and started traveling on a northward course.

The old man was as light as the bundle of herbs they had collected. Occasionally, the Hermit would open his eyes and correct Kenlahar's direction. The Hermit had suffered more than he had in the exposure to the nights cold. Kenlahar wondered if the old man would survive the dangerous freeze, but his worried thoughts turned again and again to his own dream—or vision. If he *had* seen the future, Sanra was alive, but in danger.

After what Kenlahar was sure must have been a circling, twisting route, they reached the mouth of a narrow valley, which the Hermit indicated was his home. The Hermit faintly whispered to move forward, gesturing weakly.

But Kenlahar laid him down, pulling out his small, precious bag of the Cormat's blood, and poured some down the old man's throat. The Hermit choked, but when he opened his eyes there was once again life in them. He demanded to know what he had been given. Kenlahar smiled and said that it was a herb that he had brought from the Tream.

"I must have some," the Hermit said. "You must tell me now where you got it!" But the sick man was once again slipping into a stupor and his weight was finally causing Kenlahar's arms to grow weary.

At last, on one more of the endless ridges, and as the light was failing almost totally, Kenlahar spotted a small cabin nestled at the bottom of the valley. He had reached Swamp's End at last!

CHAPTER VIII

Balor watched his friend cast a bewildered glance over his shoulder, and then Kenlahar's form melted completely into the mists. Asking himself why he did not follow, he turned away. He suddenly had a sinking feeling that he would not soon see Kenlahar again. One other in the party was also looking off into the mists after Kenlahar with a worried face. Sanra sent Balor a frightened look and he tried to smile back reassuringly.

Suddenly, the Lashitu—who had been watching quietly alone as the rear of the company—burst free and vanished into the fog after Kenlahar. Balor cried out to let him go, and the astonished swampmen lowered their bows. Balor hoped the shaman would catch up with Kenlahar. He did not like the Lashitu, but he liked even less the thought of his friend alone in the Tream.

Captain Jonla's tall frame moved among the Companions in an effort to create some order, his long dark face grim and resigned. The eerie shouts of the Qreq were approaching steadily the small, muddy clearing in which the Companions were hesitating. The People of the Cormat and the men of the Watch were separating quickly into two bands, now that danger threatened. Each man seemed to wish to die with his own kind. Balor started to move away from the swampmen and toward the gathering, arming men of the House of Lahar. From the sounds of their inhuman cries, the Qreq were closing rapidly, but Balor had yet to catch sight of any of them.

Then he felt a small, hard hand pull at his arm, and looked down to see the young swampgirl examining him with piercing eyes. "We shall lead them away with us!" she said, with only a hint of a question in her tone.

Balor nodded—it was a good strategy. "Yes, we will lead them away from the Axe-bearer." He shouted hasty farewells to -Sanra and Jonla, whom he never expected to see again, and set off at a quick run. the girl stayed on his footsteps, never lagging, however much he increased the pace. Their escort of swampmen panted, their breaths muffled in the silent swamp. Soon they had left the small clearing behind. The muddy path leading into the Tream, bounded by heavy mists, narrowed and then disappeared, and they splashed through the clinging mud of the bog. Balor abandoned all caution in picking his path, instinctively reacting to the lay of the next few yards. He only hoped that the surviving men of the House of Lahar had time to get away, and had the sense to flee rather than stay and fight.

From behind and around him, came the dreaded cries of "Qreq!" and he knew that Captain Jonla and his men had not run—and that Kenlahar and his single escort had not been left alone. He abruptly slowed his flight.

"Why do you stop?" the girl demanded, breathing hard. She pulled at his arm insistently. "They will overtake us!"

"The Qreq are not following us," Balor contradicted. He looked back down their escape route with a worried frown. "There is no purpose in running on."

"The Qreq will slay them all," the swampgirl said. "If we strive to aid them, we shall die as well. You must give up your foolish loyalties! Don't you understand that your life has been saved?"

Balor's pale face showed that he did indeed understand at last. For whatever reason, the swampgirl and Captain Jonla had conspired to save him. While he thought he was filling the role of decoy, the men of the House of Lahar had stayed to fight and delay the Qreq warriors.

Balor did not really hear the rest of her protests, but had already turned back toward the battleground. The girl watched him leave with baffled anger showing in her flushed face. The men of the swamp looked at her questioningly, for none of them had understood the argument. She motioned curtly, and they set off after him, though at a slower, more cautious pace. Unlike the men of the House of Lahar, the people of the Tream had survived not by confronting the Qreq, but by shunning their enemies.

Balor plunged forward, heedless of any danger, and was surprised by the distance he had covered in his few minutes of flight. He began to fear that he would be too late. Praying that he would not be denied revenge, he roared out his eagerness to confront the Qreq—hoping to startle them into believing a host of warriors were descending upon them.

When he burst into the clearing, he found only a small party of Qreq warriors, still hacking, without purpose, on the bodies of the dead men of the Watch. Their ghostly, unnatural skin glowed in the dim light, and their faces—showing the outlines of their skulls through the stretched skin—showed astonishment that a single warrior would dare attack them. Exhilarated by his chance to confront the enemy, Balor slashed into the defilers. One Qreq fell backward, clutching his throat, and one other was unable to avoid his sweeping strokes. The survivors turned to run from the whirlwind in their midst. Many went no farther than the border of the clearing before they dropped flat with dark shafts piercing their backs.

Balor had begun to chase them, but he heard himself hailed by the young swampgirl. The swampmen rushed by him. He realized that his blood thirst had been slaked. Chasing the Qreq with berserk abandon would not bring back his friends. Like a stabbing pain, Balor remembered Sanra and Captain Jonla.

He desperately searched the gruesome bodies, but though they were horribly damaged, he was soon able to discover that neither Sanra nor Jonla were among the dead. He counted the bodies—three others were missing. He began to calm, and even to reflect with resignation on the disaster that had overtaken the Companions.

Balor was confronted with the greatest dilemma he had ever faced. Kenlahar, his friend and bearer of the Star Axe, was somewhere in the Tream, lost and all but alone. Sanra and the missing men of the Watch were in the hands of the Qreq—he was just as certain of that.

He could wander through the Tream for a year and not pick up Kenlahar's trail. The quest of the Companions had always really been Kenlahar's alone, he thought. Suddenly, he remembered his promise to look after Sanra. He knew then that he would find her. So it was that Balor was not to soon see the glorious Outside. Instead, he was to travel toward what he dreaded most—the Warlord's Haven.

The men of the swamp were beginning to drift back into the clearing, some of them shaking their heads gloomily, and others excitedly telling of a successful chase. The swampgirl watched Balor warily as he made his painful decision. "You are not going after them?" she exclaimed.

Balor nodded absently, unconcerned now with what the girl might think. He stood off to one side looking down the trail, deep in thought. The swampmen surrounded the girl and she translated his words. A sharp debate broke out among them, and their angry tones broke Balor's reverie.

"The men of the Cormat do not wish to pursue the Qreq any farther," she said. "They say that there are too many Qreq to fight. I agree. They want either to return home; or find the Cormatine and escort him to Swamp's End as they were sent to do. But they will not follow you."

Balor shrugged, and began to draw up his packs and weapons for the long pursuit. It was just as well, he thought. He had not intended to openly fight the Qreq anyway. One man could remain concealed much better than a troop of men. He walked away, following the muddy footprints and flattened grass. Therefore, he was surprised to hear the sound of another set of footsteps falling behind him. He turned warily, and then smiled broadly at the girl. She frowned back. "I did not say that *I* would not follow you. *Someone* with caution must go with you, for stealth is what we shall need most if we are to rescue your friends."

"I will not ask you why you are willing to risk your life for us, but I accept your help with thanks," Balor said, as they set off again at a brisk walk. "Tell me your name..."

The swampgirl just stared back at first, until Balor turned his eyes. He could sense her attraction for him, but had not yet identified it for what it was. "I am called Kalese. I am the daughter of the Cormatine—the old Cormatine. Women are not accepted as leaders among the men of the Cormat. Perhaps Outside I shall find what I am seeking."

Balor looked back at her in astonishment. Truly, no woman of the House of Lahar would have ever uttered such words, not even Sanra. He began to regard her with a grudging admiration, and admitted to himself that she was worthy of leading men into battle—she had proven that by now. And, he discovered with surprise, he was glad to have her along with him. "We are not likely to come close to the kingdoms of Outside, if we follow the Qreq. We may find ourselves in the Warlord's Haven—but I doubt he will want a woman chieftain either!"

Kalese only smiled briefly, and shrugged. They continued in silence, concentrating on pursuit. The Qreq were moving fast, as if all the men of the Cormat were pursuing them. They must have been carrying their captives; for neither Balor nor the more experienced tracker Kalese, could discover signs of any prints but the splayed feet of the Qreq.

Slowly, the dogged pursuers began to gain on the Qreq. But they were fast approaching the River Danjar, and Balor grew afraid that once on the river, the Qreq would evade them forever. He strained to hear the roar of the river. Surely it could not be that far away!

Instead he heard the violent rustling in some of the tall ferns in their path. He stopped, and pressed a restraining hand on Kalese's shoulder. Turning warily, he tried to pinpoint the source of the scurrying. He drew his sword in readiness. When Kalese suddenly pointed, he jumped off the path into the heavy undergrowth and vanished from her view. There were a few minutes of tense silence, and then she heard Balor's heavy laughter. Forgetting her caution, she bounded into the jungle of growth.

Balor was standing at the edge of a harmless appearing pool of water. But a thick layer of silt carpeted the pool. In the middle of this dangerous quagmire, the Lashitu stood, trapped to his waist, and flailing his arms. "You seem to have lost your way, Lashitu!" Balor said, seeing that there was no danger of the shaman sinking any deeper.

Kalese did not deem it so humorous, and leaned out over the pool, trying to reach the terror-stricken Lashitu's hands. She fell short by over a foot. Balor, however, reached him easily. He dragged the speechless shaman onto dry land. "He will be more trouble than he's worth," he warned Kalese, but she was already calming the terrified shaman with soothing words.

"This man is too frightened of the Tream to ever wander far. He will have to go with us," she answered firmly.

"I say we should leave him," Balor insisted. "Let him keep looking for his master."

The Lashitu violently objected that he could go on, and would not cause them any trouble. But then he heard the pair's goal and protested with fanatical loyalty. "Kenlahar and the Star Axe are all that matter! The others are of little importance." Still, when they turned without a word toward the river, he followed them.

Balor rushed down the slight sloping bluffs above the river, not caring if the Lashitu would be able to keep up or not. He feared now that they would be too late. If the Qreq had boats moored on the river, which he did not doubt, they could have embarked and even left the line of sight altogether.

Suddenly, Balor was swaying over the steep banks of the river. The Danjar was free of rapids at that point, and the pounding roar Balor had been expecting to hear from a distance did not exist. Light was failing quickly, and he anxiously tried to find a vantage point on the banks. Finally he caught a glimpse of a dark sail disappearing upriver. The Qreq warship was in full sail, racing toward the Warlord's Havens. His heart sank as he saw the last of the Qreq ship vanish. They had debated and dawdled and delayed too long! he thought angrily.

Dispirited by the closeness of his race and its hopeless ending, he crouched and bent his head in dejection. Kalese stood beside him and placed a consoling hand on his shoulder. It seemed to Balor at that moment, that every choice he had made had turned terribly amiss. From behind him he heard the Lashitu's taunting laugh.

"For this hollow venture you forsook the bearer of the Star Axe! Give up this futile chase now, and search for Kenlahar before it is too late."

"Don't you understand—it is already too late! Kenlahar is gone and we cannot help him." Balor found it hard to control his anger at the Lashitu's carping. He feared that he would strike the shaman, but Kalese's hand tightened on his shoulder. Instead he said, "The Tream is wide, and Kenlahar could be far from here by now. I do not intend to become as lost as we found you!"

The Lashitu remained unaware of the danger he was putting himself in by his quarrelling. "But you do not even know if there are any Qreq on board that ship."

Balor rose and approached the Lashitu, who finally realized his peril and retreated, cringing. But Balor merely shouted down the smaller man.

"Have you considered that Kenlahar may also be their captive?"

The surprise and dismay that registered in the shaman's face revealed that he had not thought of that possibility. He closed his mouth and did no more complaining.

Balor thought the chance of Kenlahar being on board the Qreq ship was slim, and he regretted shouting down the loyal, if annoying, Lashitu. The shaman's objections were uncomfortably close to what Balor was thinking as well.

"The Qreq will have to disembark at the rapids," he pondered aloud. "Once past they will not find it easy to bypass the House of Lahar. They will need to wait for a favorable time to slip by. Nor will they be expecting pursuit. There is only a wisp of wind. The Qreq will not be moving fast, but will be depending on their oars."

Even the Lashitu was eager for pursuit now that the idea that Kenlahar might be with the Qreq had been planted in his mind. Agreed, they spent no more time in discussion. They set a swift and grim pace along the narrow banks of the river. Before he would have thought possible, Balor recognized the area of river where they had left the boat.

The three of them scrambled among the reeds, frantically searching for the sunken craft. Balor stripped and dived into the river, hunting underwater for some sign of the boat. He finally gave up his search, and returned to dry land. He saw that the Lashitu had also given up his exploration, and was sitting on the beach, glumly picking at the soil.

Kalese was walking back toward the river, her head bent down in the dimming light, and following a trail only she could see. She stopped at the river's edge. "There!" she said, pointing into the dark flow. "You will find it there."

Balor waded in and reached down. His hand immediately encountered the boat's wooden sides. He began pulling out the rocks, which had served as ballast keeping the boat under. Kalese hurried over to help him and between them, they were soon able to drag the boat onto shore. They retrieved the small sail from the bow—drenched, but still in good condition. Balor insisted on immediately setting off after the Qreq, though Kalese pointed out that it would soon be too dark to see anything but the expanse of the river and the prominent banks:

"The winds are strong to the south," Balor argued. "They will shift in the morning, and if the Qreq have reached the landings we will never catch them!"

And, indeed, it was only the hindrances of the Lashitu's inept sailing, and the inexperience of the swampgirl, that kept them from attaining the Qreq camp that night. As Balor had predicted, the winds began working against them just before dawn. The River Danjar was steadily narrowing, constricting the little ship's room to maneuver. The current working against them also grew steadily swifter.

Balor felt like railing at the Lashitu in frustration as their progress slowed, and then stopped. He was finally forced to admit defeat. The Qreq, he knew, would soon be reaching the portage causeways, if they had not already. Once on the river above the rapids they would have clear passage. Balor struck the side of the boat, and Kalese asked in sympathy, "How much farther?" "Not far," Balor said. "But it may as well be a day's distance, if we have to wait for the wind to change." "Then we will not wait," Kalese said firmly. "We have not come this far to stop now."

The Lashitu, now convinced that Kenlahar was a prisoner, tiredly agreed. Again, they started to trudge up the muddy banks of the River Danjar. Occasionally, Balor was forced to draw his sword and hack a path through the undergrowth. It began to rain again, and this time it did not stop. Their clothes became quickly soaked and then, after a few days, a sour mildew sank into the fibers. Balor thought wryly that they never need worry about losing one another—all they need do is follow the stinking rot; or if that did not work, the tattered fragments of their clothes.

Their progress seemed maddeningly slow to Balor. He was convinced that the Qreq had already reached the Warlord's Haven, while he was still struggling and straining against the clinging reeds below the rapids. He battled to maintain his original fast pace, often forgetting to consider if the other two could keep up. Fortunately for the Lashitu and even Kalese, Balor did slow down—unwillingly. Leading the way and creating paths for the two followers had weakened Balor enough for them to cope with his long strides.

As they neared the portage, Balor left the other two behind with orders to follow as quickly as they could. He crept up on the causeway, but he almost stumbled unaware into the Qreq camp nevertheless. The roar of the falls and the sun's light shimmering on the horizon had almost concealed the Qreq.

They moved noiselessly, and the rumble of the rapids would have smothered any escaping sounds. Balor threw himself down behind a tall clump of reeds, and unmoving, watched the Qreq. The fires were almost burned out, but still glowed as the night approached. Only a few Qreq warriors seemed to be guarding the huge camp.

Balor was astonished that the Qreq had dared to establish such an encampment so near the House of Lahar, and on the far side from their home port of the Warrior's Haven. The Qreq ship he had so stubbornly pursued was tied up on a makeshift dock. Now that he could see the full silhouette of the Qreq warship, Balor marveled that the Qreq had managed to maneuver the giant craft around the rapids. More and more of their camp was waking, and suddenly Balor spotted a small figure moving among the tall Qreq. He squinted, desperately trying to see who it was, and was rewarded with a glimpse of long, golden hair.

Sanra! Balor almost shouted out her name. She was alive, and moving freely through the camp! His eyes followed her passage through the waking camp until she once more sat down among a pile of bundled bodies. The figures moved awkwardly and Balor guessed that the prisoners were bound. He counted three prone forms—three men of the Watch, Balor thought. That left one man still unaccounted for.

The Qreq were all up and moving now, hurrying to complete their job before darkness fell. Balor was amazed to see them wheeling a huge wagon down the steep ramp. It slid into the water, creating waves that sent the warship reeling backwards. The crew cast a thick hawser to shore. When the warship had been positioned roughly over the wheeled cart, work parties joined to pull both ship and cart onto the ramp. The ship settled, with a groaning, creaking heaviness onto the wagon. Fascinated by this display of Qreq tenacity, Balor watched them pull the load up the causeway, inches at a time. As the ship left the water completely, it tottered to one side dangerously. The long chain of Qreq slaves stretched up the portage, and out of Balor's sight.

Balor's awe was replaced by the realization that the Qreq would not escape him soon—not at the slow pace with which they were hauling their load upriver. The small cluster of prisoners remained unmoving throughout his investigation. Satisfied that he would not lose them again soon, Balor backtracked to wait for Kalese and the Lashitu. The sun descended to the horizon and still there was no sign of the two stragglers. Balor grew increasingly impatient. Finally, he thought he heard them approaching, and was about to step forward to greet them when he caught the movement out of the corner of his eyes.

A Qreq sentry had emerged from his hidden shelter, cautiously peering downriver. Balor had just enough time to think that he must have passed the picket, unnoticed in the deepening shadows. But the sentry was showing alert curiosity now, he thought. The sentry had retreated back into his concealed niche, but Balor had no faith that the Qreq had not heard this noisy approach. The Lashitu appeared into view, making no effort to muffle his tread. Wary and silent, Kalese followed several steps behind him.

Balor cursed and ran toward the area he had spotted the Qreq last. But he was still yards away when the Qreq suddenly popped from his concealment and stepped in front of the surprised Lashitu. As the ghostly warrior raised his curved sword, the Lashitu screeched and fell backwards. Kalese hurled her walking stick into the path of the sweeping sword, but she too was thrown back. Balor jumped the last few feet, thrusting his blade at the Qreq, but the Lashitu's widening eyes unintentionally warned the ambusher in time. The Qreq turned and deflected the blow.

The Qreq had forgotten, or had dismissed the other two, so he did not see the staff in Kalese's hand as it came on his huge head. Without pausing, and without pity, Balor threw the body into the river. It bobbed once and then sank into the one of the countless small whirlpools of the River Danjar. If they found him, Balor hoped, they would believe that the guard had been caught in the treacherous currents of the river.

When he once more looked up from the swirling waters he saw that Kalese was almost falling over in exhaustion. Balor, too, was feeling the toll of his marathon chase. "This time, the Lashitu will stand watch while *we* sleep," he growled when they reached his hideaway above the Qreq camp. "Wake us at dawn," he ordered the shaman. He did not add what they all knew—that when they awoke they would be on the lookout for an opportunity to rescue the prisoners. None of them had much faith in their success, but they had to try.

The Lashitu merely nodded at his orders. He had seemed preoccupied ever since Balor had informed him that Kenlahar was not among the captives.

Balor *had* to close his eyes. He had been pushing himself too hard, he thought. Now that there was no more urgent need to stay awake, and someone else to watch, the need to sleep overwhelmed him. The last image he had before he closed his eyes was of the Lashitu gloomily watching the Qreq camp.

———————

Balor opened his eyes, somehow certain that he had slept too long. It was still light, but the air felt wrong—not like a morning or afternoon, but fresher, as if it were late night. He felt disoriented by the contradiction to his expectations. His body, too, found it difficult to accept the evidence of his eyes—he was too rested for it to still be dark. Unless…the only explanation, Balor thought, was that he had slept all the night, and all the next day as well. But where was the Lashitu? Why had he not been woken?

A surge of fear and adrenalin sent him groping for his sword and to his feet. But they were in no danger; the night was peacefully quiet, except for the constant roar of the falls. The Qreq camp was deserted, and the makeshift dock was teetering above the swift water of the River Danjar, the only sign of the enemy's presence.

Kalese lay quietly sleeping as he had seen her last, but the Lashitu was not standing guard, was not even awake. Instead he was kneeling against a bulwark he must have hastily dug, head in arms—fast asleep.

Balor howled in fury, forgetting all caution or judgment, and lifted the shaman bodily into the air, ready at that moment to throw the Lashitu as far as he could down the small cliff, into the abandoned Qreq camp. The Lashitu shrieked as Balor began to launch him into the air. Kalese woke just in time and shouted, somehow penetrating his rage and bringing him back to his senses. At the last moment, he turned instead and dropped the Lashitu roughly to the ground. The shaman's scream was abruptly stilled and he squirmed on his back, his eyes showing his frightened images of death, struggling to draw a breath.

Balor immediately regretted his violent reaction, thinking that he may have seriously hurt the Lashitu. But Kalese pulled him away from the moaning shaman. "He is not injured, Balor," she said. "Do not concern yourself with *him*. We both should have known that this would happen, but it is too late now. It is time to think on what our next action should be."

The Lashitu had finally caught his breath and now said, a little timidly, "But Kenlahar is not with them. I thought that was why we were after them. We should be looking for the Star Axe. Let us turn around now, I beg of you!"

"Is that why you let them slip away, Lashitu?" Balor's voice lashed at the shaman with scorn. "Did you think we would abandon our chase if you let them go? Then it is time I told you that I knew Kenlahar was not among them. I chose to pursue them anyway. You may not understand this, but it is the only way I can help Kenlahar now. Lashitu, if you have any counsel with the gods, ask *them* to help Kenlahar, for we cannot."

"I will join Balor in his quest," Kalese said. "From this moment on I will neither hinder you or help you, Lashitu. From this moment on we will not turn back, we will not turn aside. We are after the Qreq!"

She turned to lead the way down into the deserted camp and up the other side to the Qreq trail. Balor smiled at the Lashitu menacingly, and turned to follow her.

The Lashitu hesitated, and looked uncertainly around him. At that moment, the rickety structure of the docks toppled into the river with a loud splash and the Lashitu shouted as if he had been stung. He rushed after the disappearing figures of the warrior and the swampgirl. The Lashitu's fanatical loyalty did not, apparently, extend to being left marooned in the Tream, Balor thought. Even when they stepped up their pace, moving much faster than they had before, the Lashitu meekly followed, and did not complain.

The giant wagon had cut deep ruts into the road, and halfway to the Statue of Kings they came upon one of its massive wheels, lying broken to one side. The crushed remains of several Qreq were tossed callously about it, for the wheel had evidently only been replaced at the price of many lives. The wagon had continued grinding up the ancient causeway. Already the twin ruts left by the wagon in the hard earth of the portage were filling with dark rainwater.

They were nearing the Statue of Kings, when they heard the creaking, grinding racket of the giant cart. The rear guard of the Qreq was set foolishly within the range of the wagon's noise or the Companions would have stumbled onto them. The Qreq wagon crawled ponderously forward, while the three shadows followed.

The guard was a token precaution, Balor thought. The Qreq were overconfident. They would learn better if he could reach the House of Lahar before they did. But the uncomfortable thought entered Balor's mind that perhaps the Qreq were so bold because they no longer needed to fear the House of Lahar.

The night still had several hours of darkness, but Balor did not believe the Qreq could reach the Statue of Kings, launch the ship, and embark before light. When the Lashitu complained once more that he could go no further without rest, he made his decision. "I may be able to reach the House of Lahar in time to warn them," he whispered to

Kalese. "You follow the Qreq, and when they make their attempt to sneak by, light some kind of signal. We will lay a trap for these reckless Qreq!"

He started around the slow moving Qreq party, in a wide detour into the Tream. But his effort to remain just out of sight of the Qreq vanguard—and also away from the treacherous interior of the swamp—was constantly frustrated. Every clear passage through the tangle seemed to lead away from the River Danjar, and every obstacle seemed to lie between him and the river. His efforts to cut across the uncooperative land, and angle toward the river, were always hindered by growth. Only by exaggerating his progress toward the river, much farther than his sense told him he should, was he able to maintain his infrequent glimpses of blue that indicated the flow. He settled for keeping the murmur of the rushing water at an even level, and was thankful he did not have much farther to go.

Now that the groaning Lashitu was not slowing his advance, Balor quickened his pace. He was gratified by the trouble the Qreq were encountering. Each time he had thought that he had fallen hopelessly behind, the Qreq had confronted a new obstacle. Perhaps the Raggorak were on the side of the Companions after all! He was eager to arrive at the House of Lahar. A Qreq warship had never before sailed below the island. The Watch commander would not wish to see the warship escape punishment!

He negotiated his way up a steep muddy path, placing each foot solidly on the slippery earth before lifting the other. Even so, by the time he had reached the top of the bank he was covered by mud from falling. It seemed to him that every bush in the Tream had thorns, and every bit of dry land was infested with biting, stinging insects—as were the pools of foul smelling water. Every blade of grass burned with an itching poison, every step could turn into a quagmire.

He was amazed that the few species of plant life could be twisted into many forms. The insects seemed to stay at a stationary distance from his nose, no matter how fast he moved, how swiftly he jerked his head away. Then, if he stopped paying attention for even a second, they would strike.

Thus, Balor was not paying attention to his path. The Tream was springing its trap. Balor suddenly realized that he was lost, and his panic sent in running in the direction he was sure he had last seen the river. Before he could adjust the night was robbing him of sight. His sense of orientation, his sense of time seemed to be playing tricks on him. He should have seen the House of Lahar by now, he thought desperately. Find the river and he would find the House! But he could no longer even hear the river he realized with a feeling of dread.

Finally he stopped his futile wandering. He peered into the darkness, trying somehow to distinguish something out of the murk. By watching intently he began to see lights on the horizon. At first the shimmer could barely be perceived, but gradually its glow intensified. The Qreq had saved him by a night attack on the House of Lahar, and their mammoth fires lighted the horizons. But it was only later that Balor learned of this irony. Right now, he hurried toward the strange lights, unsure how long they would stay lit. As he stumbled through the dark, and waded through the muddy pools of the swamp, he began to have intimations of their strategy. An attack in the early morning would allow the Qreq warship to slip by unnoticed!

The banks surrounding the island were filled with the debris of past battles. Balor mounted a loose mass of wreckage upriver of the island and let the current carry him toward the House of Lahar, steering at times to maintain a distance from the Qreq ships. But the Qreq surrounding the island were not watching for someone trying to break through the siege lines from Outside.

The warships had huge torches on their bows as a means of avoiding collisions. As he neared the island, Balor realized that the smaller boats of the House of Lahar were exploiting this exposure. The little boats of Lahar were sailing without lights, and Balor caught brief glimpses of them as they darted under the prows of the enemy crafts. Already one of the giant ships was burning. The Qreq had never before attacked by night and Balor doubted that they would ever do so again.

Balor heard the sound of the river being cut neatly by the hull of a small boat somewhere very close to him. He cried out. Surprised voices drifted back across the river to him, and he yelled again, to identify himself. He was answered this time by the sound of arrows slicing through the water around him. He fell silent, and all the boat passed on. Apparently they were searching for larger prey.

Balor continued paddling toward the island, but he began to wonder now how he would convince the Watch of his identity before they mistakenly killed him!

. Wading ashore at the forest's deepest point, he slipped easily past the warriors guarding the island. When he finally strolled openly into the Courtyard of Moons, he was not even noticed at first. Gradually, however, he began to draw stares. At least now they knew he was not a Qreq, he thought.

So Balor walked up the broad stone steps of the Great Hall without hindrance. Someone cried out his name, and others took up the cheer with wonderment in their voices. He waved and entered the open doors. Marching down the long, dusty halls toward the Chambre of the Elders, all the warm, dry memories of his childhood returned. He felt an overwhelming sense of relief and safety.

But he was not meant to rest within its confines yet, he reminded himself. He wished the inner rooms had windows on the river, for the vision of the Qreq ship passing by outside even now, kept entering his thoughts.

CHAPTER IX

Several hours had passed since Balor and the High Elder had assembled on the docks with a small company of the Watch. The low roof, supported by braces placed at random along the length of the pier, protected them from the worst of the rain. But it gave Balor the uneasy feeling of waiting within a long, dark cave. Waiting for the swollen river to rise and swallow them, he thought. Three boats had been outfitted for battle, and in their prows had been stowed clay pots filled with hot coals, and covered from the rain. Occasionally, one of the warriors would step from the shelter and jump into one of the boats to bail out the new rainfall.

Balor peered into the darkness, waiting for a sign from Kalese that the Qreq were about to attempt their escape. His eyes hurt from the strain of searching in the blackness of night. From beside him, the High Elder said, "Perhaps they have passed us by already."

It was the third time, Balor noted, that the High Elder had wondered that. "No!" he insisted again. "Kalese would have signaled us. I am certain of it." Nevertheless, the High Elder's doubts were beginning to create doubts in Balor's mind as well.

The new Captain of the Watch, Tolose, added to his fears when he stopped his relentless pacing just long enough to say, "I do not trust this swampgirl." The warrior turned away again without waiting for a reply.

Balor held back an exasperated retort. Tolose was as grizzled and hoary as Captain Jonla had been, but did not have the tolerance. He would never be convinced of any integrity among the People of the Cormat. It did not matter how much Balor argued with the man—in Tolose's mind the swamp people were not to be trusted, and that was that. So instead of arguing again, Balor resumed his search for a light in the gloom.

In this time of waiting, an aura of greatness seemed to have been granted Balor by the troop. Rumors moved among the warriors that the tall, blond battle-scarred man in their midst had been wandering in the Tream for many, many weeks. It was even whispered that he had dared to journey Outside, and had returned with dire tidings for the House of Lahar. It was fortunate, Balor thought, that they did not know of Kenlahar and the Star Axe, or just how bad his news had been.

He was aware that his ragged, travel-stained clothes strengthened the wonderings of the warriors. He caught them casting him glances filled with awe. Though he tried his best to ignore the looks, he could not help himself from feeling a wry pride in his battered appearance.

A tall guard from the Chambre, who had long ago been sent to fetch the Healer Coron, finally returned to report to the High Elder. Coron had refused to leave the Hospice without first tending to those laid to his charge, he reported. "There are many sorely wounded man from the battle," the guard recited. "Further battle will have to wait."

"Is that his answer?" the High Elder demanded. "Has he no concern for the Axe-bearer? Go back and escort the Healer Coron to my presence."

"It does not matter, Elder," Balor said. "There is nothing the Healer Coron can do until after we have captured the ship."

The High Elder reluctantly agreed and called back the guard. Balor thought it just as well. He was not looking forward to the old man's questions. Coron saw too much, and never what you wished him to see.

Meanwhile, Captain Tolose continued to pace back and forth, muttering fiercely to himself. All the company overheard, with amused snickers, his profane vows—he would teach the Qreq not to take their ships downriver! With a thankful prayer to Lahar, Balor reflected that he could not have asked for more cooperation from the grizzled warrior. Though he may have been of minor rank when he had left, he had returned as a Companion of the Star Axe, and he had a feeling he would be granted everything he asked for.

As the night wore on, Balor began to fear that it would all come to naught. Perhaps, he thought, Kalese had already signaled the Qreq ship's dash upriver. Perhaps his confused wanderings in the swamp had given them the time they needed. Perhaps they had blended into the battle and escaped notice after all. Or worse, perhaps Kalese never would signal, but linger lost—or dead—dead within the Tream. But he never once thought what the High Elder had implied, and Tolose had stated outright—that Kalese had failed his trust.

He looked about him once more and saw that the High Elder was staring at him with a curious expression on his face. The night was ending, and even the troops were beginning to display little interest in the purpose of their vigil. Even Balor appeared to have lost his fascination to them. He forced himself to feign a calm confidence as the night grew late.

Then, without warning, the Needle of Lahar was illuminated by the flash of a huge fire. Invisible only seconds before, the tall column now cast a shadow down upon the roofs of the Great Hall. The warriors scrambled into the boats and cast off, and Balor found himself in command of the lead ship. As they neared mid-river, he saw the beacon Kalese had set among the rushes. The swamp was ablaze with the light of its flames. Balor wondered how she had managed to kindle such a fire among the damp fen-trees and swamp reeds, while the rain continued to pour down heavily.

In the bow of the ship, the archers deftly wrapped the points of their arrows with squares of cloth and smeared them with a thick sap. The arrows were lit in the hearth- pot and sent flying toward the eastern banks of the river. Their passage could be heard as a loud whispering hiss to those in the boats. Flight after flight of arrows were sent soaring upward and the night skies were filled with the fireworks.

Balor's eyes followed their fiery paths until they were extinguished, steaming into the river. Finally, one of the men cried out and pointed into the dark, at about amidships. Another archer carefully inserted a burning shaft into the heavy string of his bow, and every warrior watched the flaming arrow's flight, until it briefly illuminated the dark hull of the enemy warship. The next flight of missiles scored three hits on the frame of the ship. They clung there, burning fitfully.

The Qreq swiftly doused the flames, but it did not matter now. The fleet of Lahar had its bearings, and the ships sliced through the water like diving eagles, cutting the Qreq ship off far from the upriver camps of the Qreq army. Balor had only a little time to worry about how he could keep the enraged warriors from accidentally injuring one of the captives, or prevent the Qreq from purposely murdering them rather than allow them to be recaptured. Then he was in the fight and had no more time for thought.

The custom of the House of Lahar was to keep out of the range of the Qreq spears, and harass the warships from a distance with the accurate fire of their archers. But this time, the attacking boats discarded that strategy and drove alongside the giant ship. Grapples flew into the air and over the bulwarks. Though warriors of all three attacking ships prepared to mount the looming sides of the warship, none were more eager than Balor, and he found himself the first up.

By now the Qreq had recovered from their surprise, and at the top of the rope, where it strained against the bulwarks, Balor saw the Qreq sword flash down. The thick rope spiraled downward, cut through, but Balor desperately threw his hands above him. His fingers caught the railing of the ship's sides. The Qreq had already moved on, to sever another of the grappling ropes, failing to notice the warrior dangling from the side of the ship.

With a strength even Balor had not known he possessed, he hoisted himself over the side of the ship in one motion and bared his sword. For the next few seconds he was the only warrior on board, and the focus of a furious attack. Finally, other men of the Watch surmounted the bulwarks, and Balor was relieved of much of the pressure. The deck was a swirl with darting, lunging warriors, but Balor was oblivious to all others. His eyes were fixed on the closed lid of the hatch. Pressing forward, seeing and fighting only those foes that confronted him, he slowly neared the hatch.

Two Qreq saw him approach, and moved to oppose him, but Balor was too near his goal now to be stopped. With a quick, deep thrust, one of the Qreq was felled. The second Qreq's sword slashed downward over Balor's extended arm. Balor abandoned his sword and leaped at the enemy. The Qreq was unable to bring his sword around before Balor's hands closed around his throat.

When Balor finally threw open the hatch, he expected to be met by a deluge of defenders, but there was no one in sight. Cautiously, he ventured down the companion-, way and explored the unfamiliar ship's interior. He found himself in a womb of peace. He shook his head, puzzled by the absence of guards. All the Qreq seemed to be above on the deck! At every bulkhead he expected to meet an ambush by the Qreq, but there was no one lying in wait. With his heart filling with dread, he reached the after-cabins, deep within the bowels of the ship. Futilely retracing his steps, he scrutinized every inch of the ship in a furious search. There was no sign of the captives.

Captain Tolose found him sitting on the steps of the companionway. "The Qreq will never attempt to sneak by the House of Lahar!" he said with satisfaction. Then he noticed Balor's slumped shoulders and sightless gaze. "Where are the prisoners?" he asked anxiously. "Have they been killed?"

Balor shook his head. "They are not here," he whispered.

Captain Tolose sat down heavily onto the next step to Balor, as if his knees had been weakened by the news. "It appears that your friend let you down after all," he said.

Balor started at the warrior's words, alive once more to his surroundings. "You are unfair," he said. "How could she have known? How could any of us know that they were not aboard?" His voice trailed off. He had realized suddenly that he had forgotten Kalese and the Lashitu.

Hurrying onto the deck, Balor looked to the shore. The giant blaze set by Kalese was still flickering on the banks. He looked around for his crew. The last Qreq bodies were being unceremoniously dumped overboard, for there had been no quarter. Balor shouted for his crew to follow him onto one of the boats. The shock of not finding Jonla and Sanra had not quite left him. It was hard to accept that things had gone amiss again. All he could think of right now was of finding Kalese. Surely she would know!

As they neared the shore, the warriors in the boat saw a thin figure leaping frantically, outlined in the weak flames of the fire. The profile looked so much like a Qreq that all but Balor held their weapons in readiness. Balor, however, quickly recognized the skinny figure. He leaped from the prow of the boat, as the keel plowed into the sandy beach, and ran toward the Lashitu. The shaman greeted him excitedly, thanking the gods loudly that he had been saved. Balor looked for Kalese, but all he saw was the burnt-out hulks of the fen-trees, the smoldering ashes of the low brush.

"Where is Kalese?" he demanded. "Why is she not here with you?"

"That is what I have been trying to tell you!" the shaman said, aggrieved by the lack of attention Balor was paying him. "She left me here—alone."

I can see that she is not here," Balor replied impatiently. "Where is she?"

"She is a clever girl," the Lashitu said, refusing to acknowledge Balor's questions. He seemed annoyed that Balor was not concerned with his sufferings, and determined that the warrior would hear him out. "She started this inferno. The fire seared so hot I thought we would surely burn up! I had to wade into the river to escape the heat."

Balor grabbed the Lashitu's cloak. "Where did she go?"

"The Qreq tricked us," the Lashitu said. "They took the prisoners off the ship and slipped by you. The ship was a decoy while they went around by land. After the swampgirl lit the fire, and you did not come, she told me to wait for you. She told me to tell you to follow her." Balor was not very surprised by the account of the ruse, for it was what he had suspected ever since he had found the ship empty. He had been more foolish than the Qreq to believe that they would try to pass—safely—on the warship. Even the Qreq had apparently thought they could not. What he hadn't expected was that Kalese would go after the Qreq alone.

"Why did she not wait for me?" he asked, half to the Lashitu, and half to himself. For once, the Lashitu could not answer. How was he to find her in the Tream? Balor thought. There was nothing he could do but follow her—immediately. "Get into the boat," he ordered the Lashitu. "We are going after her."

"Are we not going to the House of Lahar first?" the Lashitu asked in a horrified voice.

Balor hesitated—he did not want to delay a minute. * But the crew would probably not go with him without permission. He commanded then, with an urgency that had them jumping for the snails, to return to the House of Lahar. The little boat glided through the water at full sail in response.

They arrived at the pier at the same moment as the captured warship. A reception by the Council of Elders, the Healer Coron, and many of the family awaited them on the docks. The Healer Coron smiled at the sight of his former student, but Balor was in no mood for greetings. "They were not on board," he said glumly.

"We have been told," the High Elders said. "We also have tidings that the Qreq fleet is retreating upriver. The siege is lifted." The crowd, unaware that the capture of the Qreq warship had been anything but a great victory, cheered at this news.

"They have what they came for," the Healer Coron said grimly in a low voice that only those near him could hear. "The fall of the House of Lahar will be a simple matter once the Warlord is master of the Star Axe." "Then we must go after them," Balor insisted, keeping his hope and belief that Kenlahar was not among the prisoners to himself. He suspected that the Council of Elders would not seek to rescue a woman, or even a captured Captain of the Watch. The Lashitu also did not correct the Elders of the misapprehension that Kenlahar was a captive. Balor was not about to ask the shaman for his, no doubt mysterious, reasons for staying silent, but was thankful for the favor. The Healer Coron was looking at him strangely, and Balor wondered if it was amused skepticism he saw in the old man's face. But Coron said nothing.

"This is not a matter to discuss in the open," one of the Elders reproached Balor.

"We do not have the time to discuss it anywhere else," Balor retorted hotly.

"Such an undertaking must be thought on, Balor," the High Elder said gently. "If we are to send men into the Warlord's Haven, then the matter must be weighed carefully. But do not worry, Balor. We will not let them escape. To forsake Kenlahar, would be to forsake the House of Lahar itself."

Despite Balor's worries a forum was quickly assembled in the Chambre. But his worst fears were realized when an opposition formed among the warriors to any kind of rescue mission.

"We should not send our fleet—no, not even one boat, on such a hopeless quest," one warrior insisted, implying rebellion in his firm stand. Balor knew that even the Elders could not overrule a consensus of the Watch. "Would you have us storm the Warlord's Haven?" another of the warriors shouted. "The Qreq will someday return, and if you strip us of man and weapons, the House of Lahar shall be defenseless to their attack."

"If Toraq possesses Alcress then all your men and all your boats will be of no avail," the Healer Coron said angrily, seeing that the warriors of the Watch would not budge from their defiance.

But none of Coron's arguments or pleading would change their minds. The Axe-Kith had seen no evidence of the Star Axe's power, they asserted loudly. They had fought without it for a hundred generations, and they could fight without it for another hundred generations. If Alcress was as all-powerful as legend maintained, then Kenlahar would need no help from the Axe-Kith.

Balor saw that he had been wrong. They would not follow him as a Companion, even to rescue the Axe- bearer himself. He began to make plans to go alone if need be. If he could help Kenlahar in no other way, he could at least keep his promise to look after Sanra. He had failed so far, but he could not now forsake his friends: Sanra, the quiet self-assured girl who had been the first, after Balor, to understand Kenlahar; Jonla, the confident, skilled scout, who had begun to teach Balor all he knew; Kalese, the girl of the swamps, who would be willing to give her life for his, and, most of all, Kenlahar, his first and strongest friend, and bearer of Alcress.

"Captain Tolose," he shouted. "I will not abandon the Axe-bearer and his Companions! I ask now, before all this company, for history to attend, and for Lahar to see—will you help me or no?"

The Captain of the Watch seemed ashamed at that moment, but Balor saw that the answer would be no.

The High Elder finally chose to speak. "You have a new addition to your fleet, Captain Tolose," he said mildly. "Surely you will not object to yielding that?"

"The Qreq warship?" Captain Tolose said in disbelief. But the disbelief quickly changed to relief as he saw a way to compromise. "The ship is so ponderous I would not have it among our fleet!" he said with scorn. The other warriors reluctantly agreed.

"Then it will sail in the morning," the High Elder decided. "The Companions will yet be reunited! In command I will place Balor, who has proven his steadfastness. The Lashitu, one of the last of the Companions, will go also. May Lahar give you good fortune!"

The Council of Elders rose and filed off the dais—the audience was ended. The warriors of the Watch had no time to make any more objections to the expedition, and Balor made no attempt to ask for more help. At that moment, he was grateful for any aid.

The next morning he glumly watched the loading onto the Qreq ship of a meager supply of provisions. He had been granted a skeleton crew to the man the giant vessel, and Balor suspected that he had been given the weakest of troops. Captain of the Watch Tolose had been right, Balor thought, as he surveyed his crew. It was foolish to send this token army into the Warlord's Haven. There would be no escaping from Toraq's wrath.

The Healer Coron, who emerged from the House of Lahar just in time to see them off, interrupted his gloomy thoughts. "Do not despair, Balor!" the old man said, as if he had been reading Balor's mind. "It is a noble quest, even if it fails. After all, the Warlord must not be allowed all the initiatives."

"It might be better if I went alone," Balor said, having second thoughts.

"Toraq will not believe that anyone would sail so boldly into his Haven. From what you have *not* told me of Kenlahar, I suspect the

Warlord will be looking elsewhere." The old man looked at Balor quizzically. "In this irony I find hope!"

Balor regarded the old man, wondering—not for the first time— what he knew. Only the Healer Coron had showed to see them off. Balor had never before realized the lack of faith the family had in the prophecy of the Star Axe. Apparently, the Axedelve was no more than a meaningless ritual to most of them. But because of the Healer Coron's teachings, Balor and Kenlahar had always believed wholeheartedly in all the legends.

The loading had ended at last and there was no excuse for waiting any longer. Balor shrugged his shoulders and clasped the old man's arm silently. Then he boarded the gangplank, shouting the orders to sail for Warlord's Haven.

CHAPTER X

It was early morning, about a month after Kenlahar had reached Swamp's End. The first snow of winter had fallen silently during the night. He reluctantly rose from his warm bed and hustled to the brick stove, which stood in the center of the small hut. Shivering, he sacrificed the last chips of wood. While he warmed himself, he glanced around the one room of the dwelling. Along the walls hung the Hermit's dried herbs. Scattered about the room were the bowls and baskets with which the Hermit gathered and stripped the herbs. Mortar and pestle ground the leaves into a powder. Some was mixed into potions, and most was put into bottles. The fluids were contained in huge, earthenware pots along one floor against the walls.

The Hermit would sit in a rickety, uncomfortable chair in the comer, surrounded by his paraphernalia and concocting his medicines. By now the floor was covered with a thousand different leaves and flowers, crushed under foot. The aroma of one plant would fill the room with pungent sweetness, another with bitterness, and others with odors hard to identify.

The Hermit was finally asleep, after a long feverish night. He lay, tousled among the gatherings of blankets that Kenlahar had placed over him. The room heated up quickly, thanks to the solid layer of snow insulating the cabin. Kenlahar set about fixing himself a small meal of cheese and bread. The Hermit had recovered for a while after reaching his home, but had then fallen ill again.

Kenlahar felt that he owed the Hermit his life. The Hermit had saved him when he was cold and hungry, and now it seemed that it was Kenlahar's turn. So he stayed to attend the old Hermit until he was well. He was sure now that the Hermit, an ancient man, was dying. Nevertheless, Kenlahar was continuing to learn the language, and with the help of the Hermit, was learning even more of the art of healing with the use of herbs and roots. If the Hermit died, the world would lose its most knowledgeable herbalist, Kenlahar thought.

Every day, for many years, the peasants who lived in this wild border country had come to the Hermit for the healing of almost any hurt or illness. Kenlahar had replaced the Hermit as best he could. Both had been able to teach the other new cures, but Kenlahar benefited most from the Hermit's instructions from his sick bed. After having been chased across the Tream, the four rickety walls of the Hermit's home gave Kenlahar a sense of security he was reluctant to leave behind. He was content to hold from his travels for a little while.

This morning there were no patients to heal, and Kenlahar decided to do those chores he had been unable to do before. He grabbed a bucket from its hold in the wall and went out to gather water from the small spring a few hundred yards away. As he stepped onto the porch, he stretched in the illusory warmth of the winter sun. Looking over the small clearing, he felt peace in the stillness of the scene. Snow lay pure and unbroken from the stoop on into the horizon.

His mood was broken when he passed the small hill west of the hut, on his way to the well. Its clarity of proportions made Kenlahar think that it was man- made. In his fever the Hermit had often spoken of the barrow, warning him with scowls to stay away from it.

Warding off any questions by making signs in the air with both hands, he would say only, "Evil!" Kenlahar gathered that the Hermit had once tried to dig up the grave and that something had happened. Kenlahar could not discern what, only that it had left the Hermit in great fear of the barrow. His curiosity about the mound of earth had been checked. Yet, through the long days he took care of the dying man, Kenlahar had taken to spending more and more of his time on the knoll, though he was repelled by it as well.

That afternoon, he took out the Star Axe, which he had left in his traveling pack once he had reached Swamp's End. It was one of his rare moments of peace, for he was torn between the urgency to leave, and his duty to the Hermit. He had been brooding all week and it was a rarity for him to walk the crest of the hill without a thought. But today, holding the Star Axe in his hands, he felt his spirit being cleansed by the wind, his body feeling as vibrant as the quaking aspen that grew on the mound. The blade was clean, with a bright silver color. Kenlahar searched for signs of rust, then for even a scratch on the smooth blade. It was indented on both sides, curving in a crescent, with room for a narrow haft.

He realized with a start after carrying it so long, that it still didn't seem to weigh anything. It appeared to be sharp, yet when he scraped the blade against his fingernail it did not flake the nail. Curious, he returned to the side of the shack, where the Hermit kept a grindstone. He set the blade of the axe toward the grindstone and began to pedal it into action. Sparks flew off into the snow. After a few minutes he tried the blade; it again seemed dull. As an experiment, he threw it at the nearest tree. It glanced off the tree and sheared the bark cleanly. Kenlahar picked it up and pressed it against the bare wood. Without leverage, it sank half an inch into the wood. It would cut anything but his own flesh!

Now he had the time he had wished for, so he cut the strongest fibered wood he could find and shaped a handle for the blade. A small tree at the crest of the knoll provided him with a short, thick stock. Warming the wood over a fire, bringing out the reddish sap, he formed a handle. The hardened pitch was resilient and captured his grip. When he was finished, he felt and looked at his handiwork with satisfaction. It was not as fancy as some he had seen, but it was strong and light. When he had finished attaching it, the weapon handled as balanced and light as a child's wooden sword, but with deadly effect. Slightly ashamed at his fascination with the talisman he never intended to use, Kenlahar angled it back into his travel pack and tried to forget it.

He was chopping wood with a normal axe when the rider appeared. He stood waiting as a creature that he had never before seen, but which had played such strong roles in the books, appeared on the road. Horses did not exist on the island or in the Tream, and until now the visitors to the Hermit's shack had been the poorest of the Queen's subjects.

The rider was an even stranger sight than the steed. Kenlahar had never seen such a wild display of color. The cloak was rich blue and lined with fur. The pants and tunic were a matched soft red, and yellow boots rose to his knees. The wearer of these colorful clothes was a young man whose face seemed soft and plump, in contrast to the coarse, lined faces of the peasants.

Kenlahar was shocked out of staring when he saw the look in the stranger's eyes. He recognized the look. Though that look had been reserved for him alone at the House of Lahar, Kenlahar realized that this boy probably looked on all peasants with contempt.

The stranger began to draw out his sword and Kenlahar hastily bowed his head low. When he looked up again, the noble had already dismissed him. "They said that there is an old hermit who lives here," the young man said arrogantly. "I wish to speak with him." Kenlahar suddenly felt an urge to upset this complacent young man. "He is ill, my lord."

The stranger drew back and looked nervously at the shack, "Ill?"

Kenlahar disguised a smile, but decided not to play with this dangerous young man. "It is age, my lord. Nothing more."

"Ah," the noble said, looking relieved. He glanced at Kenlahar and said, "I am going to stay here for a few days and I wish to be as comfortable as possible. If I am satisfied," he tossed a gold piece, "you'll get more. Now stable the horse. I'll want him in good condition when I leave."

"Yes, my lord." Kenlahar started to lead the horse away.

"Wait!" The stranger looked at him sharply. "You speak differently. Where are you from?"

Kenlahar's distrust of this young man urged him not to let himself appear to be anything other than a peasant. "I'm sorry, my lord. I have always talked this way. Since I was a child. I injured my mouth…" he shrugged.

"I see. You peasants can never care for yourselves." "Yes, my lord." Kenlahar disliked himself for the ease with which he fell into the role of servant. That night he fed the noble the last of the fresh vegetables and a side of ham he had been saving in the event that the Hermit recovered enough to eat it.

The Hermit was sleeping most of the time now, and he only once awoke to inquire about the visitor. When he had been told, the Hermit merely shrugged and went back to sleep, muttering that there was little the Queen and all her nobles could do to him now.

The young noble, who had not bothered to tell them who he was, ignored both him and Kenlahar, who retreated to the stable for the night. He awoke after a terrifying dream that he could not remember and pulled the Star Axe from his pack. He placed it in the straw near his head and fell into a deep sleep.

The old Hermit woke in the middle of the night, lucid and clear-headed. A few feet away, in the crude bed Kenlahar usually occupied, the Prince of Kernback slept fitfully. The Hermit wished more bad dreams on the Prince. The hate he felt for the Prince of Kernback was unusual for the gentle herbalist. He had planned all his life to replace the Prince with the Son of Lahar. The old man knew he was dying. He had had a long life, many times the span of most men. In his youth he had traveled from the very stars, and had attended Lahar himself.

He was sorry now that he had ever joined the others of the Raggorak in the overthrow of Lahar. His life since then had been spent trying to right that wrong, and atone for the deed. Slowly, over many hundreds of years, he had convinced the others of the Raggorak, subtly and stealthily, of the need for a return of Lahar or one of his descendants. Then the extraordinary birth of Kenlahar had occurred. The event still mystified the Hermit. Could the stranger really have been Lahar himself, as the Healer Corn maintained? There was no denying Kenlahar's possession of Alcress!

Now his role in the restoration of the family was fulfilled. He could not help the Axe-bearer any longer. The Hermit could extend his life unnaturally, but unlike the others of the Raggorak he had grown tired of living. He slipped his hand through the layer of blankets. There, at the bottom, he found the pitted meteorite. For an hour he debated calling together the Raggorak. When he had been under the influence of the poisonous herb, he had seen the future—and he was content. He could not call forth his brethren of the Raggorak to warn them of their fall. He replaced the meteorite under the layers of blankets, and went back to sleep.

———

The next morning the stranger had gone from the hut. Kenlahar hoped for a little while that the man had left the Borderland, but the noble appeared that evening in time to demand a dinner. Kenlahar learned to his horror that the stranger had been digging into the barrow. The one good aspect of the Hermit's illness was that the old man did not learn of the sacrilege.

Over the next few days the Hermit's condition seemed to take a sudden turn for the worse. Kenlahar was kept busy tending to his needs and those of the Border Folk, who began to show up in greater numbers as the fame of his healing powers, and news of the old Hermit's illness, spread through the Borderland. He was surprised at the reverence in which these farmers and laborers held the Hermit. In all the previous month, this respect had not shown itself; only when it became apparent that the Hermit was dying did the people make their feelings known.

Even more surprising to Kenlahar was the way this respect was beginning to be shown to him as well. One night, as the mourners watched, the Hermit woke from his delirium long enough to make a sign of benediction over Kenlahar's head. After that the Border Folk began to look on him in awe.

Early one morning, the Hermit died in his sleep. Kenlahar had somehow hoped that the old man would survive the illness—there had seemed something enduringly ancient about him.

The stranger had left the hut before light; either not noticing or not caring that the Hermit had died in the same room where he had slept.

Sadly, Kenlahar told the peasants as they arrived. The news seemed to spread quickly. By noon the hilltop was overflowing with mourners. Again the number of people who lived in the Borderland surprised Kenlahar; there were many more than he had imagined. The peasants removed the body from the dwelling and with quiet dignity carried it to the hill, a narrow path in the crowd opening before them. Curious, Kenlahar followed the delegation. There was little to see, until the body was in the ground. Then the skies were filled with the wails of a thousand women, and children threw themselves on the soft, loose earth. Even the men seemed overwhelmed, some tearing the hair from their heads.

Then suddenly there was silence. Kenlahar started when he realized that all eyes had turned to him. One decrepit old peasant slowly approached him. "You are our Herbalist, now," the man said, as if he was bestowing a title upon him.. Without asking for any acceptance, the people began to quit the hillside, leaving Swamp's End as Kenlahar had first seen it—empty and deserted.

The imperious stranger showed up at twilight again, and merely shrugged at the news of the Hermit's death. Kenlahar made preparations in secret to leave Swamp's End. There was nothing to keep him there; no duty to any but the people of the Borderland, The same kind of duty had not kept him at the House of Lahar nor, after that, the village of the People of the Cormat. His search for the secret of the Star Axe had precedence over all other callings. Besides, he told himself, he had not asked for the responsibilities that people seemed to want to give up to him.

He was awake the next morning when the noble left to dig up the barrow. Kenlahar's fear of the barrow had worn off, as if a hex had been removed. He decided to follow the stranger and watch the excavation. While the stranger jealously reserved the right to dig in the sizeable hole he had already created, Kenlahar walked idly around the barrow.

Overnight the barrow seemed to have grown in its sense of evil, yet Kenlahar no longer felt constrained from searching its secrets. He kicked at the dirt at the base of the mound; something metallic flashed in the cloud of dust. The earth seemed to peel away for him, the top layer of grass revealing beneath it dry roots and a chalky soil that made him shiver when he rubbed it between his fingers. Without thinking, he reached for the shiny object, and fell to his knees with a cry, flinging the offending object from his hand. The young grave- robber quickly emerged from the barrow's wound and irritably strode to where Kenlahar knelt stunned.

"What is it?" he asked. Kenlahar just pointed to the rusted blade of a dagger, which gleamed red in the dust. With a sudden look of joy, the stranger sprang toward the blade—but at the last second hesitated. He gingerly touched the blade and then, encouraged, picked it up. He examined it, apparently finding marks in the metal. Triumphantly, he held it up to the sunlight and addressed the heavens, "I have found it! My long search has ended!" Suddenly, he seemed to notice Kenlahar watching him. Suspiciously, he asked, "What is your name?"

Kenlahar felt he should quickly allay the noble's fears. "My name is Kenlahar, my lord," he said as humbly as he could. "I am happy that you have found what you wanted."

"Know then, Kenlahar, that you are addressing Prince Molnar, heir to the throne of Kernback! And this," he said, holding up the dagger, "is Toraq's Dirk—and Toraq's Bane! It is a most powerful weapon, to be defeated only by the Star Axe—which is forever lost in the mire of the Tream." Kenlahar was astonished by the identification of the blade. Toraq's Dirk, a curved dagger, had absorbed much of the Sorcerer King's power on the day it had turned against its master, and had become Toraq's Bane. Supposedly guarded by one of the Raggorak, the Sorcerer King was unable to acquire his most powerful weapon, even if he had known where it lay. Yet legend had it that the evil of Toraq's Bane still attracted evil to it.

Kenlahar bowed low, excited by the information he had just been given, but not for any reason that the Prince might have thought. If this man was indeed the Prince of Kernback then he was the person that Kenlahar had traveled to see. Surely a Prince would be able to supply the help that the House of Lahar needed, and surely he could help Kenlahar find Balor and the Companions! But again caution told him not to reveal anything yet. The Prince of Kernback's next words could not have been more welcome. "I command you to accompany me to Kernback. You shall be my servant."

———

When the two men began their 'journey the next morning, the Prince riding his stallion and Kenlahar walking behind him, the Border Folk lined the dusty road. None tried to stop him, though their unhappiness at his departure was obvious. Guiltily, Kenlahar bowed his head and trudged on. The people misread his attitude as weariness, and soon a skinny nag was produced, apparently from someone's farm. Its young owner pressed the reins into Kenlahar's hands. Seeing that he could not refuse the gift, Kenlahar reluctantly accepted. There seemed to be even more inhabitants of the Borderland than he had ever dreamed, and all had turned out to silently see him off. Finally, the two travelers left the lowlands, leaving the eerie watchers behind, and began to climb toward the mountains.

The setting up of the first night's camp set the procedure for the rest of the journey. The two men half fell from their mounts, staggered to level ground and collapsed on their sleeping blankets. Kenlahar, however, was soon ordered to rise again and start a fire. On the fourth night of this routine, something happened which changed the nature of their relationship. On this night, Kenlahar could not find enough loose dry wood. He removed the Star Axe from his knapsack and soon had cut a large pile. He gathered the wood and turned toward the camp.

Prince Molnar stepped from behind a tree into his path. "Give it to me!" he said, and reached for the axe with an assurance that the command would be followed without resistance; never in his life had he been disobeyed, and such was the confidence in his voice that Kenlahar almost responded to it without thinking. It was the look of greed and triumph in Molnar's face that alerted him.

"No!" he cried, and sprang backward, raising the Star Axe in readiness for a fight. For a few seconds, Prince Molnar did not change his expression. Then his face contorted in a succession of emotions — disbelief, followed by growing anger and fury. Kenlahar had seen Molnar practice with his sword, wielding it with blinding speed; now he prepared for a short struggle he was certain to lose — unless Alcress could somehow save him. But the axe had shown little inclination to do anything since that first blinding flash. He was beginning to doubt his inheritance, and he did not think he could depend on its mythical powers. He prepared himself for death.

Warily, Kenlahar watched the fury slowly recede from the Prince's face; his freckled cheeks were regaining their usual pallor. Molnar's mouth slowly quirked into a smile, but the eyes remained cold and angry. His shoulders lifted in a short shrug. "It does not matter," the Prince said in a mocking tone. "I was merely curious."

Kenlahar was taken aback by the retreat. If he did not have faith in the Star Axe it appeared that Molnar did—even if he could not yet be certain that it was the ancient weapon. But never again would Molnar believe Kenlahar's servile demeanor. What had perhaps been only casual curiosity would now turn into an inquisition. "Forgive me, sire!" he said, though neither was fooled. "It is a worthless tool, yet it means much to me. It is all I have of home."

"It is not important, I said," Molnar answered, and turned his back and bounded up the trail.

That night as he fell asleep, Kenlahar could see Molnar's eyes gleam at him speculatively in the light of the campfire. He pulled his blankets closer around him and resolved to keep the Star Axe out of view for the rest of the trip. His dreams were peaceful, until suddenly he saw a face in his dreams that he knew instinctively was that of the Sorcerer King. He struck the evil face with the Star Axe, and the weapon melted in his hands. He woke, drenched with sweat. The tingling sensation of intense pain remained. Molnar sat, as if struck, on the ground between the two beds.

The Prince recovered first. "You were having a nightmare," he said. "I tried to wake you and...a flame... leaped at me from the axe!"

Kenlahar thought he detected a mixed note of fear and loathing in Molnar's voice. The Prince was making no effort to rise and Kenlahar was sure that he could see the red gleam of Toraq's Bane half hidden beneath Molnar's legs. "I am fine now," he said, as if he suspected nothing. "I am sorry for what the...ah, axe ...might have done, for it was without my conscious will." He purposely turned from Molnar

110

and looked at the sky. As he expected Molnar quickly got up. Kenlahar thought he heard the sound of a knife going back into its sheath.

"Let us go back to sleep," Molnar said, behind him.

Kenlahar agreed and soon both were settled back in their bedrolls, as if nothing had happened. But Kenlahar was unable to sleep, and hours later rose and, with a firebrand, bent over the area where the Prince had fallen. To end all his doubts, the imprint of the curved blade of Toraq's Bane was clear in the dust. It was only with his hand on Alcress, which he no longer bothered to hide, that Kenlahar was finally able to sleep.

Soon they neared the foothills of a huge mountain, which Molnar dismissed with the name of Crakoa. But Kenlahar was amazed by its size. The Prince then brought out some filthy rags from his bags, fully as filthy and infested as the poorest commoner, and ordered Kenlahar to put them on. Kenlahar was about to refuse indignantly, when he saw the Prince bring out another set of rags and begin to put them on himself.

"The horses are worth stealing of course," the Prince said. "But we may as well make ourselves as little tempting as possible." The hills were infested with bandits, he explained. Now Kenlahar understood why the mountain range was called the Sanctuary.

"The outlaws have always been a nuisance," Molnar said. "Now they seem to have organized under some fellow named Whistler."

The road led north up the mountains, crisscrossing back and forth into the low mists. Soon, for the first time in his life, Kenlahar found himself above the cloud level. They flowed like a slowly melting layer of ice. Only the mountain Crakoa pierced the tray ocean. It was fully as wet as his native country; yet here, instead of the swamps, was a tangled growth of greenery.

Soon they had entered the lava fields. Here, the Prince explained, the Sorcerer King had called forth the very substance of the earth and sent it against the Starborn. But Lahar had called upon the Star Axe — there was no break in his story at the mention of the weapon — and sent it back. Beneath them were thousands of men, trapped forever in the rock. They had come upon the field in the bright light of afternoon. Glass obsidian nodules glittered red and black in a background of dull black lava. The trees were bright red and yellow against the uneven field.

Molnar ordered him to dismount and they led their horses onto a narrow trail in the lava flow. Without the rough, winding path their shoes would soon have been ripped apart. After a few hours the lava stretched in all directions beyond the sight of the travelers, a vast sea of jagged rock. Occasionally they would come across islands of earth, covered by virgin wood. Some were quite large and once within, Kenlahar could almost convince himself that he was in a large forest — but as they approached the summit of the pass, the oasis became fewer and fewer.

Finally it seemed to Kenlahar that they were headed downhill. Then there was no doubt. The trail suddenly veered severely down a steep slope. It was frightening, for the barren terrain seemed to emphasize the steep incline. The Prince and his horse went down it without hesitation, so he followed without comment.

Halfway down, Kenlahar could touch the side of the mountain on one side and drop a pebble onto the trail beneath from his other hand. He felt dangerously top- heavy while the horse swayed precariously over the drop. Every time the horse tripped slightly, Kenlahar's heart would seem to stop briefly, despite the blasé, weary attitude of his nag. Luckily, the skinny horse simply followed the other horse, and Kenlahar had to do little except try and stay on.

Soon, as they descended again into the mists, even the side of the mountain disappeared; all that could be seen was the trail, twisting before them like a ghost.

The Qreq chose this moment to attack. Out of the mists on both sides of the trail came eerie cries of "Qreq!", and following them he saw the albino skins of the enemy flash in the dull gray mists. The Prince immediately drew Toraq's Bane, but Kenlahar was too stunned to reach for the Star Axe. "Use the battleaxe!" he heard Molnar cry out as the war party of Qreq split. Half of the enemy force headed for each of them. The frightened horse saved Kenlahar for a few moments by bounding recklessly down the trail, but out of the mists another party of Qreq moved to intercept him. Reluctantly, Kenlahar removed the Star Axe from its sheath. But he did not need its power.

Out of the mists came the ragged shapes of the farmers of the Borderland. The Bordermen were silent, but deadly; their weapons crude, but effective. What they lacked in skill, they made up in numbers and determination. Out of the mists they came, surrounding and cutting off the Qreq. They began to close in with an eerie silence to their deadly strokes. It was not a battle, Kenlahar thought, but a massacre. Kenlahar watched in shock, and the Prince in open-mouthed amazement, as the farmers cut off the Qreq's only routes of escape. The Qreq ceased shouting their war cries, and concentrated on their fight. Soon they quit fighting, and ran, thinking only of surviving. But the Bordermen showed no mercy.

When the slaughter was done, the farmers bowed as one and disappeared one by one into the mists. They carried off their dead and wounded in their arms. Too late Kenlahar realized that they were leaving. "Wait!" he cried. "Let me heal your wounded!"

"Let them go," the Prince said. "They are not important." Molnar had dismounted and was examining the bodies of the Qreq. He did not seem surprised by their deliverance—perhaps he believed that it was his due as heir to the throne. Nor did he seem concerned with the deadly potential of his subjects.

Kenlahar, however, was surprised and did notice. One of the last of the Bordermen gestured at the Prince threateningly behind his back with a scythe. Silently, Kenlahar shook his head, and then the man was gone. There was no sign of their presence but the bloody bodies of the Qreq.

Molnar had begun to question Kenlahar about their attackers. "What are they?" he asked, kicking one body curiously. Kenlahar had often wondered what made the Qreq so strange. As a healer he suspected a hereditary disease—or one given them purposely by the Warlord—that made them unnaturally quick and tall, and obedient; but which had the ugly side effects of loss of hair, color to the skin, and all body fat. But he had never seen a Qreq up close before, much less examined one, so he had remained unsure.

Here, Kenlahar thought, was his chance to tell his story. The evidence to support him was lying on the ground—his appeal might even have a chance now. Perhaps the Prince of Kernback would give the House of Lahar the help it needed.

But he was too shocked by the attack to talk. Over and over again he asked himself why the Qreq should have strayed so far from their Havens to attack two men. Perhaps, Toraq had maintained a watch on the barrow, in case his dagger should be found. But that was to assume that all the legends were true and that the Hermit had actually been a Raggorak, guarding Toraq's Bane!

Yet Kenlahar believed that the Dirk had not been the only motive for the attack. He was certain that the Warlord not only knew that the Star Axe had left the House of Lahar, but knew where it was!

The two continued the journey speechlessly. As they once more approached the lower lands, the air began to smell different—dry and fragrant. The terrain showed a lack of moisture. Jigsaw-barked pines stood tall and alone, with only low scrub brush at their bases. It was a hot day, and when they reached a swift river they both plunged into it. Afterwards the Prince changed back into his colorful clothes and Kenlahar into his own traveling clothes.

There seemed to have been a shift in status, and for the first time the Prince was pleasant to him. Molnar no longer seemed in a hurry, and they spent the rest of the day fishing for the huge trout in the stream. "We are on the outskirts of Kernback," the Prince said. He began to talk lovingly of his kingdom.

After' the Raggorak had finally been overthrown, Molnar admitted, the Kingdom of Kernback had fallen into a dark age. But with the ascension to the throne of his family, the kingdom had grown magnificent once more. As Molnar talked on, Kenlahar began to sense the truth behind the words. The quick succession of rulers told of times of great turmoil. Later he was to see the lands and cities going to waste—a great decimation of the population had occurred. The mighty city-state that dominated the Outside, was in these later centuries, just a village compared to its former bustling metropolis. Yet it still remained the center of power, and all who wished power must travel to Kernback.

Nevertheless, the Prince was in a mellow mood and Kenlahar felt it was time to tell his story. Molnar listened without interruption, his eyes glowing at the passages dealing with the Star Axe. He did not seem to doubt the tale, nor was he frightened. To the people of Kernback and its dominions, the Sorcerer King was no more than a half forgotten legend—a bogeyman with which to frighten their children. They had forgotten that his evil made the worse evil of their villains seem petty. At the end of the story, the Prince exclaimed, "Do not worry, Kenlahar. The Kingdom of Kernback will save the House of Lahar! Tomorrow we shall see the ivory walls of my city. Any doubts you still have will disappear when we stand before the throne."

The afternoon had passed with the telling of the two tales, and they prepared for bed. But Kenlahar did indeed have doubts, and he grasped the Star Axe in his hands protectively as he fell asleep.

CHAPTER XI

Molnar was impatient to leave early the next morning, announcing grandly that they were now within the dominions of Kernback. But it was not until after a hard and dusty day of riding that they began to sight tended, structured farmlands. The few inhabitants seemed to melt into the checkered countryside at Molnar's approach. The evasion was discreet, but it was noticeable. As the two tired and filthy travelers neared the first of the large manicured estates, only one of the tenant farmers came forward to greet them. The farmer apologized profusely about the need for harvesting that had drawn the others away, but even Kenlahar could tell that he was not telling the truth. Kenlahar also saw that the man was terrified, though the Prince was virtually alone and undefended. Prince Molnar, all charm and graciousness, waved away the explanations.

This breed of farmer, Kenlahar observed, was far different than his proud, but much poorer cousins in the Borderland. The man was well fed and clothed, but fawning and servile—even to Kenlahar, a stranger dressed in little better than rags. The man led them toward a pine lodge, set beside a small, clear stream at the center of the estate. The master was away, he said, and nervously explained that this was Herald's Manor, the land of the noble and munificent Sar Devern. The Prince of Kernback, of course, was always welcome at the Herald's Manor.

The empty dining room was spacious and the long table was set with glittering gold and silver. But Molnar insisted on informality and simple fare, and they were taken instead to the workers kitchen. The kitchen drudges sprang to work, terrified, but pleased by the honor of the Prince's presence as well. Midway through a luncheon of what seemed to Kenlahar to have the proportions of a feast, he saw the reason for their fear.

A thunderous approach of horses was accompanied by a roar of pain from Molnar. The Prince spat out the shattered pieces of a tooth. The kitchen slave who had served the bread cowered on the floor before him. When the soldiers entered, an ominous quiet hung in the air. The leader of the troops seemed astounded at the sight of Molnar, but immediately recovered from his surprise and bowed. "My Prince!" Then he noticed the looked of pain in Molnar's face. "What has happened?" Molnar waved a hand toward the girl, and said through tense lips, "This slave served me bread with a stone in it!"

The commander of the soldiers hesitated, and then reluctantly shouted out crisp orders. Molnar's vicious tone had left him with no choice. Several soldiers took her away roughly.

Next, Kenlahar was beckoned for. "You know the art of healing," Molnar said. "Heal!" The Prince of Kernback was becoming more and more imperious as they neared the city, Kenlahar noticed bitterly. He wondered what would happen to the girl.

Within minutes he had extracted the rest of the tooth. Molnar bit down on a fluff of cloth and nodded to the leader of the troop. "Sar Devern. I appreciate your appearance. But—" he raised an eyebrow, "what is the need for soldiers?"

"My Prince," the scarred warrior answered. "Much has happened since you left. Strange things…

His voice trailed off and he looked at Kenlahar with a question in his eyes. "We were on our way to investigate the latest of the reports. Something has destroyed our border post at Sige Tomar."

"Ah—brigands," Molnar mused.

"No, my Prince. These brigands were not human." "I see," Molnar said, eyeing Kenlahar with the same expression as Sar Devern's. "I believe I know of what you speak. I must return to the city at once. I will need two of your freshest and fastest mounts."

"I shall form an escort immediately," Sar Devern said, saluting and turning to leave.

"No," Molnar barked, stopping the old soldier at the door. "Go on to Sige Tomar. I do not wish an escort, or any fanfare. I want to surprise my mother, the Queen." From outside came the scream of a woman, which was suddenly broken off. Kenlahar shuddered, but Molnar seemed as unconcerned with the servant's execution as he was of the panic the reports of massacres had created in the farmers.

———

The next morning, on schedule, the troop set out for the Borderland. Kenlahar and Molnar rode out through the gate just behind them, but turned down the road in the opposite direction.

The road became wider and smoother, and crushed red lava stone rose in a cloud, covering everything that moved through it. The two started to meet other travelers, who scurried off the road at Molnar's approach. Moving swiftly along the road at first, soon even they were clogged in the traffic of carts, livestock, and humans.

Out of the flat farmlands, in the far distance, rose two hills. Neither was tall, yet they seemed enormous on the level plain. On their peaks were the White Walls of Kernback. The white ivory which coated their stones came from a species of tusked animal so long extinct' that none could remember the creature's name, the Prince explained. The blinding glare of the reflected sun off the ivory was a formidable defense on sun-filled days, Molnar boasted. From it came the proud cry of the citizen of the city-state: "Cast down your eyes before the White Walls of Kernback!"

Kenlahar was indeed forced to turn his eyes from the sight, for the glare hurt even from this distance. The road split, and most of the side traffic went on to the north; a very few travelers turned south. But Molnar went straight, by way of a narrow path that wound between and behind the two hills. In this untraveled, deserted region, Molnar finally turned to face the sheer cliffs. The shadows rose swiftly from the plains, as the sun went behind a cloud, up the reddish cliffs, until only the White Walls remained, brilliantly lit—then their glare also winked out.

The disguised portals of a staircase were revealed from under the rubble of an overhang. Molnar bounded up the secret staircase two steps at a time. Kenlahar, with a tired sigh, began to follow as fast as he could. The granite steps were dusty and narrow, and circled in a tight, steep spiral. The air was stale and what little light there was came from a small shaft far above. Kenlahar was breathing deeply from the exertion and coughing up the thick dust as a result, when he noticed the black gap the stairs created to his right. In the dim light, with his thoughts turned inward, he had been negligently stepping only inches from the deep hole! From that point on, he trailed his hand along the wall.

Molnar had apparently left him far behind, so when Kenlahar reached a small opening to the left of the stairs, he gratefully turned into it—escaped the thick dust, the yawning hole—and postponed for a little while the meeting with the Queen. Kenlahar could see no purpose for the tiny room; it was a featureless square, except for the curious height of the entrance and the lack of any dust.

As far as Kenlahar could tell the staircase was endless, and it seemed to him that he had been climbing for hour upon hour. Muscles he thought had been toughened by his long trek now protested at his new test of his endurance. But when he had rested, he moved on. It was only his hunger and thirst that drove him upward. The dust caught in his throat, and his belly cried out for food.

He had once again turned into one of the small rooms for a rest when he heard Molnar's returning footsteps. "There you are!" the Prince said. "What is taking you so long?"

As they marched on up the steps, Kenlahar noticed that despite Molnar's best efforts, he too was breathing hoarsely, and no longer seemed interested in going on ahead without Kenlahar. So, at Kenlahar's pace, they reached the seventh and final of the small openings. The dim light, he now saw, had come from a conical shaft which now revealed darkening skies.

Molnar paused and ran his fingers over the stonewalls. He nodded to himself in satisfaction and motioned for Kenlahar to join him. He swept Kenlahar behind him with one arm, and making one last mysterious hand movement over the face of the stone, squeezed back against the wide entrance. The wall started grinding toward them and then, at the last moment, swung away—blocking the staircase and created an opening the wall. The new doorway was curtained off.

"Thus even our secret passages are defended," Molnar said proudly. "Only one, or at most two, grown men may enter the halls of Kernback through these entrances."

Molnar was whispering. Kenlahar, in the same hushed tone, asked, "Where are we?"

"Where?" the Prince echoed, and smiled. "We are at the entrance of my mother's domain. Now, wait here. Do not enter until I call for you."

Molnar vanished through the curtains. Presently, Kenlahar heard muffled voices, then Molnar's distant, but unmistakable voice calling his name. Unable to imagine what lay beyond, Kenlahar drew a deep breath and parted the curtains.

He emerged on the floor of a huge crater, stretching from one side of the mountain peak to the other. He stopped, in awe of the man-made volcano. The lip of the crater towered over him, instilling in Kenlahar a sudden irrational fear of being buried alive by the massive cliffs. The smooth walls curved away into the dark, and night skies sparkled at the center of what had once been solid rock. The floor was smooth and seamless and the black polished surface reflected the stars above, creating a sense in Kenlahar of being suspended in space. With a shudder he saw the red moon of Bantling hanging directly overhead.

"Kenlahar!" Molnar's impatient call brought him back to his senses. The staircase had deposited the two travelers near the throne of the Queen, which was spotlighted by a circle of torches. The ring of light seemed to cease just a few feet away from the throne.

"Step forward, Kenlahar, so that we can see you," Molnar shouted, though Kenlahar was already very near. He hesitated—it took all of his courage to step into that circle of light. Yet finally, he walked through the shimmering wall of torches.

"There you are!" Puzzled relief showed in Molnar's face.

Strewn over the enormous high-backed throne was a many-hued pile of blankets. As Kenlahar approached he began to distinguish a person beneath the blankets. First an immense, round face and then two plump hands emerged from the shapeless mass. Molnar was the only person visible to Kenlahar, but he doubted they were alone.

Prince Molnar turned to the bundle of blankets on the throne. "Mother, this is Kenlahar. He had journeyed far in his search for his brother." He glanced sideways at Kenlahar. "Balor was the name, I believe."

"My son," emerged a soft, wheezy voice. "Why do you...bring us...this person?" The Queen seemed unable to finish a sentence in one breath.

Flamboyantly, as if what he was about to say was greatly amusing, Molnar said, "He is my gift to you, Mother."

"Do not tease me, Molnar." The panting, dry voice was imbued with venom. "I will not care who rules after me, for I shall be dead. Perhaps I shall take you with me as well."

Molnar paled, and for the first time since Kenlahar had met him his swagger disappeared. "I am not mocking you, Mother!" He removed his pack from his back, and brought out a velvet bag. Untying the strings, he poured the precious stones into the Queen's outstretched hands. The wheezing breath grew louder as the contents of Molnar's pack overflowed her hands and fell onto her voluminous lap. "Are you pleased, Mother?"

"You have done well." Her plump fingers dug through the treasure.

That is nothing, he said, pointing at the wealth with contempt. The fingers stopped groping and the moon face turned expectantly toward him. He drew a curved blade from its scabbard; the metal was pale and cold in the torchlight. He uttered a short laugh. "Toraq's Dagger! *Now* what do you think of your son?"

"You have done well, indeed."

Molnar laughed again. "Yes, it is well, and still not all. There is one treasure more valuable than any other! Did I tell you, Mother, that

Kenlahar comes from a land deep in the Tream—a place called the House of Lahar?"

Kenlahar became conscious of the weight of the Star Axe around his neck. Molnar was going to betray him, he saw, in order to impress that thing on the throne. He began to back away from them.

The Queen had leaned forward, jewels falling from her lap unheeded. "You have the Star Axe?"

At that moment, Kenlahar vanished into the dark shadows. Too late the Queen and Molnar saw their error. "Seize him!" she cried and collapsed in a coughing fit, while the Prince desperately shouted orders.

Kenlahar ran across the gigantic throne room searching for a way out. As he had suspected, the darkness had concealed many guards, who were even now lighting torches all around him. Their strategy soon became obvious. The torches began to form a ring around the perimeter of the crater. Kenlahar halted and, crouching, removed Alcress from under his jerkin.

Why was he carrying the Star Axe if he never intended to use it? he thought. Why had it chosen him, when he had chosen the path of peace? He did not know what powers he might unleash if he used the Star Axe—or if he could control those powers once he had unleashed them.

Even in the increasingly violent course his life had taken, he had not yet seriously injured another man. He had not set out with the intention of not using it, but the fates of the Raggorak had kept him from using Lahar's battleaxe. He would not start using it now, though it meant his death. He re-sheathed the Star Axe and looked up to see the guards complete their circle. The ring of torches began to close around him.

His mind made up, Kenlahar got to his feet and started running toward the only exit he knew of. The encirclement had not yet closed beyond the throne, and Molnar was standing where Kenlahar had left him. Gauging the progress of the guards, Kenlahar picked up speed and burst into the spotlighted area. As he hoped, the guards had kept a respectful hole in their circle. Prince Molnar only had time to utter a short exclamation before Kenlahar pushed him from his feet, and then he was beyond the throne and the guards.

The curtained doorway was closed off. Desperately, Kenlahar heaved at the stone door, but it would not budge. He ran his fingers over a portion of the wall, as he had seen Molnar do, but it was a futile end to his gamble. He turned to meet his pursuers—and since he had rejected the use of the Star Axe, his death.

Suddenly, a few feet away, another door swung open. Kenlahar sprang through just as it began to swing ponderously shut behind him. Molnar arrived and hesitated, stopping to judge the width of the rapidly closing exit. Then it was too late, and his furious shout was abruptly cut off as the door snapped shut.

Kenlahar breathlessly turned to look at his new surroundings. In the corner of the room a young girl gaped at him. She was dressed in rags, which contrasted with the luxury of the chamber, and Kenlahar assumed that she was a servant. The walls were covered with thick tapestries, and the floor was filled with cushions and rugs, the Queen's colorful blankets. There did not appear to be any exit from the room.

Suddenly he felt a hand on his arm. He looked down at the girl questioningly. In response to his look she led him to the wall and held a tapestry aside. Kenlahar began to speak, but she held her hand to her mouth. So he said nothing and ducked behind the curtain after her.

The girl led him down a long narrow tunnel. Again and again they descended short flights of stairs, which opened to yet more long halls. Kenlahar lost all sense of direction and soon he was not certain any longer if they were going deeper into the mountains or outward to the surface. They encountered no other people. Finally a blank wall confronted them.

The wall slid aside as Kenlahar and the girl drew near. A large fireplace, filled with burning logs, took up one whole side of the room beyond; the room felt freezing cold, nonetheless. The bare stonewalls and floor had innumerable cracks from the constant changes in temperature. The room was large, and empty of furniture except for an enormous desk in one comer, its every cubbyhole filled by strewn parchment. Kenlahar's eyes were taken by the sight of a man so that

that the stool he sat on to work at his massive desk almost came to Kenlahar's waist.

The man had his back to them as they approached. He turned, his pen held delicately in long fingers. "Ah—Kenlahar. You have arrived at last!"

Fascinated, Kenlahar watched the man unwind and stand; he seemed as absurdly slender as he was tall. The long arms gestured at the young servant girl. "You must forgive us," the man said. "But the Queen will allow only very young, very deaf girls to attend her." The girl nodded to his hand motions and left the' way she had come. "Yet they understand enough to hate her," the man continued, and waved his arm hospitably at the fire. They stood near it, warming themselves as they talked. The girl soon returned with a tray of food.

"I have already seen how servants are treated in your kingdom," Kenlahar said.

"The royal family of Kernback was once vigorous and humane," the tall man acknowledged, "but now it is dying out. The present ruler has few of her predecessors' strengths and none of their humanity. Her son, Prince Molnar, will someday be just as fat as his Mother, but will have none of the humanity or strengths. Perhaps only a new dynasty can save this ancient city."

"Who are you?" Kenlahar finally managed to ask, through a mouthful of food.

"I am Karrack, the Queen's physician—a healer as you are, though perhaps a bit more sophisticated in my medications." He paused, waiting politely for Kenlahar's next question.

Kenlahar supplied it, "How do you know who I am?"

"I know much of what happens in the Queen's dominions," the physician said. "Your presence here is an example of that. It was I who sent Prince Molnar to the barrow of Toraq. I feel responsible for what happens to you! And I believe your next question will be, why? An answer to that question would require too much time for now. So if you are through playing who, what, why, where, when, and how, you had better get as far from Kernback as possible."

The physician turned from the fire and walked back to his desk, evidently dismissing Kenlahar from his attention. The wall slid aside.

Kenlahar was at a loss. The entire interview had taken less then five minutes—the tall physician mystified him. "But where shall I go?"

The tall man turned from his desk and said shortly, "You will find the help you need in the mountains, Kenlahar."

Once again the young servant girl solved his quandary, by appearing at the opening and motioning for him to follow. He knew that he did not have any choice but to abide by Karrack's advice. Kenlahar couldn't blame the doctor for choosing not to hide him somewhere among the secret corridors. What a fool he had been, Kenlahar thought, to have so blindly followed the treacherous Prince Molnar into the city!

———

Karrack watched the wall slide shut, and opened the top of his desk. His most precious possession—a shapeless gray rock—slipped into his hands. He greeted the visitants one by one, until four of the Raggorak had replied. The Healer Coron expressed surprise, and the Cormatine annoyance, that it was Karrack, and not the Hermit who had called the meeting.

"I have been waiting for word from him," he said. "Why did he not tell us of the Axe-bearer? When Balor reappeared at the House of Lahar, I feared all was lost!"

"The Hermit is dead," Karrack announced. "Kenlahar arrived at the city this night. Prince Molnar, who was holding Toraq's Bane, accompanied him. He helped the Axe-bearer on his way and then I guessed the Hermit felt his duty was done. He has allowed himself to die."

"I was afraid he would do that," the fifth and last of the Raggorak said. "He has never forgiven himself—or us—for the exile of Lahar. But it removes all my doubts about Kenlahar. The Hermit would never have allowed himself to die, unless he knew Kenlahar would succeed."

"You will soon meet him yourself," Karrack directed at the fifth man. "He has left Kernback. He will be headed for the Sanctuary Mountains. Watch for him."

"I intend to stay with him for as long as it takes! Kenlahar has learned all he needs to know; has been hardened enough. Now we must maneuver him into a situation where he must resort to using the Star Axe. Perhaps the Healer Coron's training of the value of life will serve to force him to wield Alcress!"

CHAPTER XII

Kenlahar followed the servant girl down one empty corridor after another. Dust and rubble from the cracked, crumbling, walls had carpeted the floors with a thick layer, attesting to their ancient age. Kenlahar noticed that the walls were covered with painted murals, which astounded him. The family of Lahar did not replicate life on objects; no doubt the Elders had once banned it—for forgotten reasons. Fascinated by the pictures, Kenlahar began walking almost at the girl's heels in an effort to catch all the features of the faces in the light of the single torch.

The representations of people in the murals were a kind of stiff, formal caricature—it fit Kenlahar's impression of the city folk. The rich colors, of reds and purples and greens, were amassed with such profusion that the tints seemed unnatural. There was none of the subtlety of line and color that Kenlahar remembered from the House of Lahar.

He exclaimed loudly at the sight of one of the figures. The servant girl turned and motioned for silence—indicating eloquently that they were near people and could be overheard. Kenlahar pointed speechlessly at the face on the wall. It was a dark face, with black hair and beard, and gaunt cheeks. The man was obviously surrounded by worshippers, and in his hand he held what Kenlahar knew to be the Star Axe. If the face had been clean-shaven, he would have looked exactly like Kenlahar!

The girl nodded, almost bowing, but Kenlahar could see no surprise in her eyes. Instead, she once again signaled for quiet and led on. Kenlahar followed apprehensively. Now he could hear people on the other side of the walls, and he marveled at the hidden hallways that honeycombed the city, and yet remained unknown to its citizens. The sounds of a bustling, populated city—the hawkers' shouts, the bickering of shoppers, the cries of children—reached his ears. The passageway ended abruptly at a dirty, faded wall hanging.

The girl made it known that he was to stay quiet and wait; then she went through the curtain. Kenlahar resisted the temptation to peek behind it, and the girl reappeared quickly, carrying a filthy, bloodstained cloak. As Kenlahar gingerly donned the garment, the girl pantomimed that he was to linger a few steps behind her. Then they went through the wall hangings.

Kenlahar found himself in the busy marketplace of the city. The houses were tight in upon one another, and the steep slope gave the impression of the buildings being stacked on top of each other. He had emerged from behind a butcher's stall. The meat cutter looked at him with a misleading casualness and Kenlahar nodded slightly, but the man did not respond. Kenlahar hurried after the young servant girl, who was already immersed in the crowd.

He found it all but impossible to both keep up with the nimble girl, and also make his way through the crowd, without stumbling into the shoppers. All the people—men, women, and children—seemed far more capable of avoiding collisions with each other he thought. But the bewildered, frightened fugitive seemed to have lost the ability, in his lonely wanderings, to dodge. Everywhere he turned he confronted someone, and he was sure that people were staring at him curiously. It was like a nightmare.

Inevitably, he slammed into someone. The man was almost two heads taller than Kenlahar, and he heard the stranger's breath forced out of his chest. His breath stopped as well when he saw the uniform of a Queen's soldier. The man said good-naturedly, "Watch it there, young man!"

Kenlahar mumbled his pardons and hurried away. He caught a glimpse of the frightened face of the girl staring back at him, and he willed himself to walk and not break into a panicked run. Don't look back, he told himself; but at the last moment the urge grew too strong and he gave in to the impulse.

He saw the soldier staring at him over the heads of the crowd, with a dawning suspicion growing in his face. When Kenlahar stared back at him, that suspicion seemed to change rapidly into a certainty. The puzzled eyes hardened and seemed to drill into Kenlahar, and the face set in a scowl. The soldier turned and waved to someone out of Kenlahar's sight.

The servant girl was now leading him into the thick of the crowd, and once in its midst he did not require persuading to discard the bright red butcher's coat. With an easy, fluid motion, the girl plucked another loose cloak from one of the many outdoor food stalls. The little girl also clipped a purse from the belt of a passerby, Kenlahar noticed. He was thankful for the new coat, for his hooded swamp cloak was all but shredded away.

Kenlahar put it on quickly. He was anticipating the paths of the other people now, and blending in inconspicuously. But it was too late. He soon saw that no matter what direction they emerged from the crowd into less populated, thinning parts of the throng—especially near the gates—patrols of soldiers were keeping a close watch on all the departing shoppers. Again and again, the girl and Kenlahar were forced to retreat back into the crowd's center. But the day was ending, and the people were beginning to drift slowly home. It would be an hour yet before they were all gone, but the market was already emptying noticeably. By now, even the escape to the butcher's stall was blocked off.

A cover to a stall slammed shut behind him, and Kenlahar jumped. It was obvious when he glanced at the girl that she would not be able to get him out of this trap. She had reverted at last into a frightened little servant girl, and Kenlahar felt ashamed that he'd expected her to extricate him again. It was time he quit following and made his own choices, he told himself. But there seemed to be no alternatives open to him. All he could think of was of somehow bypassing the patrols and he hand signed to the girl; first, a scooping movement, and then a soaring motion.

The girl seemed to understand something from these ambiguous signs and excitedly nodded her head. She rushed off and almost left Kenlahar so far behind that he lost sight of her. It did not matter. Kenlahar soon had a suspicion of where the girl was leading him. He could smell it before he actually saw it.

All the waste and slop of Kernback flowed through the culvert she showed him, but it was at no spot deeper than a few feet, or wider than it was deep. He noticed with distaste that it was so murky that he could easily conceal himself in it. But he would not get into it until he had to, he decided. They began to follow its course toward the walls.

This time they were able to venture out of the crowd much farther than they had before. Eventually, they emerged from the market entirely. Kenlahar had begun to hope that they would escape detection when he saw a patrol approaching. As he reluctantly waded into the culvert, Kenlahar thought he caught the ghost of a smile in the little girl's eyes, just before he lost sight of her. He made a resolution not to submerge into the noisome liquid until he was on the verge of being spotted, and crouched down under the edge of the culvert. That patrol veered off, and he was left alone.

Before he went on, Kenlahar hastily bundled what was left of his package of herbs and the jug of Cormat's blood into the remains of his rain-cloak, now one of only two reminders he still possessed from the House of Lahar. After a moment's hesitation he included the Star Axe.

He held the bundle over the refuse and waded down a steepening decline toward the distant walls. It appeared for a while that he would be able to walk through with no trouble. The number of people the soldiers had to search kept them busy; the increasing darkness helped conceal him, and a tendency not to get too near the stink by the townspeople aided him.

In the end it was not the soldiers who stopped him, but the culvert itself. As he approached the walls, Kenlahar saw that the conduit went underground. He hesitated at the tunnel, but eventually began to carefully descend. The incline grew suddenly sharper, and he struggled to maintain his footing in the sludge. The roof of the sewer left just enough room for his head, but the stench was overwhelming. Finally he reached the bottom, and Kenlahar felt in front of him an iron gate. The gate was evidently designed for men, and the way was securely blocked.

Angrily kicking the barrier, he felt, to his surprise, the bars give way just a couple of feet from the bottom. The sewage had corroded and weakened the gate long ago!

Outside he could see the moons of the Sistern in the night skies, and for a while he pressed his nose up against the bars, trying to catch the sweet night air. Then he wrapped his possessions even tighter in his bundle and prepared to dive under the gate. Taking a deep breath, he plunged into the flow. He kicked under, making a sloshing sound in the thick murk, and held his eyes tightly shut. Feeling his way with his free hand, he pulled himself under the shards of the gate. He felt his bundle catch on something sharp, and tried desperately to free it. Finally, just as he felt his air giving out, he pulled at it violently—and felt it give. Then he was up, gasping for breath.

Panic-stricken, Kenlahar searched the tattered remains of his makeshift pack. The Star Axe, the jar of Cormat's blood, the herbs, were gone—it was all gone! He dived back under, forgetting all his misgivings. His hands scraped the bottom, which was a thick layer of sludge. Inch by inch he felt along the floor, but each time he came up empty.

Finally, he forced himself to calm down. The current was not strong, and the Star Axe could not have gone far, he thought. He was out of the view of the walls and it was growing steadily darker. But it would not have mattered if he could have been seen, for he realized now that his life was joined to Alcress. He would search until he found it. That judgment soothed him, and he was oddly certain he would find it.

On the next dive his fingers touched something large in the grit and washings. His hands closed around the circular neck of the jug of Cormat's blood. Encouraged by this discovery, he allowed himself a brief rest, and watched as one of the Sistern disappeared entirely behind the mountains. The Chalk Plains below the White Walls of Kernback stretched out to the tall peaks, which looked near enough to reach in a short walk.

When he began his search again, the Star Axe seemed to leap into his hands. It had drifted several feet beyond where Kenlahar had first looked, but something seemed to guide him to it. He put its cord around his neck and tucked the sheathed blade next to his chest, where it had lain safely for so long, and vowed to never remove it again until he had discovered its secret.

He ventured from the base of the walls, tentatively at first, then made a dash across the white powdered plain. He was able to stay out of the sight of the sentries, and kept up a strong pace that first night. But the dried sewage was irritating him, and his eyes watered with what he feared was an infection. He found a tall crop of corn to spend the day in, and gouged a bed in the soft furrows of plowed earth. After some debate with himself, he doled out a few drops of Cormat's blood for each eye.

The next night he made steady progress toward the mountains, hindered only by the fences and hedges of the vast estates owned by the city-state's nobility. The fruits and vegetables he found growing in plentiful variety were almost impossible to eat in their unripe and raw form, but he found enough food to eat to fill his stomach.

Yet he knew that he could not be satisfied with just surviving or escaping discovery. His search for the key to the Star Axe seemed to him no nearer resolution when he had left the House of Lahar. His frustration grew the farther he ran from the city of Kernback—for he was somehow sure that the answer lay somewhere behind its White Walls. Somewhere in its ancient libraries could be found a clue to the power of Alcress.

Early the next morning he reached what he recognized to be the well-tended estates of Herald's Manor. The mountains loomed over the land, but Kenlahar knew he would not reach their safety that night. He looked for a place to hide for the day.

His body felt sore and filthy and his eyes were taken by the sight of the clear, clean stream that ran through the estate. Nearby, the giant manor house loomed. Taking a chance, he plunged, clothes and all, into the crisp flow. Kenlahar did not see the men on the banks of the stream.

An arrow pierced his shoulder, paralyzing his right arm. He struggled to stay afloat, holding back a scream of pain. A voice drifted over towards him lazily, "What are you shooting at?"

"I don't know." This voice was edgy and suspicious. "I'm sure I saw something swimming in the creek." Kenlahar was trying to keep his efforts to stay afloat quiet.

"Come off playing Queen's Guard, then," the lazy, drunken voice said. "What would a poacher be doing in the creek? I still have a little wine left, so drink up."

"But I really saw something this time…"

The voices drifted away and Kenlahar crawled onto the bank, painfully pulling himself to the shelter of a toolshed.

The morning of the next day passed while he slept, and it was not until the next afternoon he woke—to the shouts of the manor's workers. They had stumbled on his trail of blood and one of them had remembered the shooting of the night before. They were fast approaching his hiding place. Already feverish from the open wound, and the infections caused by the sewage, Kenlahar ran blindly in the direction of the hills. Long after the farmers had quit their search, he ran.

Panic and fear drove him on and on, sure that pursuit was only steps behind him. Instinct and Karrack's terse words sent him into the mountains. It was not until he reached the first of the foothills and looked across the impossible distance to the next one that his adrenalin charged energy finally gave out.

CHAPTER XIII

The captured warship, majestic and imposing in the featureless swamp, sailed up the narrowing River Danjar day after day. Despite his misgivings, Balor felt the grandeur of his craft and the thrill of his adventure. His spirits were as strong as the winds that blew at his back and filled the giant black sails. All that disturbed, him was that he had not yet devised a way to free the hostages once he caught up with the Qreq.

But he doubted that they would overtake the Qreq before their fleet reached the Warlord's Haven. The crew he had been given handled the unfamiliar craft clumsily, and there was not enough men to manage the huge sails. He settled for having only a fraction of the sails up. Besides that, he knew that the Qreq would be using their banks of oars when the wind died, but the men of the House of Lahar found rowing with the massive oars a hopeless task.

Balor explored the interior of the huge ship. The Qreq must have been used to even smaller spaces than the men of Lahar. Even the small crew found it difficult to get used to the narrow hatches, the low roofs. Most took to sleeping on deck, rather than face the little cubicles the Qreq had slept in. But Balor found the interior of the ship a fascinating glimpse of life the Qreq warriors must lead. They lived like insects, he thought, burrowing in warrens below the decks or below the ground.

The jagged, rain-washed gulleys and mounds of muddy silt that characterized and contoured the Tream began to flatten out. The pale swamp reeds, and scraggly fen-trees—all that grew in the Tream— were being supplanted by lush, thick growth. Balor soon saw that the terrain would shift. Rain had ceased to pound down on them, and eventually stopped falling altogether. It left the men of Lahar with an ironic and uneasy sense of loss. Yet moisture still seemed to hang in the air, shimmering visibly in the hot midday sun. The Lashitu, obviously unhappy at having been forced to go along, but keeping quiet for once, spent most of his time hanging listlessly over the side of the ship.

Finally, even the wind died. The air seemed to close in on the intruders and Balor felt that he would suffocate in the dense, damp atmosphere. Suddenly, he looked up and felt a spurt of dread. The banks were moving forward! He jumped to his feet and saw that the ship was drifting steadily backward. How long had he been lying there? he asked himself. How long had he been content to just try and breathe! The crew seemed to have melted at their posts onto the deck, and lay sprawled and panting for breath.

Balor forced himself to put some energy into his voice. He shouted urgently at the drowsy men to get back on their feet and man the oars. For a few seconds he thought he would face a mutiny of inaction. Then, one by one, the men slowly took up the oars.

At first, their efforts to row were hopelessly irregular, and there was a great deal of useless flailing at the water. But eventually the massive warship began to make a desultory progress up the river. Though he felt the effort draining his body of all his strength, Balor would not allow himself to rest, but instead paced vigorously across the quarterdeck. The ship actually seemed to be making some headway! he thought. And now that it was moving forward, it was easier to maintain the movement.

The state that had enervated the crew and its captain passed. The shock they had felt from the change in the environment—from the barren land they knew as the Tream, to a land of jungles and inhospitable darkness—also faded. The crew was goaded by fear and excitement to keep pulling at the oars. They caught glimpses of strange, wild creatures in the gloomy growth, but the jungle was so thick it was impossible to see anything clearly.

They were approaching a wide, broad curve in the river, which teased Balor with visions of boundless vistas on the other side, when the Lashitu shouted and pointed to shore. One of the huge, endlessly dripping trees had suddenly burst into flames. The ship was already midstream and fast approaching the curve—then they were past the burning tree and into the bend. Finally, Balor reacted to the sight and commanded the astonished crew to reverse their hard-on advance.

It seemed to Balor to take an eternity to slow the ship and reverse the momentum. For a while it appeared that they would sweep on around the turn, and at their furthest point upriver Balor saw the masts of many ships pointing over the trees. The crew was finally impelled by the sight to turn the vessel around. There was no need for Balor to order them to row to the fire. They turned toward it the minute the ship was reversed. They discovered a small cove cut into the bank, invisible from the river, concealed by overhanging branches. It could barely accommodate the enormous vessel, and the landing party was able to jump from the ship onto the high banks. Balor immediately sent several men toward the Qreq moorings to scout out the surroundings.

Kalese was waiting among the shadows of the trees. She stepped forward almost shyly, as Balor let out a loud hallo and swept her up in a hug. "Kalese! Once again you have saved me," he said.

"I have been waiting for you," she said in an annoyed tone, though Balor could see that she was pleased with his greeting.

Though he was not really surprised by the swampgirl's speed, Balor asked, "How did you travel so far on foot? I thought I would never see you again!" "The Tream is my home," she said, shrugging. She looked about her at the thick growth and cloying soil in distaste. "It has been difficult to find a path through this wasteland."

Balor laughed, amused by the irony of the swampgirl finding the lush jungle primitive, and relieved at finding her in this wilderness. "Have you caught any glimpses of my people?"

She frowned, and said in a disappointed tone, "I have not been able to get close. From afar I have counted five prisoners; one girl and four men, but I did not recognize any of them from the distance."

"Five?" Balor asked. "Are you certain of your count? At the camp below the Statue of Kings I counted but four."

Kalese answered confidently, "Three bound; and the girl and one man walking free." Balor shook his head, puzzled by the news, but he was not given the time to think about this contradiction. One of the men he had sent out to spy came running back to the ship. "The Qreq are torching a village and leaving. They seem to be fighting something, but we could see no one."

The skies over the forest were suddenly filled with black clouds of smoke. From Kalese, Balor learned that the Qreq had landed on the shores of a little village on the riverfront. The swampgirl seemed perplexed as she described empty huts that were no taller than herself. The giant Qreq had kicked the little hovels apart like abandoned toys, she said.

"Let us investigate this village a little closer," Balor said. They rowed from the little harbor, and sailed cautiously around the bend in the River Danjar. They entered an inferno. The dwellings were already crumbling into cinders. The men from Lahar, with Balor and Kalese leading, marched into their remains, striving to approach without being seared at the same time by the heat. Balor looked around him in amazement.

Everything was in miniature! He stooped to pick up a knife, which had a hilt no longer than his little finger. A few of the hovels Kalese had described were left miraculously untouched by the fires. They were crude dwellings, barely distinguishable from the forest growth, sometimes leaning up against the forest itself. The huge leaves that had formed the roofs had been trampled under the feet of the Qreq, and the stick walls had been burst by Qreq flailing. Balor only recognized them as living places because of the scattered implements.

Yet several Qreq dead lay about the clearing, with small arrows protruding from their bodies. Apparently, the Qreq had turned their anger on a deserted hamlet, for there were no other dead.

Then suddenly, the mysterious citizens of the village surrounded the party. When the men of Lahar first saw them, they were standing silently and unmoving at the edge of the forest, unnoticed by the expedition. They held tiny bows that Balor knew to be deadly, and carried nets on their shoulders. Their loin- clothes were made from the bark of trees, hammered to a pliable softness. Balor realized with a sudden intuition that to these people, the warriors of the House might appear no different from the Qreq, and he feared that they would suffer punishment for what the Qreq had done.

"The Mabati!" Kalese gasped in her own language. "You know of these people?" Balor asked.

"We call them the Mabati—the Little People. There are many legends concerning them among the People of the Cormat. Some of our people even claim to have seen and talked with the Mabati, but I thought them touched or lying. They are the most ancient of all peoples, though not counted as one of the Five Peoples. Yet I have always been told that they are a people, worshippers of the forest."

One of the little men, an older man with white flecks in his patchy beard, stepped toward Kalese and barked, "Mabati..." her word for his people, at himself, the others. Kalese nodded, and slowly spoke more words in the language of the Tream. The old man haltingly replied. Kalese turned and translated, "He says that he knows we are not Qreq, but asks us why we have one of their ships."

"Tell him that it is a prize of war...that we are enemies of the Qreq and pursue them."

The old man seemed excited and pointed to himself. Kalese explained, "His name is Grandfather and he is a friend of the people of the Tream. The Qreq are his foes as well. The destruction of the village means nothing, but the clumsy Qreq have harmed the forest and that cannot be forgiven. Then he says something that sounds like a ritual: 'We endured in forgotten days, and we will endure ever after.' "

Balor turned back to look at the man more closely, but he and all his people had suddenly vanished. Several of his men let out shouts of surprise. "Wait!" Balor yelled, but they were gone. He shuddered and wished at that moment that the Qreq would attempt to carve a path through the forest.

The men of Lahar were anxious to be back on the ship, nervously peering at the veiled forest. Balor gave the order. The path back through the rain forest was covered by plants that entangled their feet. They waded through inches of falling leaves, as wide as their path. The trees did not sprout branches until far up their tall lengths. Then the growths arched together to block out most of the light. The green moss covered the naked, straight trunks, entwined by clinging vines. Balor could hear rain above, though none penetrated to them. The falling leaves—their passage among them creating a noisy rustle—told him that there was a strong wind above. But within the forest it was quiet and still. Around the trunk of each tree was a halo of bright green ferns, which opened up like flowers. It fell dark quickly in the rain forest, and there was little time to set up the night's camp.

"I just wish the Qreq had to hack and fight their way through this forest by foot, instead of sailing through with such impudence," Balor said.

Kalese just nodded her head absently.

They had no time to waste now, Balor thought, they were fast approaching the Havens and he had not yet found an opening in the Qreq defense. His hope was that the Qreq would make yet another stop before they entered the Haven. For once within the Warlord's dominion, Balor had little faith that he could produce a rescue. He thought of and then rejected a hundred plans. Each scheme seemed wilder than the other, as his mind sought to come up with new ideas, until they became too outlandish to even consider. His mind kept supplying him with the schemes, anyway. There was simply no way of invading the Qreq stronghold, he thought.

The debris of the Qreq fleet left in their wakes indicated that the men of Lahar were sailing a steady day behind the enemy. Balor was content to let that gap remain, for he still had no plan; something that would allow him to infiltrate the Qreq ships. Again the terrain was changing, with odd little patches of barrenness interspersed among the jungle green—as if that portion of the forest had been poisoned. At last, this wasteland began to dominate. Now, even the dampness in the air vanished, and all that remained was the heat—a dry, searing heat that seemed to bake the ship.

The Desolation, Kalese called it, and Balor agreed with the name. This was the land the Warlord had chosen and made his own. Nothing grew in that desert, and no animal lived. The edges of the jungle had been ravaged for food, and wood, and Balor saw how the Warlord fed his people, and enlarged his domain at the same time. He understood also why the Little People were so deeply enraged. With growing

139

dread, and lessening hope, the men of the House of Lahar, and the girl from the Tream sailed deep into the Desolation.

CHAPTER XIV

For two dry and horrid days the ship of Lahar sailed through the dismal wasteland of the Desolation. Far in the distance they beheld the heavy clouds drifting over the giant expanse of the Sea of Dead, source of the River Danjar and port of the Warlord's fleet. At the head of the river they espied the Qreq anchorage—Cralock Bere, its tall spires, like sharp daggers, visible for many miles. A haze floated over the stronghold, a shimmer of heat from its forges—for the city was the foundry of the Warlord's hordes. The black fume of its furnaces billowed out of smoke shafts day and night, tainting everything near the stronghold.

Balor reflected, to his horror, that Sanra and Jonla were somewhere in that netherworld. He had been avoiding thinking of what they must be going through, but the sight of the Qreq hell had prodded his awareness. Yet he could not just blithely sail into the stronghold and pluck them free! It was a city of Qreq, and only Qreq walked its streets; there was no way of passing unnoticed among its denizens.

The ship had caught a good wind before dusk and they were sailing rapidly toward the evil port. The crew began to mutter among themselves as Balor delayed his orders to turn back or aside. Kalese came to stand beside him as he stared at the looming sight of the foul lairs. Soon she realized, as did the crew, that Balor did indeed intend to sail boldly into the harbor. He ordered most of the nearly rebellious men below the decks. The few that remained were told to garb themselves in heavy cloaks, though the night was hot and humid. They were the tallest and largest of the crew, and Balor thought as, he looked over them, that they could pass for Qreq—if only because the Qreq would assume that they were.

Kalese, for one, agreed that there was no other way of penetrating the enemy city. The Qreq would feel safe in the middle of their own domain, she said. They would never suspect that anyone would be mad enough to dare invade *their* stronghold. She agreed to stay in the shadows, but refused to go below.

The ship hobbled into port with few of its men available to manage its course. It seemed to Balor to take an eternity, and he felt flagrantly obvious in his deception. But Kalese's surmise had been right—the Qreq paid no attention to just another Qreq warship, for there seemed no end to the ships, or the piers attendant to them. Balor saw that the Warlord had not sent even a fraction of his strength against the House of Lahar. The Warlord was plainly interested in more than the tiny little Island of Laharhann.

Perhaps Kenlahar would find no help in the Outside, Balor thought. Perhaps it had already been conquered and there was no help to be found. And perhaps the House of Lahar stood alone against the Warlord's dominion. It seemed that, at the least, Kenlahar would find the Outside already fighting the Qreq, and unwilling to send help.

The trespassing warship had no difficulty finding a place to moor, or any trouble blending in. The docks seemed deserted, and the fog rolling in served as cover. Balor stepped off the gangplank with five men at his back, feeling dangerously foolish, but putting on a heavy show of assurance for his even more frightened men. Behind, he left Kalese, with orders to sail if he had not returned before dawn, and escape if she could.

It was eerily silent on the docks, and Balor soon had a sense of passing through the same area over and over again. The ships were strangely alike in their ordered rows, with the streamers of fog drifting across the bows, and their sterns extending into the darkness. Few Qreq walked the docks, and those they passed did not acknowledge the bundled intruders. For once, Balor was glad of the hostile and sullen nature of the Qreq warriors.

For hour after hour, the small party scrutinized the wharfs, searching for some sign of their comrades. As dawn neared, Balor decided to continue the hunt until light and then stow away somewhere on the piers. He would not leave the stronghold without Sanra or Jonla and the other men, he vowed. But he could not ask the men following him to risk almost certain detection. He sent them back to find the ship, and emphasized that Kalese was to cast off without him. He could not begrudge their chance at escape, though he suspected that Kalese would not leave unless she had to. The men started back without argument.

Balor continued his frenetic exploration long after he should have been looking for cover. Finally he was rewarded with the striking sight of a man pacing the deck of one of the many ships. The man had his head down, but there was no mistaking him for a Qreq. Balor saw that he still wore the dark rain cloak of the House of Lahar. There didn't seen to be any guards around the man, so Balor took the risk of hissing at him. The man jumped and Balor saw his face peer out into the dark — it was Jakkem! Balor hesitated, but there was no help for it; he could not choose whom he would contact first. "Jakkem!" he said, this time with an audible clearness.

Jakkem started again, and stared right at Balor, but he still couldn't seem to see who was addressing him. "Balor! Is that you?" Jakkem almost shouted, then hushed his volume and looked furtively about him. "How did you get here?"

"Yes, it's Balor," he answered tensely. "I have no time to explain. Where are the others?"

A sly look seemed, for a moment, to cross the big man's face. But Balor thought he must have imagined it, for there was no mistaking the joy that filled Jakkem after that. "They are on this very ship," he said eagerly. "The Qreq let us out one at a time. But how will you save us? Where are your men?"

But Balor had already slipped away. Walking with what he hoped appeared calm, he mounted the ship's gangplank. As he thought, the guard was just about asleep. It was a simple matter to overpower him, for he was not looking away from the ship but toward it.

The thick fog was aiding him now, and Balor was sure that he could not be seen from very far away. He ran up the gangplank toward the hold, ducking away whenever a Qreq form started to materialize in the murk. The entrance to the hold was mysteriously unguarded and he plunged into it. The knowledge of the desperateness of his goal only inspired Balor to speed through the hatches. With his new knowledge of the Qreq warships he ran toward the area where he hoped he would find the captives.

He rushed around another corner, into a sleepy guard with his weapon bared—but the Qreq never had a chance to respond, and went down. Balor sliced at the leather straps holding the door, and threw it open. Jonla was already at the door, alert and ready as usual. Two of his men lay sprawled on the filthy floor of the room, unwilling or unable to get up. Sanra stared at him from a corner with frightened eyes. Balor was shocked silent for a few seconds by the sight of their condition. They were pale and filthy, and their hair seemed to be falling out in patches. Balor tried to conceal his shock, and his aversion to the odor. For a few moments the image crossed his mind of the ghostly Qreq.

"Balor?" Jonla whispered uncertainly.

"Yes, Captain Jonla, it is I," Balor said, recovering from his shock. "Are you able to walk? We have just seconds before they discover the missing men. And it will be only minutes before the fog lifts and it becomes light enough for us to be seen by all."

"I can walk," Sanra said in a hoarse voice, rising to her feet shakily. Jonla reached down and pulled one of the men to his feet and leaned him against his shoulder. The man seemed to be in an uncomprehending daze. Balor helped up the other half crippled man, and they hobbled out into the corridor. When they reached the deck, Balor glanced out. It was a little lighter out, but the fog was thicker than ever, and more of it was rising from the lake's surface.

The prisoners blinked dazedly in the morning air, while Balor held them back, for they were in a quandary. One large man, heavily cloaked, passing as a Qreq in the dark and haze, had with surprise and luck, managed to get aboard the prison ship. But Balor had no illusions how all five of them, some weak and injured, could escape the same way. The only possible route, he thought, was by water. He spied a small boat tied to the stern. He pushed them toward the boat, and the wounded were lowered by their arms into it. "Hold here for a little while," he told Jonla. "I must try and find Jakkem."

"Jakkem!" Captain Jonla exclaimed. "Does Jakkem know you are here? Then we are already caught, for Jakkem has joined the Warlord — if he wasn't always his agent."

Balor asked just one more question as he slid down a rope into the rowboat next to Jonla. "Why has he not raised the alarm?"

Jonla had no answer, and pulled at one of the oars. Balor joined him, pulling at the other. They rowed between the sterns of the Qreq ships and steadily approached the place where Balor had left his captured ship. Dawn was breaking now, but he began to hope that they would reach the ship before it was too late. It seemed too easy — against all the odds, he had sailed into the Warlord's very headquarters and taken his prizes and was about to get away with it. He wanted to shout in triumph.

Then the night erupted with the cries of the Qreq, and Balor knew that their escape had been discovered. His heart sank. Once the Qreq started looking, the little group would be quickly found. One of the sterns of the Qreq ships pulled out in front of them, blocking off their escape. On the deck of the ship Balor saw Jakkem, with a grotesque smile on his face. Qreq warriors swarmed down its sides, and the traitor directed Qreq to bring them to him. In the distance, to near that it hurt, Balor saw the familiar lines of his ship, still quietly moored beside the others.

The Companions did not try to escape for there was nowhere to go. They were surrounded by three other rowboats, and put up no resistance as they were towed to the Qreq ship. They were hauled roughly up the bulwarks and placed before Jakkem.

Jakkem was pleased. "I was hoping you would free them," he said in an undertone to Balor. "Now, perhaps the Warlord will listen to me about what I have brought him. Surely this will reach his ears! He'll finally hear what I've been trying to tell him — that if he doesn't yet have the Axe-bearer, he does have Kenlahar's best friend, and his woman."

He turned and ordered the Qreq to set sail for the Warlord's Haven. Before he commanded them to be taken below he said, "What I don't understand is how you hoped to get far—but I'm sure the Warlord has ways to finding that out. Tomorrow I will present you to Toraq, and I—I will be rewarded."

"So *you* were the spy all the time!" Balor said. "I should have known. That is why you accused Kenlahar, to cover your own tracks." The ship was already underway, and with a start of surprise that he tried to conceal, Balor saw his warship coming up. There did not appear to be anybody aboard, and it could have been deserted. Balor raised his voice as they passed the ship and attempted to make himself as visible to the warship as possible. *"Well, Jakkem!* Where are you taking us now?" Meanwhile he was silently cursing Kalese for her stubbornness in not leaving. Perhaps the sure knowledge that he had been captured, and could not escape would frighten her away at last. He didn't think so, though she would have trouble with the crew.

"The Warlord had already commanded me to bring you to him. He was very angry that he was not told before, and grateful to me. Now I have you also, Balor!" Jakkem was excited and Balor could see that he was also scared. They passed the ship now, and out of the corner of his eye, Balor thought he saw the slight figure of Kalese in the shadows.

"If I had known Kenlahar was the Axe-bearer, I would have killed him that day," Jakkem said, obviously regretting the missed opportunity. He walked over to Sanra and began to run his hand across her face. "I should have killed him anyway."

Captain Jonla reached across and knocked the traitor's hand away. Jakkem just smiled, and then ordered two Qreq to take Jonla below. "Teach him not to get in my way," he said. "I will teach Sanra to obey, myself."

"I thought that you loved Sanra. Why have you betrayed her?"

"She means nothing to me now," Jakkem answered, and Balor saw the depths of his hate, the dregs of his love. Spite dominated Jakkem now, and Balor remembered how the traitor had been shunned at the House of Lahar. But so had Kenlahar, he reminded himself, and he had not become a betrayer. He appealed to Jakkem's greed.

"Remember that you are going to present them to the Warlord. You don't want to harm them. Toraq may not like it."

Jakkem hesitated at this, and then nodded to the guards. Before Sanra and Balor were taken below, he gestured at the ships. "I want you to see the might of the Warlord, that you may despair. Up to now, he has sent but a pittance of his power against the puny navy of the House of Lahar. He has larger, greater prey. Soon we shall sail to the Kingdom of Kernback!"

———

Later, Balor was brought back up on deck to listen to more of Jakkem's gloating. They sailed past pools that boiled with noxious fumes, and cruised up and along the coastline. Balor did not know what to expect of the Warlord's Haven, but after the Desolation he was uneasily sure that it would be more evil. He was astonished when distance away he saw the lush greenery of the Havens. As they drew near, Balor saw that it was a well-tended forest, breathtakingly beautiful and peaceful.

The Warlord had created a Desolation for his subjects, and was striving to expand his destruction. But for his own home he had designed a paradise. They were met at the single pier by clothed Qreq, the first time Balor had ever seen that phenomena. They appeared almost human, he thought. Sanra and Jonla and the other prisoners were brought up, dazed and sluggish, and marched up the dock onto a path of soft green grass that wound up the steep hill to the citadel. It was like something out of one of the books Kenlahar always read, Balor thought. A fairyland.

The castle was of eldritch grace and fragility, yet seemed possessed of an inner strength. They walked down its narrow, confusingly twisting passages into an inner, sunlit court. *This* was the center of the Haven's beauty, Balor thought. This is where all the allurement emanated from; the masterpiece of its designer. It was shaded and restful, a miracle among the ruins of the Warlord's rule. Somehow it was cool, and sweet smelling. A few hundred feet away it was sweltering.

The beauty of the delicate white spires, and translucent walls confused the Companions. This could not be the abode of Toraq! Banners flew from each tower, battle-scarred and stained. Balor saw the tattered remains of a flag from the Island Laharhann flapping prominently among them, and knew then that this was indeed the Warlord's creation. An entire crew would have had to be slaughtered to capture such a prize, he knew.

The master of the garden destroyed the illusion of beauty. By a serene pool was a giant throne. On the throne sat a huge, enormously fat Qreq warrior, with a horribly ugly visage. The huge Qreq had wide eyes set deep in his skull, and puffy jowls bunched up beneath them. The veins of his arms and head stood out in a blue network.

"What have you brought me," the creature demanded in a booming, menacing voice. Smaller, agile Qreq scrambled about him like maggots. Off to one side sat a radiant appearing man, with one hand skimming the water of the pool. He was a small man, and dark, with heavy curls in his black hair. His eyebrows were raised in a quizzical expression, and there was a hint of amusement in his eyes. But the man said nothing.

Jakkem seemed unnerved by the sight of what he took to be the Warlord, and was stammering. "I have brought the prisoners you requested, my lord."

"Who are they?" It asked in a bored, and disinterested manner. He seemed to be concerned only with the food the Qreq servants were bringing to his side.

Jakkem stuttered even more. "They are the friends of the Axe-bearer."

"Ah, yes," the giant Qreq said. "You will be rewarded—by becoming my servant." As Jakkem's face paled, and Qreq turned his huge head partly toward the man by the pool. "Take them away and care for them," he said, apparently dismissing the whole matter from his mind.

"Yes, mighty Warlord," the man said, coming close to mocking him, but the huge Qreq did not appear to notice. Balor almost laughed at the look in Jakkem's face. The man smiled at the Companions and led them into the castle. They were given rooms more luxurious than any they had seen. The man chattered the whole time, in a richly scornful voice, as he described the significance of one object, the history of another. The Warlord had plundered the kingdoms for centuries to collect this beauty, he explained. The man seemed to know everything there was to know about the Warlord's domain.

But he would not answer questions, replying when they asked him for his identity only that they must eat and bathe and rest before he would think to answer any questions. The Companions gladly did as he requested. The dark man was the only help they had, but he moved so quickly and surely that he always seemed to be where he was needed most.

They were given new clothes and a meal, and, finally, they were all seated at last. The three Companions were lost for a while in the enjoyment of the luxuries—the rich textures of the new clothes, the grainy feel of the wood table, the sensual smoothness of their glass goblets. The dark man laughed happily as he looked upon the satisfied faces of the men of the House. Only Sanra seemed uncomfortable, and Balor caught her warning look.

"Now then," the dark man said. "Tell me of your journey!"

Balor answered for the prisoners. "We will tell you of us, if you will then tell us who you are and how you came to be here."

"Of course," the dark man readily agreed.

So Balor told of his long pursuit and of the hell the captives had endured. But he left out all mention of Kenlahar or the Star Axe. When he had finished, the man said, "Tell me everything or I cannot help you!"

"Help us?" Jonla broke in eagerly. "Will you help us escape?"

"I have some sway over the Warlord's edicts," the dark man said mysteriously. "Come! You said you would tell all. What of Jakkem's report—and what was the reason for your wanderings through the Tream? I have to know all."

Balor was grim as he said, "We will say no more until we know who you are, and what role you play in this land." The captives looked at Balor apprehensively, but did not add anything to his story. For the first time, the pleasant young man's face showed irritation, and a hint of ugly anger. Balor knew then that his caution had been proper. *"Who are you?"*

The man tossed off his impatience. "I am the planner, the designer of the Warlord's Haven. It is my creation. But I am as much a prisoner of it as you are." "You still do not tell who you are, or why you would help us," Balor insisted.

"I tell you what I wish to tell you!" the dark man said heatedly, and his audience was taken aback by the change in the man's manner. The host seemed to have a dangerous anger, and a deadly impatience. Their host sensed this and relaxed again. The room was restored to its amiable atmosphere. "You do not trust me?" he asked innocently.

"No, I do not." Balor rose to his feet. "Tell the Warlord that his little trick will not work. Send us back to your prison, for we will not tell you what he wants." "I see that Jakkem was right," the dark man said thoughtfully. "You *are* hiding something. Perhaps the Axe-bearer would not wish to see you suffer." He must have sent a signal, for the room was suddenly filled with Qreq warriors. "I told you the truth when I said I would not tell the Warlord what you told me. You see—I am Toraq!" He waved for them to be taken away, and his laughter followed them all the way to their prison.

Down below the graceful towers, the Warlord concealed his true intentions, just as underneath his beautiful facade, he concealed his evil nature. Rooms of torture, of engines that burned, of instruments of degradation, filled the lower corridors of the Havens. Qreq young scrambled by them by the thousands, destined not to see the outside world until fully grown, and never to see the beauty of the gardens. In the breeding dens of the dungeon were the homes of the horrid women of the Qreq, who were never seen.

Balor was not unused to small rooms and narrow passages, but Toraq's warrens gave him an entirely different, uncomfortable feeling. The walls dripped with rancid moisture, the floors were maddeningly uneven. As the Qreq children swarmed by them, under their legs, and over their heads, Balor shuddered at their leathery touch. He felt suddenly queasy from the amount of food he had devoured.

The Companions were thrown into a room more foul, more dismal than any they had yet suffered. They found the two other soldiers already there. After a few hours the two men were taken away and the survivors never saw them again.

CHAPTER XV

Balor explored the crevices of the dungeon with his hands, for there was no light to investigate by. He had already experienced some of what the other captives must have endured up to now. They had been eager for his news, and had shaken their heads in amazement at his audacity. On their part, they told him the story of their capture, and it filled in the gaps in the Lashitu's tale. But they said little about what had happened since. They would only say that they had learned to sleep as much as they could. Balor could understand why—he had lost all sense of time in the lightless cell, thought the others assured him that not much more than a few days could have passed. Every morning the prisoners were given gruel and stale bread.

Balor continued exploring, looking for an escape. But he stopped suddenly when his hands encountered the furry body of a huge rat. He jumped back with a shout, but Jonla excitedly asked where he had felt the animal. In distaste Balor listened to the scurrying of the rat, its squeals of death when Jonla caught it. In surprise he saw Sanra eat the carrion as well. He declined the offering. The Warlord seemed to know exactly how much food and water he had to give the captives to keep them barely alive.

They had just been fed the noisome food, which Balor gave distastefully to the others. So it was that Balor was healthier than the others at first, but the sudden deprivation also seemed to hit him harder than the other two. It wasn't long before he too was eating food he would have scorned and left untouched a scant few days before. He could easily have allowed himself to starve to death, and he thought perhaps that that would be best for the Axe-bearer. Perhaps then he could not ever be used against his will as a weapon against Kenlahar.

But the Warlord did not leave them in their deep prison long. The doors opened and they were tied and wrenched from the room. They were dragged from a dark, musty cubicle to the deck of a Qreq ship. Toraq apparently intended to take the captives with him wherever he journeyed. They were placed in a giant open cage, which was hung dangling from the mast of the Warlord's flagship. The sea was filled with ships. The entire massive fleet of the Qreq had been assembled before the Havens.

Balor saw Jakkem standing beside the Warlord as they sailed east of the Havens, answering his master's every need. For a full day and night they sailed along the barren coast, until at the dawn of the second day they entered the mouth of one of the many small rivers filling the Sea of Dead. The little river could barely hold two of the massive warships abreast, even at its mouth, so the fleet was forced to sail up the river one by one, in file. Looking down the bars of his cage, Balor could see the bottom of the river. Soon he overheard the name of the river. It was Shallowspill, and it flowed, it was said, from the very walls of Kernback. The invasion of the kingdom had begun.

The Shallowspill was narrow and shallow, but it was also an ancient river and flowed sluggishly. The galleys had shallow drafts, to accommodate the oars, and were just narrow enough to fill the width of Shallowspill. Balor realized with somewhat of a shock, and reluctant admiration, that the ships had been designed with this trip in mind. The black sails stretched back down the river like a line of the watch, an invincible armada.

Balor looked back on a confused jumble of warships at the bottleneck of the river. Majestic, but ponderously slow, the line of ships still looked invincible in the full morning's light. Balor knew that the ships were filled with swarming masses of Qreq warriors.

For three days they sailed up the never changing river, and the land around that marked the boundary of the rain forest. On either side of the river stretched, for hundreds of yards, rounded, washed pebbles.

Where this gray boundary to the river's floods ended was a featureless brown, cracked mud. A few dried, once hardy stocks of bushes pointed raggedly out of the dessert, brown petals and leaves piled high around them. It was especially desolate against the backdrop of the green forest.

As they neared this clear line between two very different lands, the flagship slowed and from beside the Warlord, Jakkem ordered the fleet to slow. Toraq wished to land briefly before they entered the forest, he announced, for his spies had warned him that they could not stop once within. The warships behind the flagship suddenly began to move forward around them.

The Qreq could not believe what they were seeing, and neither could Balor. One craft passed the flagship, ignoring the bellowed commands to stop. By now Balor had recognized his ship, and was astounded to see Kalese standing clearly in sight on its bridge. She was looking at the cage with a mixture of sorrow and triumph. Balor guessed her mind, and roared out his approval.

With a finesse that the men of Lahar would have found impossible a few weeks earlier, the crew sent the ship sideways into the current, and into the path of the still moving flagship. The lead ship rammed the rogue ship, grinding ponderously into the side. The Qreq had not suspected the move, and were unable to stop. The captured warship slowly settled to the bottom—and the flagship joined it, bow first. The crew of the rammed ship had already abandoned it and was running for the forest.

Finally, the Warlord reacted and sent men to shore to pursue the saboteurs, but Balor saw most of them reach the forest boundary. None of the Qreq who followed them into the forest returned. The ships finally settled with their decks only a few feet below the surface of the river. The bottom of the cage was awash with water, and the captives were thankful now that they had not been left below decks. Balor laughed as he saw the Warlord wading about the deck, up to his waist in the water.

"Cut that cage down and throw it into the river," Toraq shouted, livid with anger.

Ironically, it was Jakkem who saved them. "Remember who they are, my lord!" He pleaded desperately, sure that his fate was tied up with the prisoners. "Remember the Axe-bearer!"

"Yes, yes," Toraq said. "You are right." Balor saw that Toraq had' succeeded in controlling his rage, but that he had not liked being mocked, or corrected. Balor knew that Jakkem would not save them again.

The traitor ordered the party transferred to another ship. And so it stood, hour after hour, while the Qreq warriors dived into the river, to chip and hack at the hard wood of the sunken ships. The captives could see that they were making no progress in clearing a path.

Finally one of the Qreq timidly approached the Warlord and informed him that the way was impenetrable, and would be for many days. The fleet could sail no further.

Toraq exploded and for several minutes most of the Qreq around him visibly shook in fear. Finally, he calmed down. "I will not be denied my triumph now. I have planned and waited too long for this. They must not know we are coming! The longer we wait the more chance there is of their finding out. Have the warriors disembark—we will march to Kernback."

"But my lord," the Qreq who had informed him of the impasse now protested. "We have no wagons to carry our provisions. Nothing to carry the siege machines!"

"Nevertheless, we march," the Warlord said impatiently. "We can march to Kernback before the ships are raised. Have each man carry what he can. We'll relay the provisions by foot if we must. Send the ships back for wagons, with as few men to manage the ships as can be spared." The Qreq turned to do as he was ordered, for no one dared contradict the Warlord more than once. "Wait!" Toraq called him back and looked at Balor with a gleam in his eyes. "Have fifty ships with full crews set sail for the House of Lahar. I want it destroyed once and for all."

The prisoners from the House of Lahar stared at the Warlord in horror. The Island Laharhann would never be able to turn back such an assault! If Kenlahar did not soon return with help, he would be too late. Toraq laughed, satisfied by their discomfort at last.

The unloading of the ships was taking much too long for Toraq, and he sent the first companies of warriors off into the forest, loaded down with the first of the unloaded supplies. They were told to set up depots and return for more of the provisions. When the first sortie did not return, he halted his forays and waited. They did not come back that first day, nor the next, and the supplies continued to pile up on the banks. By the time the wagons finally did arrive from the Havens, Toraq had decided to lead the huge army into the forest himself.

The Qreq surrounding the cage, and out of the hearing of the Warlord, were whispering nervously among themselves about the malevolent spirits that resided in the evil forest. Once within the green ocean of growth, it seemed to close in around them. The Qreq were forced to cut a path through it. As though they had entered an older, more fundamental world, the army fell silent and wary. Even the Warlord seemed a little uneasy as they carved a road through the forest and pulled their engines behind them. Balor knew the Little People thought of the forest as cool, shady, and restful. But now it seemed menacing. The whole forest seemed to shudder under the tramp of the Qreq invaders. Balor welcomed the hostility, hoping that it would overwhelm them, and bury them under its strange plant life.

A tree came crashing down behind the leading wagons onto a cart full of weapons, crushing it in two. A new path had to be hacked around its mammoth length. Other trees were felled by the Qreq, but would not fall as they were meant to. Instead of falling away from the road, they would fall unpredictably into their path. Balor suspected that these were not accidents, and that the "malevolent spirits" were flesh and blood. He saw nothing, though he scanned the forest intently.

But Sanra's eyes were sharper. She grabbed his arm tightly, as frightened as the Qreq. She had no idea what was causing the accidents. "Do you see that?" she hissed. Balor looked in the direction she was pointing, but he could distinguish nothing among the trees.

"There...look!" she insisted. As Balor stared, he slowly discriminated the form of a small man from the surrounding jungle. He had apparently had a mistaken notion of what the color and size the Little People would be, and had passed by the figure. Then, as he still watched, it seemed to disappear into the background.

As thought the disappearance of the figure was meant to be seen only by the Companions, and was the signal for an attack, a guard near their cage fell back with an arrow piercing his neck. Invisible attackers wounded those in the area of the cage. The survivor jumped from the target of the wagon to the ground for shelter.

The Warlord, at the lead of the column, was meanwhile was surrounded by his own attackers, and only Jakkem noticed that the brunt of the attack was centered around the cage. He started running back, but as the arrows landed in clusters about him, Jakkem finally dived under a different wagon, as had most of the Qreq already. The prisoners were the center of the storm, but none of the arrows seemed to land too close to them. Toraq was sending squads of Qreq into the forest after the unseen assailants, but the strategy did not seem to lessen the barrage of missiles.

Sanra grabbed Balor's arm again, and he turned to see the crew of his ship, or those few that had survived, rushing toward them with Kalese in the lead. Arrows cut down most of the Qreq who rushed to confront them, and the wedge of attackers overwhelmed the last of them. Kalese leaped onto the wagon and sliced at the bars of the cage again and again. The bars splintered, and Balor pushed the weakened Sanra out into the arms of one of his men. Jonla went after a moment's argument, and then Balor was out and free.

The freed Companions started for the forest, but the concentration of arrows in the area of the cage, had freed other Qreq to converge on them. Balor felt the fever of battle and revenge fill him as he saw Jakkem leading a troop towards them. He stopped to pull a spear from the dead hands of a Qreq warrior, and turned to meet the traitor.

But they were already very near the forest, and they would not escape if he hesitated, or stopped to fight. Kalese pulled at him and shouted angrily. He became aware that he would be jeopardizing them all by holding back. He threw his spear with a shout at Jakkem, and turned to run, without seeing if it had landed. But he knew without looking that he had missed.

They did not need to go far into the interior of the forest to escape pursuit. The Qreq who followed were cut down at the ragged border between the dense growth, and the rough trail hewn by the Warlord.

157

No enemy penetrated very far. Sanra and Jonla were very weak from the time they had spent in the small cages of Toraq. They reached a tiny clearing; just a gap where a huge tree had once grown. The Lashitu was waiting excitedly under the boughs of a dripping, bowed tree. Sanra and Jonla collapsed, as the knowledge and relief of their escape hit them. Soon she was asleep in safety of the grove, and Jonla was soon dozing beside her. They did not need to fear the Warlord any longer, Kalese told them. The Qreq could not reach them now. Kalese insisted on letting them rest, though Balor was insistent in helping the Little People harass the column. Still, Balor remained with the swampgirl. And they sat talking in undertones.

"The Companions are together again at last!" Kalese said smiling.

"We are Companions in name only," Balor said. "The one we were meant to accompany, the one we vowed to protect, is alone."

"No!" Kalese said. "We are still very much Companions—to each other. There are roles for all of us to play. Shall we be satisfied with just escape from the Warlord?"

"What else can we do?"

Kalese's words were fervent. "We can slay the Sorcerer King! Let us pursue him, and harry him, and harass his Qreq, until we are killed or he is destroyed!"

Balor stared at her in shock. Up until now he had not even considered it possible to slay the Warlord himself. Surely that required the Star Axe!

"I agree," he said at last. "Let there be no peace for us until either he—or we—are in the grave." The battle had not ended, but had lessened in intensity. The Warlord was once again making headway. Every few hours one of the small men would pop into the little hole and report the progress of the battle. For every Qreq that would fall, there seemed to be many more to take his place. In the muffled forest, its rustling life shocked by the violence of the battle, Balor looked down on the sleeping shapes.

"How did you manage to escape the attention of the Qreq at Cralock Bere?" he asked Kalese, still amazed by what she had done.

"When you did not return by noon," she said, "I knew that you had been captured. The crew would have forced me to leave, but for the fact that there was no way of sailing away with arousing interest." During all the time the warship had sat docked on the piers of Cralock Bere, she told him, a Qreq warrior had never approached them. The sheer numbers, the hundreds of ships, had protected them from any curiosity. Most of the other surrounding ships had remained bare and deserted as well. When the docks of Cralock Bare had suddenly filled with thousands upon thousands of Qreq warriors, she said, they had not moved. But each Qreq had seemed to know which was his own ship, and theirs had never been approached.

"Then I heard and saw you on the flagship. I didn't have to harangue or kick the crew onto the deck this time. In the confusion, and concealed in our cloaks, we set sail with the other ships." Like a mote of dust swept up in a wind, they had sailed with the giant fleet, powerless to turn back or aside. "When the men saw you, and the other two, in that cage, they insisted on ramming the flagship. We waited until the forest to make our move, which was fortunate. Apparently, the Little People saw us, for they were waiting for us just within the first trees.

"It is strange," Kalese said. "I have never seen more than a few of the Little People together at one time, but there must be many of them. They are angry at the desecration of their world. The Warlord will not find it easy to make it through."

Talking of war and of revenge moved Balor to join the battle. Over her objections, he left Kalese behind to look after Sanra and Jonla. He began to make his way through the thick growth towards the sounds of battle, and soon almost tripped over one of the Little People who seemed to materialize at his feet. The little man beckoned and Balor followed, and soon a path emerged out of the tangle and confusion, where there had not been one before.

They entered a small break in the forest, room perhaps for five of the crouching Little People, though Balor's giant frame strained its limits. All but one of the small ones stepped back into the forest, and Balor was left facing the old man called Grandfather again. The wrinkled face broke into a smile at the sight of him, and the old man said something in his strange clicking language, and then in the guttural tones of the Cormat. With Balor's small understanding of that

159

language, and with much gesturing, they were able to understand a little of what the other said.

Grandfather pointed toward the battle and then at the leaves in the tree above and then at himself; then at the stock of the tree, and again at himself. After much repetition of these movements, Balor realized that the man was apologizing—telling him that there were too many Qreq, and not enough of his own people. The Warlord would escape!

Balor bowed respectfully. The little man seemed to understand the motion and bowed awkwardly back. The warrior of Lahar hefted his borrowed sword and also pointed to the battle. The forest man nodded and _ smiled, and they set off for the outcries together. Before they could leave the clearing, Balor heard Kalese call out his name and she hurried up to him. Balor was more impressed with her than he ever had been before. He knew that he could not have followed the wandering trail. She had left the sleeping Companions in the care of the Little People, she explained. She wished to join in the fight.

The Warlord had left a trail of dead behind him* but the Qreq still kept coming, numberless and multiplied from many years in his breeding pens. Toraq did not even seem concerned. Half of his army could be destroyed, and it would still be the greatest, mightiest army the world had ever seen. But Toraq was frustrated by his inability to even see his assailants.

Balor wanted to confront the Qreq, and even the Warlord, but the little forest men would not show themselves. Balor was ineffective with the little*bow, and was frustrated by his inability to get close to the enemy. Kenlahar would have been horrified by his blood thirst, Balor thought with sudden insight. But he had suffered too much at the hands of the Qreq to feel any mercy now.

As the Warlord neared the end of the forest, and view of the plains of Kernback peeked between the last of the trees, the Little People launched their fiercest assault. The last of the Qreq columns were heavily shorn of their marchers. But once the Qreq were milling on the fields, Balor saw from the forest edges that a massive number of the Qreq warriors had survived.

The Warlord surveyed the forest intently for several minutes, then he motioned to one of his commanders. Soon several bands of Qreq dared to approach the forest again, though a barrage of lethal arrows met them. They retreated, carrying with them only wood. A bonfire was lit, just out of range of the bows of the people of the forest, and Balor realized with horror what Toraq was about to do.

The Qreq, by the hundreds approached the massive fire and pulled burning logs from its flames, without regard to their safety. Balor and Kalese watched as the Qreq rushed toward them with the burning embers. The forest did not catch easily, but the Qreq were persistent and eventually the leaves of the trees started to fly into sparks, the trunks into flames. All along the border of the forest the flames were becoming too intense to endure and Balor and Kalese had to retreat. He knew what would happen if he emerged on the plains, so he retreated just ahead of the fire, not away—perhaps incredulous that anyone could do what the Warlord had done. The Companions knew that the Little People would die if they could not extinguish the fire.

The fire seemed to gain in speed, roaring high and loud behind them. Soon Balor saw that the fire would become too fast to escape, and he veered toward the river. There was no time now to look for the others. There may not be enough time to save Kalese and himself, he thought. Finally his steps brought him to and over the banks of Shallowspill. The inferno seemed to be sucking all the air above him, but by lying still and almost submerged in cool water, they were able to survive the heat. As Balor looked back, he saw some of the last survivors of his crew running just steps from the fire toward them. He shouted his encouragement from the banks. Then the fire engulfed them and leapt from the tops of trees to the tops of others on the opposite shore.

He heard Kalese gasp from beside him, then the heat made him duck under the flow of the river. He was certain that all was lost. In those few moments he reached his fullest measure of hate. The Warlord would die for this! He was, crying bitterly, and angrily berating himself over the roar of the fire. Only Kalese could hear him, and she stared dazed, but unhurt as the flames swirled upward into the evening skies.

Balor remembered the Little People's boast of being the first of all the peoples—and how they would be the last. They had not reckoned with the inhuman and unworldly power of Toraq, he thought with sadness.

The next morning they finally dared to crawl on shore. Overnight it almost seemed as if the Warlord had doubled the extent of his Desolation. Balor and Kalese, with a single mind and purpose pulled still warm stumps out of the soft, crumbled earth. Soon they were paddling up the river on their crude raft, too tired now to even rise from its rough wood planks. Side by side they lay, with their hands and feet trailing in the water.

Occasionally they drew their hands through the water. Their progress was slow, but they continued their pursuit with an unspoken determination. The acrid smoke of the fire, a smell that Balor had once thought benign and comfortable, now assaulted their senses. Soon they could breathe only shallowly through their mouths in a futile attempt to avoid the penetrating smell. Each breath seemed to burn his lungs, and his eyes were often closed for long minutes.

A cool wind began to whip across the water, striking their exposed dry faces like a soft caress. Balor wished they could just drift, close their eyes and drift, but right now the wind was just another hindrance to paddle against. The banks began to rise above them, with soft rolling mounds of earth, covered by feathery tufts of grass. Balor fought the oncoming urge to sleep, to crawl onto that warm carpet of grass and move no more.

Through watery eyes he looked beside him at the battered form of Kalese. Her long dark hair was singed, and curled from the heat, her face and arms smudged from the flying ash and charcoal. Balor noticed with an unwanted and hidden revulsion that her feet were blistered and swollen. But the swampgirl made no complaint, the expression on her stoic face did not change or twist from the pain, nor did she moan or cry out when Balor accidentally touched the infected soles of her raw feet. Balor marveled at her persistence, and vowed to endure the pain as long as she did.

So they went on, crippled and exhausted, only because there seemed to be nothing else they could do. Balor thought his mission a failure. He had heard nothing of Kenlahar since the Companions had been separated in the swamp. He feared that his friend was lost, or captive, or dead. The Warlord would not have dared act otherwise. Of all the original Companions, he thought, he alone had survived. But Balor still had one goal as long as he still lived. He would kill Toraq, he pledged, or never return to the House of Lahar.

They moved upstream steadily, even in the sluggish flow of Shallowspill. Then, to their dismay, Balor and Kalese began to notice that the level of the river was dropping—inexorably—in depth, every few minutes. The rhythmic reduction of water finally emptied the shallow river. At last, as their raft encountered more and more obstacles, they were forced to scramble up the banks. Hastily, they filled their water bottles from the rapidly drying stream.

On foot they continued to follow the path of the Warlord's horde. The two thirsty trackers soon began to come across small oases in the flat grassland. Tall trees, filled colorfully with dying leaves, surrounded cool springs of water. But they found each of the springs poisoned, littered with the bodies of small animals. Kalese shook her head in puzzlement. Why would the Sorcerer King make the only water available undrinkable? she asked Balor. It made no sense to him either, especially when they began to come across the bodies of Qreq warriors, dried and shriveled in the glaring winter sun.

Around the last well they sighted a band of Qreq. The warriors were fighting among themselves under the small, sparse trees. The two travelers stood back and watched the battle in amazement until there were only a few, exhausted Qreq survivors. As these tired victors stooped to drink from the little trickle of water, Balor and Kalese crept up on the unsuspecting warriors. Engrossed in the spoils of their bloody fight, the Qreq did not watch behind them—what need?

It would have been impossible to creep up on the Qreq if they had been on watch. The dense growth around the little tepid pool of water was thick and bounded on three sides by an impossible barrier of thorns. The pool was a small remnant of the rainy season, and would soon dry up. But the life in and around it clung desperately to its sustenance. The surface was still, broken only by small insects skittering from on floating bits of slime and moss to another. Normally no one would have drunk from it, but now it was the only water in a waterless land, in a dry season. The Qreq guards were slain easily by the two furious, thirsty Companions.

Again, Balor and Kalese filled their water bags, and in their turn poisoned this spring. Balor did not recognize the figure reflected in the pools. It was a gaunt face; a body no longer stocky and muscular. His blond hair hung around his neck in a tangled mat. His clothes were in tatters. As they went on after the trail of the Qreq, the dead seemed to multiply on the trail of trampled earth. Many of the bodies had already been devoured by scavengers, some dragged far from the bed of Shallowspill. But the trackers saw that the Warlord still followed its course, perhaps hoping vainly that it would begin flowing again. The two Companions tied strips of cloth across their faces to block out the noisome smell of the decaying bodies.

Soon the two knew from the freshness of the dead, that they were at last nearing the Qreq horde. They dropped to the cracked mud of the riverbed, and began to creep toward the undisguised noise and lights of the Qreq army. They watched the procession, waiting for a chance to rush the Warlord's guard. Balor and Kalese only wished at that moment to get as near to the Sorcerer King as they could before they were sighted and killed. Neither had any hope that they would succeed.

CHAPTER XVI

Kenlahar woke up as if from a very bad dream. It was dark—neither of the Sistern moons had yet risen, and the Bantling would not rise at all that night. The torn clothes left from the House of Lahar provided little material for a bandage, but Kenlahar ripped up the last of his green scout cloak, under his new coat, and pressed it hard as the pain would allow against the arrow wound in his shoulder. Taking out the flask of Cormat's blood he poured it sloppily onto the grimy bandage and tied it firmly. He shook the jug, and found that it was over half empty.

Suddenly, he heard footsteps going right by the heavy undergrowth he had crawled into before he had collapsed. As the footfalls stopped only feet away, Kenlahar tried to control his breathing and his urge to run.

"We could search for years around here and never find anything," he heard a rough, alcohol-ravaged voice whisper. With a start, Kenlahar recognized the voice of the man who had shot at him from the bank of the stream at Herald's Manor. "Remember that Gartort boy? He disappeared in the mountains and they never did find him."

"Him and many others," another voice answered. This voice was smooth as honey, and it seemed to Kenlahar that he caught a hint of teasing in its tone.

"He was just the last of them. Apparently you haven't heard about those others."

There was a silence and Kenlahar imagined them looking furtively around them. "I may be new around here," the rough voice said. "But I've already learned a few things that the Queen's soldiers might want to hear. Like how some of the local troops never came back from patrols." There was a dramatic pause as the heavy voice hammered up his knowledge—or was he trying to hint at something to the other man? "Some of them never came back though they had the best local scouts- like you!"

The other man didn't say anything at first; then under his breath he said, "You should learn to keep what you know to yourself, son." Kenlahar could tell that the term "son" was not one of good will.

The hard voice came back subdued, but only for a moment. "You know everything around here, old man." Now the term "old man" seemed full of scorn and menace. "Tell me, what reward is there in staying quiet?" The hint of blackmail was back in the voice.

"Let me tell you something, *son*" There was the sound of what Kenlahar imagined to be two men squatting on the ground, and a creaking groan from one of them. The man he assumed was the older cleared his throat. "They say that this band of outlaws you hear about are not outlaws at all. The nobles of Kernback may dismiss them a brigands, and hunt them down like animals, but the Mountain Tribes are one of the Five Peoples of Lahar, and, though they do not know it yet themselves, the most dangerous. They do not accept the domination of the Queen. Because they rebel against Her authority, they are called outlaws."

"Well, why doesn't the Queen's Guard clean them up?"

"Why, son, what I told you is only rumor! To send Her armies would be to admit that they exist. It is also a rumor that those who go up to the mountains never go back—and that includes soldiers."

"Give me a few troops and I would take care of them!"

"You would need more than a few soldiers. Whistler and his gang have more than ten thousand men and they know these mountains like you know your own home. They probably have their eyes on us right now."

The rough threatening voice was a little uneasy. "How come you know so much, old man? You know, I bet there is a big reward for one

166

of those outlaws!" The menacing voice had finally made his threat known.

"You shouldn't ask so many questions, son," the smooth voice said, dismissing the other man in his tone. There was a silence, then a quick rustle of steel on leather. Then there came noise of what sounded to Kenlahar uncomfortably like flowing water. Kenlahar felt himself about to pass out again, but just before he did he heard, "I told you that those who go to the mountains don't go back! You should have listened to the rumors, son." There was the sound of soft, unmelodic, whistling that faded, then disappeared. It was the last thing Kenlahar heard before his awareness slipped away.

When he awoke once again it was morning. Immediately and instinctively, he put his hand down to his wound and felt the dried blood. He had stopped bleeding and his fever was gone. He wondered if he had dreamed what he'd heard the night before. His mind seemed to be working clearly again—the pain seemed to make him more aware. But he distrusted the feeling. It was not difficult to know that he needed water most, and, after that, food.

When he tried to remove the bandage, he found it caked to his skin. He feared that if he persisted, the wound would start bleeding again. His attention turned entirely to his thirst. His mouth was dry and he had an idea that he needed a great deal of moisture after losing that much blood. His mind continued to build up reasons why he needed water, even as the overpowering urge got him to his feet and started him in the only direction of which he was capable—back downhill.

He had only gone a few steps before he stumbled on the body of a man. So he had not been delirious the night before! He looked about him expecting to see brigands surrounding him. Running from the body in horror, his caution was forgotten. He staggered and rolled and collapsed again and again, amazed that he was not being injured by the constant falling. But his thirst overwhelmed any scratches and bruises he might be getting. It was forested country, with outcroppings of rocks that he maneuvered around wildly. Looking back down the mountain, he was surprised at the distance he had traveled the day before. Now the same instinct for survival propelled him downhill.

Kenlahar knew the creek was there before he actually heard it. A few short days before he would not have believed that he would smell water, but the scent of it now was strong. The stream was at the bottom of a steep gorge. A small glacier filled the little valley. The water of the creek had carved graceful bows in the snow, the red sunset shone through its rare arches. This time though, the beauty of the mountains was lost on him.

He contemplated the steep slope, knowing that he would have to climb down it soon or he never would manage it. Then he heard off to his left a trickle of water. Within seconds, his mouth was underneath the small waterfall. It was only a choking fit that caused him to quit drinking.

Later, he was able to concentrate on what he should do next. His mission had been a failure. He could not return to the House of Lahar without help, nor did he know the fate of Balor and Sanra. But before he started thinking of long-range plans, he told himself, he had best dwell on his immediate needs. The water was a real find. It would keep him alive for a few days, if he didn't freeze first. But he would not last very long without food. He reached over to the comforting water a few inches from his head and took another long drink, but already another need had replaced his thirst. The water could not fill his empty stomach.

Then he heard the familiar sound of somebody whistling a tuneless melody. Whoever it was, was coming downhill on the same trail Kenlahar had made going down! Kenlahar hesitated, then making more noise then he wished, crawled under another patch of dry bushes.

This time he got a look at the man. The stranger was dressed in a material that Kenlahar guessed was made from one of the local animals. On his belt was a knife and a row of pouches. His knee-high boots were of the same tanned leather. He walked easily down the same slope that Kenlahar had stumbled down earlier, and though he was not a small man, he had a small man's economy of movement. Kenlahar was startled to see that except for a mane of white hair, the man looked no older than middle-aged.

Kenlahar held his breath. But the man stopped directly in front of his hiding place and, still whistling, bent to the ground. Then the stranger smiled. "Come on out, son."

Kenlahar disentangled himself from the thorny bushes without taking an eye off the man. Though the stranger had not drawn a weapon, by now Kenlahar did not trust anyone. He made ready to run. He did not believe he could overcome this opponent in any kind of fight!

"Relax, son. I am a friend. Probably the only friend you have, right now. There is a big bounty on your head." The man's voice was soft, and brought back memories of the short struggle between the two talkers the night before. He stood relaxed, but Kenlahar knew that the stranger could be dangerous.

"How do I know that?" Kenlahar asked.

"If you could not trust me, you would be dead by now."

Kenlahar was forced to admit the truth of that, and he was inclined to trust the lop-sided grin that the man gave him.

The brigand laughed. "All I ask is that you do not try and knock me over the head when I am not looking. Meanwhile—" Suddenly he was very serious. "I think we had better leave. The Queen's soldiers are becoming much more adventurous lately." He turned and set a brisk pace back up the hill.

Kenlahar did not remember much of that journey. His wound soon started to bleed again, and his legs began to give out on him. Before, he had been urged on by fear or thirst. Now he just wished to rest and sleep—or die. The stranger had no sympathy. He said nothing, only whistled. But the urgency in his pace pushed Kenlahar to his limit. The last thing Kenlahar remembered was the scrawny, white-haired man putting him over his shoulders. Then he blacked out.

When he awoke, he was comfortable for the first time since he had left Kernback. The stranger was hunched over a fire, stirring a stew that smelled good enough to persuade Kenlahar to move from under his blankets. But he was learning. This time, before he moved or made his consciousness known, he surveyed the camp.

It was a small glen, bounded on one side by a steep embankment. It was level for just a few yards before it dropped off into the dark. The little plateau was named Misty Vales, he learned later. Through the ever-present fog, he could make out the distant lights of a small town or outpost of the kingdom below. On either side, the campfire illuminated the lower branches of tall trees, and in the middle, a few short steps away, was the campfire. Finally, he yawned loudly and grunted, "The stew smells good."

The outlaw did not turn around, or seem surprised. "Glad you did not try to get away. I should hate to kill you after all the trouble you have put me through." He dished some of the stew into a large bowl and brought it over to Kenlahar.

The well-worn blade of the man's knife was easily accessible, he saw. But Kenlahar had no intention of attacking the brigand. For some reason, he trusted the man. He started eating, put off a little at first by its heat. But he was too hungry to care if he burned his mouth. After a couple of bowls full, he finally sighed and leaned back. Now he noticed that the man was looking at him with a grin.

"I'm glad you can eat like that. I had thought the injury was more serious. Now, son, let me take a look at that wound. I do some of the curing up here in the hills."

Kenlahar remembered back to the night before and the voice saying "son" just before the fight. "Do me a favor and don't call me "son." I remember what you did to the last man you called that."

The man didn't blink an eye, but continued to peel away the crusted bandage. "I had a feeling you were nearby. That is why I had to kill him."

"I was close enough to hear the blood flow! I thought you killed trespassers to the mountains."

"You were that near?" the brigand asked companionably. "Well, son, you keep very quiet. Not many escape my attention. But do not worry—we harm only those intruders who mean us harm."

"Who are you?" Kenlahar asked. "Is it true what you said about the Mountain Tribes?"

"They call me Whistler. Your other questions will have to wait until I finish bandaging your wound. Now quiet." The Whistler seemed to have some skill. But the potion he used burned, and Kenlahar winced from the pain. He wondered if he had once again fallen into the hands of someone who could help him. It seemed that at every stage of his journey men of goodwill, who could just as easily have been enemies, had helped him along. It was almost as if someone or something was guiding his quest for the secret of the Star Axe, and watching over him in times of danger.

Finally, the Whistler looked up at him with a crafty speculation in his face. "You heal quickly, son."

"Do you know who I am?" Kenlahar asked abruptly, not wishing to reveal the miracle of the Cormat's blood.

"Well, son," the Whistler said, bemused by the question. "I know the Queen's Guard are after you, and is all I need to know. But I also think that you do not come from these lands." The older man looked at the young man and warned, "The outlaws do not like foreigners much. But if you are an enemy of the Queen they will accept you as brethren."

After awhile, when the Whistler did not volunteer any more information, Kenlahar prompted, "Is it true what you said about the outlaws?"

"Most of it I made up," the Whistler said, and Kenlahar's face fell. The Whistler watched the effects of those words on the young man. "There was some truth in what I said yesterday. These mountains are full of others like me, who have run from the madness of the Queen. We have even organized into the Seven Tribes of old. But that is mostly for show; we are an independent lot. Barely able to communicate with each other because someone or the other soon feels uncomfortable talking longer."

As the Whistler fell quiet again, Kenlahar saw to his surprise that the old man was genuinely upset set the state of affairs. "But you are the Whistler!" he said. "You are their leader, aren't you?"

"If you can call me that!" the Whistler said in a discouraged tone of voice. "Oh, we get together for our own defense, but it is every man for himself even then. We can't seem to agree to stay together for any length of time—or for each other's benefit." Now his words took on the flavor of a fanatic and he leaned forward to look Kenlahar in the eye. "If we had someone to rally behind, we might be able to lay down our differences. We all know we should, but our pride always gets in the way."

171

Kenlahar looked away uncomfortably. Why was the Whistler telling him these things? When the Whistler once again spoke he was almost pleading.

"We have to throw off the yoke of the Queen. All of us have suffered her lash, and most of us have been conscripted into her armies. Her armies always need men, for one dies fast under her rule."

Kenlahar remembered the prince's pride and boasts of the armies of Kernback, and he contrasted Molnar's professed love of war—whether for honor, or wealth—with what he was hearing now.

"They fight for glory, these nobles of Kernback," Whistler said. "They fight for honor! And at the end of the day, the lords decide who had the most wounded, and dead, and that army retires from the field of battle. And when night falls, they go to their manors, while all the land between burns—*our* crops, *our* homes. We are the men who face their cavalry charges, and the lances point for *our* hearts. It is no wonder that we seem cowards when we break and run. But the day will come when we shall rise. Someday soon we will destroy their manors and pull apart their walls and armor piece by piece!"

Kenlahar was astonished by the intensity in the man's voice. The Whistler had seemed so cynical, that he had not suspected the depths of feeling in the old man. Suddenly the Whistler got up and walked to the edge of the precipice. Kenlahar got up to stand beside him. Below he could see the flashing of torches, and soon became aware of the sound of distant horns. Looking farther down he saw a small army of blue-cloaked soldiers. They made no attempt to be quiet, but marched confident in their numbers. They did not see what Kenlahar saw.

On either side of the column of soldiers a line of dun colored shapes lay concealed. Then he saw the column disintegrate into a disordered mass, and a few seconds later the shouts reached him. Kenlahar could not see the arrows flying, but he saw the soldiers dropping and firing toward the hills around them.

Beside him, the Whistler cursed. A small remnant of the column was escaping in an orderly retreat. Kenlahar saw the figure of their commander shepherding the last remaining soldiers together. They were intent on backing out of the trap. One by one, the retreating troops were falling, but others closed ranks. Kenlahar saw now that the bandits had left the rear of the battle open. Despite his hatred for the Queen, Kenlahar felt respect for the small figure of their commander circling the troops and waving them on.

And then he leader was down, and the others broke and ran—to be chased and killed, one by one. The Whistler let out a sigh from beside him. "That was close!"

Kenlahar realized that the entire skirmish had taken place in just a few minutes time. The Whistler had returned to the fire and was piling green wood onto the flame. Soon the hollow was full of smoke, and Kenlahar's eyes burned from the haze. But the smoke never seemed to reach the Whistler.

Within a few minutes, another man entered the glen. This man was dressed in animal skins as was the old man, but these were greasy and dirty. The man was dark under his even darker filth. Every person Kenlahar had seen since leaving the House of Lahar seemed to have dark, swarthy coloring. The tall blond warriors of the House would stand out among these people. Perhaps it was best for him that he had been born dark after all, he reflected.

The two outlaws crouched and whispered for a while, and Kenlahar saw the man squinting at him curiously. Then the man hurried from the campsite. A few minutes later, two men carried a body into the hollow and tossed a wounded soldier in front of the fire. They backed away and joined a circle of men that had appeared to surround the glen. Kenlahar ignored the intent glances in his direction and went over to crouch beside the Whistler.

He began to ask the man a question, but the Whistler waved him silent. Kenlahar realized then that the wounded soldier was conscious.

"Why have you entered the Mountains of Sanctuary?" the Whistler said in a surprisingly harsh, and menacing tone.

The officer sat up and Kenlahar knew that this was the gallant leader of the escaping troops. Kenlahar recognized Sar Devern with a shock. Though the wounded man answered the Whistler's question, he was looking at Kenlahar with steady eyes.

"I was looking for a fugitive of the Queen's justice."

I "Well, you have found one, rightly enough," the Whistler chuckled. "You have found an army of them!"

173

"There is a rich bounty on his head," Sar Devern said.

"You are in the Mountains of Sanctuary," the Whistler said angrily. "We would kill any man who would take such an offer."

"There will be more soldiers," Sar Devern warned. ' "As long as Kenlahar is free." The crowd began muttering at that.

"There will be other soldiers even without Kenlahar," the Whistler answered, frowning fiercely at the whisperers.

"No, there will not," the officer began to say, and then coughed. A line of bloody spittle ran down his chin. "I am authorized to grant amnesty to people of the mountains."

"In exchange for what?"

The soldier did not answer, but nodded toward Kenlahar. The old man grunted and looked sideways at the young man. The man with the dirty leather skins entered the circle of fire. "We should accept, Whistler." Kenlahar heard others sound in agreement.

"Oh, you think so, do you?" the old man said disdainfully. "Have you forgotten what they did to your wife, Ohmaar? And you," he said turning sharply and interrogating the circle of listeners. "Have you forgotten how they have hunted us like animals?"

A calm voice came from the anonymity of the crowd. "No, we haven't forgotten, Whistler. And that is why we want to accept while we can."

"I call for a vote of the chiefs of the Seven Tribes," Ohmaar said. Others quickly took up the call.

"There is not need," the Whistler said. "We shall do as you say, Ohmaar, though there is nothing to go back to. You will be back here if you live for you have known freedom too long. You were not fit for the life of a Queen's subject or you would not be here now! I for one, will wait for the ones who come after you have left. This place will always have its outlaws. If not you, then someone else. I will not barter my life for another!" Kenlahar saw that the Whistler's words were having some effect, but Ohmaar broke the spell. "You will not sway us from our decision, Whistler. Do you follow our wishes or not?"

The Whistler turned to Kenlahar with a look of despair. "I am sorry, Kenlahar."

Then he turned and asked, "How are we to deliver him?"

Sar Devern replied eagerly, "I will take him back." He tried to stand but fell back with a moan.

The Whistler smiled without much mirth, "I don't think so."

"I was to return within a few hours or the deal would no longer be recognized."

"Where is the rendezvous for the exchange? I will go to tell them of our decision before anyone else is killed. I will tell them that you are coming with your charge as soon as you have recovered."

"I was to deliver him to the outpost at Sige Tomar," the officer said through his pain. The old man nodded and walked from the clearing without looking back. Ohmaar mentioned something to a couple of the nearby men, and they came over to bind Kenlahar.

CHAPTER XVII

On the morning of the forest fire, three surviving Companions were found sprawled on the fields. They were dragged into the Qreq camp at the break of the smoky dawn. One by one, the prisoners were brought forward and thrust into the Warlord's tent. They faced the Sorcerer King with their hands tied in front of them, and their heads hung in weariness, to answer to their crimes.

Jonla stood numbly, listening to Toraq's angry ranting, defiantly silent. Sanra, in turn, was impassive and her mask of unconcern and resignation did not break, even in the brunt of Toraq's insults. The Warlord seemed to find no satisfaction in the provocation of these two unresponsive prisoners. They had been captive before—too long captive—and both knew enough not to answer back. They could gain nothing but their own destruction by anger. Already, they had won a great and unexpected victory over the Warlord, and they were content to die with their part played out.

The Lashitu, however, did not understand this. The Warlord did not greet this prisoner with abuse, but with honeyed words. He responded just as Toraq hoped he would respond. Proud and unbending, the shaman accepted the hospitality without question, as his due. He did not realize the hazards of his new status. From the moment he was brought forward, the Lashitu had begun to create the means to his own—horrid—doom.

Whatever happened to the Sorcerer King would happen to him the moment he drank the magic wine and the seasoned cakes that were brought before him. Then began an echo, though the Lashitu did not know it, of the dinner that had taken place in the fairy castle of the Warlord's Haven.

Whereas the other Companions had seen through the Warlord, the Lashitu foolishly believed the fair countenance and words of the Sorcerer King, and could not see the base spirit that lay seething beneath. Believing that no one so beautiful could also be evil, the shaman bowed before the Sorcerer King. Thus did the Lashitu fall under the spell of Toraq.

"At last! One of the Companions understands that I only wish to help them," the Warlord smiled. He was reclined on a throne cushion, across a table full of food and drink.

"I apologize for what my friends have done," the Lashitu said, his tongue loosened by the tainted wine. "But all they have done, they have done for the sake of the Axe-bearer."

"I should like to meet this Kenlahar as well," the Warlord replied. Toraq was making little effort to show sincerity, and malice sparkled in his dark eyes. "All need not be lost to the ruin of war, Lashitu. You and I understand that. If I could but meet with the Axe-bearer but for a moment, I am sure that we could come to an agreement—perhaps to save the House of Lahar? Can you help me in this, good Lashitu?"

The Lashitu could not see the evil in the Warlord's eyes, the contempt in his words. All he could focus on was the bewitching smile, on the impossibly handsome face of the Sorcerer King. At the urging of Toraq, the Lashitu took another long draught of wine and began to relate the travels of the Companions. He told all he could remember, unaware of the danger to his friends. Toraq let him ramble on late into the night, satisfied to hear even the trivial and patient with the repetitions. He prompted the Lashitu for any information the shaman forgetfully omitted.

Finally, the effects of the drugged wine began to wear off and take their toll. The shaman grew sleepy, and his words slurred and slow, his head dropped to his chest.

The Warlord spoke scornfully to his unconscious guest. "You are forever mine, Lashitu. Our futures are bound together from now on. My fate is your fate, and you will know this. But you will not be able to help yourself, for when I command, you will obey!" With this he spit on the sleeping form and called for Jakkem.

"Take him and put him on the seat of a wagon. Watch him, but do not hinder him. He is mine now, just as you are mine, Jakkem."

After the Lashitu had been carried roughly from the tent, the Warlord called Jakkem back to his presence. The traitor stood uncomfortably before the reclining Warlord, while he devoured what remained on the once laden table. None of the warriors of the Warlord's army had eaten for almost two days now. Toraq was aware of his new servant's hunger, and relished the torture.

For a few seconds, the thought of killing the Warlord and redeeming himself passed through Jakkem's mind, but then Toraq looked up at him with an amused smile, as if he understood the man standing in front of him. The traitor froze, and the Warlord let him think for a while that he had undone himself.

Finally, the Warlord said, "I want you to lead the attack on the House of Lahar. I want it destroyed, once and for all, Jakkem. My spies tell me that the navy is still at anchor. You should be able to catch up with my ships before they leave Cralock Bere if you hurry."

Jakkem hurried from the tent, and boldly commanded one of the few surviving horses to be brought to him. By the time the Warlord found out, Jakkem reasoned, he would be far away. Besides, the Warlord would probably approve. Jakkem did not like the expanse of the Rolling Hills, the scorched blackened earth of the fire, the exposed desert of the Desolation. He wanted to move through it as quickly as possible. He preferred to have something close in around him at all times. Some kind of wall—of stone, of wood, it did not matter, as long as it protected him. That is why he had been a Quarrier, why he liked the Warrior's ships so much.

Things were not working out the way he had planned. The Warlord was not invincible; the Warlord made mistakes. He had seen this with his own eyes. He doubted he would survive the long journey to the Sea of Dead anyway. Jakkem was feeling the cold for the first time in his life. The once protective layers of fat had slowly shrunk from him. He felt no satisfaction in his new slimness. He was aware that his, at that moment, worthless life, depended on the-final destruction of the House of Lahar. The Warlord had made that clear. Toraq obviously thought that too much had gone amiss, and that most of the annoyances seemed to be emanating from the small island on the River Danjar.

The burning of the forest continued, until both sides of the river had been destroyed altogether. But only the three, already captive, Companions had emerged from the inferno. Not one of the Little People had chosen to escape the deadly fire, and the heat had been so intense that all signs of their bodies had burned. Frustrated in not seeing the victims of his revenge, the Warlord had some of his men sift through the ashes for some evidence that the genocide had worked. Nothing could be found.

The Warlord finally commanded his army to march onward to the north. Soon his frustration was transformed into a livid anger, as the slow progress of the Qreq army became more and more trying. The Qreq grew nervous as his anger grew; making more mistakes that delayed the column. They began muttering among themselves at Toraq's display of human weakness. Perhaps their master did not know all! Perhaps he could be defeated! The forest phantoms—and they must be spirits for none had emerged from the hellish fire—had destroyed a large measure of their comrades in the massive war horde.

But Toraq was not concerned with this loss. He had anticipated and had prepared for much worse. Nor did he care particularly what the thoughts or feelings of his Qreq were. Discipline had been bred into his minions—they may question him, though even this was unheard of until now, but they would never disobey him. The armies of Kernback would not be able to withstand the numbers of even those Qreq remaining. But Toraq was impatient with the ponderous advance of his horde.

There was nothing unusual about the Rolling Hills, nothing unusual about the brown grass, the sweep of the hills. Yet the limitless expanse of never changing terrain, gave an effect more alien than anything the Companions had yet seen. It took an instinctive grasp of where the knolls met, to find a suitably level path. None of the Qreq seemed able to avoid dead ends.

Jonla and Sanra watched the Warlord's growing anger from their place at the back of one of the creaking wagons. At first they had been tied painfully at the wrists, and were pulled by the cart. The old, almost fondly remembered cage, had been shattered in the attack within the forest, left behind in the holocaust. But after many miles, neither Sanra or Jonla could stay on their feet. It became impossible for their muscles to continue to adjust to the jerky motion of their machine. They were half-dragged, their wrists bleeding from the cruel pressure.

Finally, the Lashitu, who had at last woken groggily from the seat of the same wagon, objected to this treatment of his Companions. With ironic grace, Toraq acceded to the demand, if only to keep his new servant happy. The two prisoners were thrown brutally on top of the jagged cargo in the back of the groaning wagon.

By now, Jonla and Sanra had endured more than they would once have thought possible for any human to endure. Yet, they lived still, perhaps only because the Warlord still wished them alive. Sanra had forgotten what Kenlahar even looked like. Jonla was her world now—both a protector and someone to protect.

In their dazed condition they did not question the Lashitu's treatment. It was inconceivable to them that the shaman could turn traitor as well. Now their feet as well as their wrists were tied in the constricting bonds of sharp ropes. They hovered in the delirious region between sleep and painful awareness.

Another of the massive wagons suddenly collapsed near the Sorcerer King. The Qreq, aware of his observation of his impatience, scurried to replace the giant wheel. As the rest of the army began to slowly bypass the crippled wagon, Toraq angrily strode down upon the obstruction, as if by his anger he could make it fly into smoke. He ordered it pushed, or pulled, or lifted—whatever it required to remove the obstacle immediately from the path. The wagon was turned over with a crash, and it rolled down a gully, slowly and ponderously at first, and then with increasing momentum. Some of the Qreq warriors looked at the crushed provisions that lay strewn over the hillside hungrily, but none of them dared to pick up any of the food while the Warlord still watched.

By the next morning the horde had fully invaded the rolling grasslands and hills that marked the southern borders of the kingdom of Kernback. Yet, they sighted few people, and none of the few inhabitants they did find, were men of fighting age. Confused by this mysterious absence, the Warlord sent out advance parties to slay all those who might report the presence of the Qreq army. The patrols had an easy job—the land was emptied of life, fallow of cultivation. They encountered only a few lonely, decrepit shepherdesses. One of the hapless residents was brought before the Warlord.

The elderly, frightened captive howled out her belief that all the ancient legends and prophecies were coming true. Toraq saw that the old women had been so frightened-that she had gone out of her mind. Still, he was able to glean some truth from her ravings. All of his opponents were now clustered before the gates of Kernback engaged in civil war, he discovered. He would crush all his foes in one battle, he thought with satisfaction. His victory was assured. Until he arrived, let them murder each other!

Then, once again calamity struck the Qreq. The strong, sure flow of Shallowspill, which the massive horde had so far followed and survived on, suddenly ceased. There turned out to be little other water to be found. As they came across small springs in the grassland, fighting broke out among the Qreq who would gather around those few wells—each one with enough water for only a few men—and that they would forego all intentions of marching on Kernback for a sip of water. Only by moving onward, striking for the very source of Shallowspill, could the Warlord save most of his army. Even then it would be a race before they all succumbed to thirst.

Toraq ordered all the wells poisoned but one. The remaining spring he surrounded with his strongest and most loyal followers, with the duty to bring him a steady flow of water. It was the most severe test of loyalty he could have given his warriors, but he had wrought well. Even when the Warlord stooped to drink his fill from the last well, the Qreq did not object. "To Kernback!" he cried. Since the moment they had been conceived every Qreq warrior had heard this war cry.

"Behind its walls you will find the water you need!" This added motivation sent the Qreq onward at a desperate pace. Even the Qreq were quick to realize that their only hope of surviving was in reaching the city. The Sorcerer King would show no mercy, they knew. "To Kernback!" became a forlorn rallying cry for the dying Qreq.

One by one, the weaker ones began to fall as they marched, and the Warlord watched his once magnificent army whittled by the harsh and glaring sun. It was infuriating to be beaten by a mistake, by an action not even meant for him. Impossible to foresee! Without fighting one real battle, the Warlord had lost almost half his warriors.

The trail was specked with bodies, which seemed to feed all the scavengers of all the far-flung lands. Yet the Qreq horde was still the largest of armies ever assembled under any banner. In his fury, Toraq ceased sending out scouts, ceased watching his rear. He no longer cared if he was sighted. All he wanted was to engage with the people who had so disrupted his carefully wrought plans. He would overwhelm them with the desperate thirst of his numberless Qreq creations!

He pushed his men to a faster, harder pace—before all of his imposing army dropped dead from thirst. He sent out the giant Qreq of his personal guard with whips and staves to drive them onward.

For the first time, Jonla and Sanra were glad they were prisoners, for they did not have to march like their captors. But they received no water. Then, they saw a strange thing. A frightened messenger rode up to the Warlord's column and jumped from his horse. Though the Companions could not hear what news the man bore—they saw the look of fear that passed momentarily over the angelic face of the Sorcerer King.

Now the Qreq were beginning to look behind them in dread, and by listening to their fearful murmurs, the prisoners were able to lean', the cause of their dismay. Something—no one could say what or who— had overwhelmed the Qreq Company guarding the Warlord's private spring of water. The only supply of water in all the grasslands was poisoned! It seemed the Qreq had enemies in back of them 3.s well as in front, enemies who had slaughtered Toraq's strongest and most trusted men!

The two prisoners exchanged glances and began to whisper hopefully again. The Lashitu overheard and shushed them from his perch on the wagon. "The Warlord seeks peace!" he angrily lectured them. "Such incidents can only annoy Toraq."

The two bound captives looked at each other in dismay. The shaman had gone mad at last. They said no more that could be overheard, as the Qreq horde continued on to Kernback—now spurred by the Warlord's own thirst as well.

CHAPTER XVIII

Kenlahar woke with blurry - sight and couldn't remember at first where he was. Then the realization of his danger shot through his body and he woke completely. He was set against the embankment of Misty Vales, his hands and feet tied securely. As his head cleared, he found that some kind of celebration was going on in the glen. For the first time he saw the women of the mountains, dancing with the men. One of the men came over and tilted his head back roughly, pouring a vile tasting fluid down his throat. Kenlahar gagged on the strong wine, with a violence that made the man laugh. The man walked away, and Kenlahar noticed for the first time that Sar Devern was still beside him.

Sar Devern was wrapped in a blanket, shivering feverishly though it was a warm night. It did not look to Kenlahar as if the soldier would live through the night. The Mountain People had done little for him, perhaps all they could do, but it would not be enough. He spoke the officer's name once, then again, but the man would or could not answer. If he only had his potion of Cormat's blood and some herbs! Kenlahar thought. Some medicinal herbs would undoubtedly be growing in these parts. Kenlahar made up his mind to try to help the injured man.

"Ohmaar!" he shouted, though the man was nowhere in sight. Someone else came over and demanded what he wanted. "I think I can help this man. I've had some training."

"Why should you?" the man asked suspiciously.

"It is what I have pledged my life to," Kenlahar said simply. "Do you not want him to survive? Do you want to take me in yourself?" Just then Sar Devern groaned, and the man crouched over him, to stare at him dispassionately.

He apparently saw the Kenlahar could do no harm, for he muttered his approval. He shouted out to one of the men to find Ohmaar, and bent to untie Kenlahar. Several other men came to stand over him, watching him with speculation. Kenlahar knew that it would be impossible to escape, but he had not been intending to try. He asked for a few things, in increasing importance, until he asked for a knife.

There was some argument and discussion among the men about this request, but he was finally given it. As Kenlahar hoped, his request for the jug of Cormat's blood, which he saw tossed aside, only a few feet away, was not even questioned. The men had left his feet tied, so he hobbled over to the injured man, and collapsed beside him. He drew himself into a position where he could move freely.

"Roll him over," Kenlahar ordered. Just then, Ohmaar entered the clearing.

"What are you doing!" he demanded. The man who had given Kenlahar the knife hastily tried to explain, but Kenlahar interrupted.

"I am going to heal this man. I need the knife to remove the splinters from the shaft of the arrow. And I need to clean his infection."

Ohmaar looked at him, considering this. Again Sar Devern cried out in pain, though he had not been touched. As with the other man, this seemed to decide Ohmaar. He gruffly gave his assent, though he cuffed the other man for not consulting him before giving Kenlahar a knife.

The soldier's wound was minor, once the bleeding was stopped and the infection cut away. Kenlahar poured a little of his precious Cormat into the wound to stop further infection and speed the healing; by the time he had finished, some of the color had returned to Sar Devern's face and he was breathing evenly, without the unconscious moans he had been uttering before. Kenlahar could see that Ohmaar was impressed by the rapid recovery of the officer. He had pretended not to watch, crouching by the fire some distance away, but he kept glancing sideways into the corner where Kenlahar worked.

Finally, the man came over and extended a bloody hand, grunting, "Can you heal this?" Kenlahar gingerly peeled back the filthy bandage. Two of the fingers would always be useless, he saw, and Ohmaar was in danger of losing them all to infection. The hand had a serrated cut across four knuckles.

Kenlahar was reluctant to use any of the remaining Cormat on a man who was willing to sell his soul, for a life under the Queen. Still, he produced the flask and poured another precious capful into the wound, and bound it up in a clean bandage. "The pain is gone!" Ohmaar exclaimed in astonishment. Then a greedy look crossed his face and he extended his hand. "Give me the potion!" he demanded. "You will not need it any longer."

Kenlahar stuffed the flask under his shirt. Angrily, Ohmaar struck him across the face with the good hand. Only a commotion further down the trail saved Kenlahar from a further beating. With a final menacing glance, Ohmaar turned on his heel and vanished from the glade. A few minutes later, the keening of women drifting up the ledge warned Kenlahar of a tragedy. A dozen men entered the clearing, carrying a body.

Kenlahar knew who it was before he saw him. He forced his hobbled legs under him and staggered to the body. He grabbed the flask and bent over the form of the Whistler. He lay with a long arrow piercing his chest—dead. Kenlahar forced himself to think clearly, and touched the body. Angrily, one of the men of the mountains began to push him away. "Wait!" Ohmaar's deep voice commanded. "Let him be."

The body of the Whistler was still warm. He had been dead for only a few minutes! Kenlahar shook the flask, trying to measure its contents, and really trying to gauge its power. Could he restore life to a dead man? The potion had done miraculous things in his hands. And it was doubtful he would ever have a chance to use what was left of the Cormat.

He poured half of what was left onto the wound—and most of the rest he poured down the lifeless throat. At the last moment, by instinct, he reserved a few drops and tilted the flask back to catch the dregs in his own mouth. As before, the potion seemed to explode in his head, and he was suddenly certain of how to proceed.

Not really aware of what his hands were doing, he clasped the dead man's head between both hands and began to *will* the life back into the mountain leader. It seemed to him that he could see inside the soul of the Whistler, but nowhere was there any spark of life. He was witnessing the disintegration of the body. Soon there would be nothing to revive.

He drew back in frustration, and explored his own mind for a clue to the life he found there. He felt, or saw, the fragile spark they called life deep within himself, and called forth much of it—sending it spinning down into the dead body. Life and death fought for what seemed an eternity. Then death seemed to win, and darkness fell on him.

When he awoke it was morning. For a minute he kept his eyes closed and savored the sounds of birds and of a fire crackling. Life seemed sweet that morning, no matter what happened next. Then he remembered the night before and sat up.

The ledge was full of busy, happy people. An old lady tending the fire saw him and fell to her knees. The others quickly followed her example. Kenlahar was astounded, and Ohmaar's voice barely pierced his surprise. "May I approach, Kenlahar?"

Dumbly, Kenlahar nodded. Ohmaar approached with a deference Kenlahar would never have thought f possible, and thought embarrassing at this moment. A few feet from him, Ohmaar fell to one knee and bent his head. "Forgive me, Kenlahar. I did not know who you were!" The man produced the Star Axe from behind his back and laid it at Kenlahar's feet. "I thought to save you with more of the potion," he explained. "I searched your pack and found this instead."

"You know of Alcress?" Kenlahar asked, still surprised by the reverence with which the man had handled the talisman.

"It has been the hope of my people, of all the people of the kingdoms, that you would come," the man said. "The Whistler knows the ancient tongues, and translated your name to us. Why did you not reveal yourself to us before, Son of Lahar?"

"Whistler!" Kenlahar reacted at the name.

"Yes—he is well, and has even begun to walk. He is now calling the Seven Tribes together."

Kenlahar's joy at being alive, the impact of the sudden worship, was beginning to wear off. Uneasily, he asked, "Why has he called the Tribes together?" Ohmaar seemed surprised at the Question. "Why, to hear your wishes, Ken-Lahar, and to follow them!"

The truth was not quite as simple as Ohmaar's explanation. The outlaw had assumed that Kenlahar's "wishes" would be to attack Kernback. After all, had not the Queen chased him all the way into the Mountains of Sanctuary, would she not have had him killed if he had been caught? More importantly, that is what the outlaws had been waiting for, for many, many years. All they had needed as a champion, and now they thought they had one. All his protests, all his denials, would not change their minds. For did he not bear the Star Axe? they had asked.

The chieftains of the Seven Tribes had met for a while, and then had left to muster their men for battle. They never asked Kenlahar for what he wished. He found himself in the role of a leader who did not lead. A spiritual leader of the army of the Star Axe. He did now know what they would do if he protested strongly, and he never did test his power. He had come to find help for the House of Lahar and he had succeeded beyond any of his old fantasies. If it meant that he had to conquer Kernback first, then he would so. But he sensed that even this conflict was not the true conflict, and the unsuspecting men of both armies would soon be embroiled in the larger war with Toraq, the Sorcerer King. Through all of this he had not yet found the secret of the Star Axe!

Kenlahar loosened the tight and itching collar of the heavy ceremonial robe of a chieftain he felt obligated to wear. The weight of the robe pulled at his neck and was heavy on his shoulders. Even the cold mountain air could not penetrate the thick cloth. The crisp air, and the miles of snow, was belied by the clear blue skies and warm sun. In the tent, only an occasional waft of cool air told Kenlahar what the weather was really like.

The tent was stifling and crowded. The staff of his hastily assembled army was coming and going constantly. That the meetings were held in his tent at Misty Vales was more show than anything else, and Kenlahar was bored. He could hear the laughter of the common soldier in the other tents, which spotted the mountainside wherever level ground could be found or imagined.

He sat out of the way of the bustle as the tribes arrived one by one to add their footprints to the muddy snow. As the days passed, Kenlahar even managed to dissolve much of the embarrassing homage. One or two of the military men would even talk back to him! He knew nothing of war, and by all rights they should have told him to mind his own business, he thought. But he was the Axe-bearer. Thank Lahar for Whistler and Ohmaar, he said half aloud.

Several of the soldiers looked up from their tables of maps and looked at him curiously. But then the man who held the Star Axe was not supposed to be like other men, Kenlahar thought ironically. Whistler was the only one who was completely honest to Kenlahar; the only one who he could trust to give him the bad news as well as the good. As if the leader could read these thoughts, he appeared at his shoulder. "Kenlahar?" he said. "Did you ask for me?"

Kenlahar remembered that he had mentioned Whistler's name aloud a few minutes before, and took his chance to ask, "Have you heard from Sar Devern yet?" He was becoming worried. Sar Devern had set out for Kernback over a week ago to plead for a parley.

Sar Devern had turned out to be the first person Kenlahar had met since he had left the House of Lahar, who he felt was loyal to *him;* not to the symbolic person he seemed to represent to all the others, either as a healer or as Axe-bearer.

With the help of the blood of the Cormat, the wounded — from the slightly hurt Kenlahar, to the mortally wounded Whistler — had recovered with miraculous speed. Sar Devern had been humiliated by the betrayal that had led to Whistler's ambush! Kenlahar believed him when he said that he had not known it was a trick. The old soldier had vowed to Kenlahar that he would not return to serve in an army where the officers were forced to lie and betray. He pledged his fealty to Kenlahar, though he said he could not yet join the army of the Star Axe.

"I have long known how the Queen has treated the people of Kernback," he said. "But my family has served the nobility of Kernback for many generations. Herald's Manor was a gift to my father from the

Queen's father for saving his life. But never before have I been asked to betray my honor. I will serve you Kenlahar, but I cannot raise a weapon against the throne."

Still, Sar Devern had been looked on with undisguised suspicion and hate by the mountain folk. They would not even allow the soldier to wander free and unhindered until Kenlahar demanded it. Indeed, Sar Devern would have been executed if it had not been for Kenlahar's patronage. But the soldier became an invaluable ally to the lonely Axe-bearer, who learned to trust him completely. Kenlahar was surprised to find in the young soldier the same horror of war he felt as a healer.

So the two of them had hatched a desperate plan to avoid the cataclysmic battle that was shaping. Late one night, they had walked beyond the furthest sentries—Kenlahar escorting Sar Devern unchallenged by the guards—and the two men had clasped hands. Then Sar Devern had slipped off into the night. Kenlahar had known it would not be easy for the renegade noble to make it through the hostile foothills, and the equally hostile manor estates, but Sar Devern had insisted on trying and Kenlahar had given in. The Axe-bearer would sacrifice much to avoid war. And if anyone could make the journey it would be Sar Devern.

"Has he returned?" Kenlahar asked again.

"No, sire. No one has seen him," Whistler answered darkly. "Perhaps he has not returned because he chooses not to."

"No, he will come back if he can." Kenlahar was sure of his assessment; more sure than he was of the loyalty of much of the gathering host of men. For weeks now the foothills had been filling with the families of men who had heard of the rebellion and rushed to join it. When Kenlahar saw the hordes of people, all of them so disenchanted with the Queen that they wished to overthrow her regime, he realized that they might succeed. Indeed, it seemed that only the nobles and the townspeople—who had little choice—and the well paid, pampered professional soldiers of her Guard, remained loyal to the Queen.

Representatives of all the Five Peoples of old were assembling in the Sanctuary Mountains. From the Exiles, those legendary followers of Lahar, came the Axe-bearer; Kenlahar was still amazed by the irony of his old home being a legend to all others. From the Borderlands came the farmers and craftsmen. From the manors and estates of Kernback came servants and slaves, eager to join the crusade. From the coasts of the far north came the Mariners, those proud and aloof descendants of the Starborn. Kenlahar even saw some of the People of the Cormat, who he had learned trafficked more with the Outside than the Elders had ever suspected. Since the Seven Tribes no longer counted themselves as subjects to Kernback, to the Five Peoples had been added another.

Over these last few weeks Kenlahar had watched the massive buildup of men and arms with more and more uncertainty. Despite all his attempts to avoid bloodshed, the time was coming when he would have to choose to use his rightful legacy as the bearer of Alcress—if he ever discovered its secret—or deny his heritage for the sake of his Atima. The dissonance this created between his ideals and the needs of his followers was making him moody and preoccupied as the time set for the march to Kernback neared. If only Sar Devern would return!

Ohmaar entered the tent, still discussing the details of the march with his aids. To the gruff, plain speaking mountain man had fallen the chore of ordering the armies. Kenlahar had come to feel better about Ohmaar, but could not quite forget how Ohmaar had once treated him. Kenlahar knew that he could trust Ohmaar in the same way he had once trusted the poor Lashitu—as bearer of Alcress, and only as the bearer of Alcress. At the moment, the mountain man seemed frustrated.

"Where are they all coming from!" Ohmaar exclaimed. "I wonder who is left to harvest the food and tend the manors? We would be better off without all this rabble. The Seven Tribes are all we need— with your help and the Star Axe."

"I do not know if I will be able to help you, Ohmaar. I do not know how to use Alcress."

Ohmaar did not seem at all concerned. "It would not have been given you if you could not use it," he said in a tone that brooked no questioning. When Kenlahar asked for news of Sar Devern the old surly look momentarily passed over Ohmaar's face. "What was the purpose of his journey?" But Kenlahar turned away without answering. He did not see the sullen look his commander gave him. "We march tomorrow if you will give the order," Ohmaar announced.

Kenlahar almost laughed at this apt definition of his powers. He gave the expected command, for he saw that he could not postpone the inevitable any longer. "See to it that the women and children do not suffer the revenge of the Queen. Leave as much food behind as you can." "They will eat as much as they ever ate under the Queen," Ohmaar said.

So they left the mountains before Sar Devern had returned. Kenlahar glumly rode at the head of the army where all could see him and be inspired. He had laughed when Ohmaar had asked him to do this. Still, his men seemed in good spirits, sure that they could not lose with the Axe-bearer leading them. They marched unhindered.

Apparently the Queen had chosen to retreat behind the White Walls of Kernback. Since the time of Lahar, the massive battlements and steep cliffs had never been surmounted. The White Walls seemed to wink at them with flashes of light as the host of rebels approached, and Kenlahar could see the lances of the Queen's guard glinting far above. The huge ramps that led to the twin gates had been removed. The gates were unreachable even with tall ladders. Only the source of the Shallowspill flowed from the walls, and down the cliffs, falling to the Chalk Plains with a misty roar. As they neared the city, even the water began to sputter to a stop. Soon the walls gleamed wetly, but no water fell over their surface.

The rebel army camped below the twin hills, ready for a long siege. Kenlahar soon learned that with its own source of water, and the tons of grain that Queen's Guard had stockpiled by years of taxation—at such a cost to the farmers of the estates—that Kernback could hold out for many months. Kenlahar was the only one who seemed worried by this prospect. By the time the city fell, the Qreq could have long ago crushed the House of Lahar.

Ohmaar advised him to blockade the city. It would reduce the casualties, he explained. But Kenlahar saw the long, empty months stretching in front of them. He envisioned the House of Lahar under assault, conquered only days before he finally arrived with help. "No one has been able to maintain a blockade for this long in the last few generations," Ohmaar continued. "But Kernback traditionally can withstand a siege for no longer than half a year without help. Help has always arrived in time before now. But there is no one to rescue the Queen this time!"

Half a year! Kenlahar heard with dismay. Then when he heard the estimate Ohmaar gave of the deadly toll famine and pestilence would take of the common people of Kernback, he abandoned his reluctance to attack. He knew that the nobles and the soldiery, the ones he wished to reach, would be the last to starve. He saw that the men of his army were eager to attack. He was still tempted to follow Ohmaar's advice, but again he remembered the desperate plight of the Island Laharhann. He told Ohmaar that he wanted a frontal assault. "We can starve them if that fails," he said.

From beside him, the Whistler, who had become a sort of unofficial advisor, smiled, "If I know the Queen's Guard, they are the ones who will attack first."

"What do you mean?" Kenlahar asked. He had thought that the Queen's Guard would stay behind their walls.

"Their greatest weapon is their cavalry. The armored nobles have never lost a battle," Ohmaar explained.

"They do not fear us," Whistler added, grimly. "But this time we shall not run from their charge. This time they will learn not to take us lightly!"

Kenlahar followed Ohmaar on a tour of the fringes of the camp. Rows of sharpened stakes, planted at an angle, surrounded the army. The men were busy creating what seemed to Kenlahar almost a re-creation of the Tream. The broken and swampy terrain was being mimicked by deep ditches and hidden troughs full of water. "The kings and queens of Kernback have always relied on their horsemen to maintain their vast territories," Ohmaar said. "No infantry has ever stood against them. I do not intend to have us break and run this time!" He smiled briefly. "At least, not until we are ready."

Kenlahar looked at him questioningly, but the commander did not seem to notice. When Ohmaar had first shown up in the mountain camp in his greasy buckskins, Kenlahar had not realized the respect the other soldiers felt for insignificant looking man. As they walked from tent to tent, the men hastily rose to their feet at their entrance—bowing to the Axe-bearer, receiving curt instructions from Ohmaar.

By the next morning the defenses were constructed, the men lined up on the Chalk Plains in ordered columns, waiting in eerie silence for the Queen's Guard to emerge. From the huge gates, long wooden ramps were lowered. The nobles rode down the flimsy ramps, swaying and clattering noisily. Their bearing was arrogant, confident that they would disperse this rabble with a single charge of their lances.

Kenlahar watched from the rear, with the Whistler beside him. He could hear the distant voice of Ohmaar repeating the instructions he had given the night before. "Aim for the horses! Dismount and finish them!" Then his voice was drowned by the sound of a thousand hoof-beats. The Queen's Guard charged straight at the long lines of rebels. Kenlahar flinched long before the moment of impact. No one could stand against the force of such an attack! As he feared, the men on foot were driven back. Kenlahar saw that they were retreating over the cleverly concealed bridges spanning the traps. But they appeared to be in a rout.

The triumphant cavalry gathered again for one last, finishing blow. The rebels seemed to be milling nervously, uncertainly before them. Though the archers brought down many more horses this time, the nobles rode on fearlessly, secure in their invincibility. Then the very ground seemed to open up under them. The fastest and strongest mounts of Kernback went down in a pile of flailing legs. With a roar the infantry ran forward to finish them off. Kenlahar saw a Borderman open the visor of a noble's helmet while he lay pinned under his horse, and drive in his knife ruthlessly in up to the hilt.

Other nobles, helpless without their horses, were trying to reach the gates, but the lighter armored men of the Star Axe quickly caught up with them. Few of the aristocracy of Kernback would survive that day! Only a very few still remained mounted. They formed a wedge that drove for the city, but one by one the men at the edge of the wedge were pulled from their saddles. It slowed pitifully just before the beckoning doors.

Kenlahar saw the red leather jerkin, silver iron rings flashing in the sun, of the Prince of Kernback, in the center of the nobles. He was laying about him with devastating circular sweeps, hanging over his stirrups, with one hand extending to the grip of his saddle.

Then they were near enough to the city for the archers of Kernback to become effective. The rebel army fell back before the hail of arrows. The last remnant of the once proud cavalry clattered up the ramp. The wooden structure was dropped to the plains below. The gates clanged shut. The first battle of the siege for Kernback had ended.

CHAPTER XIX

"The power of the nobles is destroyed forever!" Whistler shouted from beside Kenlahar. Once again the healer's training and senses were stunned by the savagery of a battle between man and man. Now his army owned the Chalk Plains, and men moved freely below the walls, carefully out of range of the archers. The siege engines were pulled forward and lined at intervals along the cliffs. In the spaces between, men clustered, carrying ladders that were meant to be stacked one on top of the other. In theory these precarious structures would reach even the tops of the White Walls.

As the shielded engines were pushed forward and the first of the ladders were placed against the cliffs, Kenlahar turned away from the bloodshed. With the Whistler attendant, he toured the tents of the wounded and immersed himself in the work of healing. No one questioned Kenlahar's decision to stay away from the fighting. No one thought of doing so. Yet Kenlahar was aware of the incongruity. He told himself that he did not know the secret of the Star Axe. That he was preserving his Atima. But these explanations no longer seemed to be adequate. His old fears of cowardice were returning.

Reports from the battlefield told of the attackers being thrown back again and again. But eventually the heralds gave tidings of victory. One of the towers of the White Walls had fallen. From this foothold, other parts of the battlements were falling. And always leading the way, he learned, was Ohmaar.

Whistler interrupted him as he worked on the wounds of a young border farmer. His face was downcast and worried. "What has happened?" Kenlahar asked, fearing that the battle was lost, despite the excited murmurs of the soldiers. Before Whistler could answer, the body of Ohmaar was brought into the tent. The wound was fatal, Kenlahar saw immediately—beyond even his healing powers. The gash in Ohmaar's neck was deep and jagged. Kenlahar poured what little of Cormat's blood he still had onto the wound. But it was too late—Ohmaar never woke again.

Kenlahar rose from the bedside with his head hung in sadness. What good was his Atima if he could not save his friends? A sense of disgust with himself filled him and would not go away no matter how hard he tried to dismiss his cowardice. He had been hiding behind his role of healer too long! Because he had neither wished to kill or be killed he had stood back while many others killed for him and in his name. It was time to fight his own fight. "Call a halt to the attack," he ordered.

"But, my lord, we have won it!" One of his attendants protested. Whistler was not in the tent when Kenlahar made his startling command. But there was no need to fetch him, for he came rushing back, ready to argue fervently. When he saw Kenlahar's face and manner, his objection was muted.

Kenlahar slowly, almost reverently unsheathed the Star Axe in his hands. It seemed to be pulsing, with a power demanding to be released. "Come with me," he said to Whistler and they walked to the now peaceful and confused battlefield. He marched to the very gates of the city. The scattered fighting—the Guard had not disengaged and was probing the apparent weakness of the rebels—ceased as he approached. Contrary to his commanders' warnings, no one made a hostile motion from the walls. He stood vulnerable below them.

"Prince Molnar!" he shouted, and on the hushed plain his voice carried to all. "I challenge you to single combat! Show yourself!" He said nothing more, but stood gloomily introspective between the greatest armies that the world had seen.

Finally, the huge doors above creaked open a few yards, just enough for a narrow ramp to be extended onto the battlefield. One by one, a small delegation negotiated down the swaying board and gathered at the bottom. At the rear of the small party, Kenlahar saw the Prince of Kernback, now wearing a crown. Molnar had changed—had matured fully into a man. His plumpness was gone, and with it the deceptive softness. Now his face was drawn and haggard. No one could mistake him for a weakling. His bearing was proud, disdainful even in defeat.

When all of the delegation had finally reached the safety of the Chalk Plains, the doors opened a little wider and a man was lowered with ropes, limply to the ground. Two of the Prince's attendants dragged the man towards Kenlahar. They dropped him cruelly. Without a word they walked away.

Kenlahar recognized Sar Devern, who seemed barely conscious of his surroundings. His traditional garb as Herald of Kernback was torn and tattered. Kenlahar could see no obvious wounds, but all could see that he had been hurt badly. A cold anger filled Kenlahar, unlike any emotion he had ever felt before. This anger did not confuse him or make him tremble, but seemed to focus all his fury at the Prince. Molnar paled at his look and even stepped backwards in surprise.

Then Kenlahar knelt beside the old soldier and cradled his head in his lap. He knew that he had been right to come forward at last. Soon the bloodshed would be ended—one way or the other. Sar Devern opened his eyes at his touch and said wearily, as if reporting a simple message. He did not seem aware of the import of his presence. "The Prince of Kernback has rejected your proposal of a duel," he said almost formally. Then the sight of Kenlahar revived him and he sat up. "I think he has changed his mind now," he laughed painfully. "He did not think much of your army. Now he knows better!" He managed to smile.

"Will you join us now?"

"I did not want to betray my Queen, but she is dead. Molnar is now King! I owe them nothing more."

Torture had removed all the loyalty Sar Devern had once felt, Kenlahar saw. He did not have to ask how the Queen had died. He remembered Molnar's fear and deep hatred of his mother, his yearnings to be master of all.

Kenlahar also knew that his healing had little to do with what happened next. Sar Devern rose slowly to his feet and stood swaying, scornfully facing Molnar. The King could not hide his surprise. Kenlahar realized that Molnar had meant to give him a corpse. The men of both armies gasped at the miracle, attributing it to Kenlahar's powers of healing. What had been meant to dismay Kenlahar turned into a symbol of his godhood. The Axe-bearer, though, knew it was nothing more than a manifestation of Sar Devern's own strong will.

The King of Kernback now approached alone and unprotected, glancing nervously at the revived Sar Devern. "Have you come to taunt me?" he asked.

"I have come to offer you one last chance at single combat. Let us end the slaughter. With either of our deaths, there would be no more purpose in fighting. It is *our* battle, Molnar—others have fought for us too long."

Molnar's eyes filled with a hopeful desperation. As Kenlahar had hoped, the King knew that he had lost the battle. Here was a chance to save his throne in one stroke of the blade! He looked at the Axe-bearer with a calculating glance, and seemed to sense the weakness of his opponent. Had not Kenlahar admitted his unfamiliarity with combat? And he could not have found the secret of the Star Axe or he would have used the weapon long before now. The spirit of defiance would be stilled by Kenlahar's death. Then he would possess the Star Axe. He smiled and said, "I accept your challenge."

A circle of level ground was prepared for the duel. Kenlahar noticed that no one seemed very worried about the outcome. They did not expect him to lose. After all, was he not the Axe-bearer? Kenlahar could not tell them that the Star Axe was to him no more than an ordinary battleaxe, and that he did not know how to wield any weapon! If he was killed, then he had condemned all his followers to slavery.

The Whistler was giving him last minute instructions. He alone seemed to sense Kenlahar's fear and uncertainty. "The battleaxe can deal cruel blows, Kenlahar," he whispered hurriedly. "It will shatter the armor into the wounds, where they will fester. But you are going to have to deal the fatal blow quickly. Strike hard and strike first! You must overwhelm him, for he shall have a sword and will be swifter. The battleaxe is not a good weapon for defense."

199

Kenlahar tried to listen carefully. Even these simple instructions were new to him. He had been carrying the Star Axe for months and had not wondered once how to use it as a weapon, not once had he practiced. He had just assumed the power of Alcress was something deeper than that, something spiritual, and that actually striking out with it would never be necessary. Now he regretted the lost time.

The Whistler had outfitted him with a light, tough leather jerkin, and had given Kenlahar his own shield. A helmet was hastily fetched from some soldier of the army of Alcress. As Kenlahar placed it over his head, he felt the warmth of its owner, lining the inside of the helmet. He felt foolish wearing the armor, as if he were masquerading as a warrior. They walked slowly to the marked boundary of their battle field. The Queen's Guard had emerged peacefully from the city to join the rebels around the circle. The crowd gave way before Kenlahar. Before he stepped into the ring, Kenlahar was given one last bit of advice by the Whistler. "Trust Alcress, Kenlahar. Trust the Star Axe!"

To all but Molnar, and Kenlahar himself, the King looked foolishly confident. The multitude fell silent as the two men stepped into the field of combat, and circled each other slowly. The Star Axe felt heavy in Kenlahar's hands for the first time, but he knew it was only his worried imagination. He remembered the Whistler's admonishment to strike first. But, as always happened when he was faced with conflict, he could not bring himself to strike first. Molnar sensed this and grinned wolfishly, circling his unthreatening and frightened opponent without any effort to defend himself.

Suddenly, Kenlahar's eyes were blinded momentarily by a reflection from the White Walls of Kernback. Too late he remembered the ancient warning, "Cast down your eyes before the White Walls!" The sun had emerged from behind the clouds, and the King had cleverly maneuvered Kenlahar into facing the city at the same moment.

Instinctively, Kenlahar threw up the shield, and the metal boss in the center of the barrier deflected Molnar's blade. Kenlahar defended himself again and again with the shield, while the Star Axe trailed on the ground uselessly. Finally the sun once more ducked behind a cloud and Kenlahar scrambled away from the White Walls.

Molnar stopped moving altogether and lowered his own shield. He taunted Kenlahar to use his own weapon. When Kenlahar did not respond, he pressed forward and again Kenlahar was forced to defend himself. The King backed away and grinned. Then, contemptuously, he threw down his shield and drew Toraq's Bane from its concealed sheath.

The men of both armies stopped their shouting at the sight of the deadly blade. It winked red in the midday light. All recognized Toraq's Bane, and the King's Guard started cheering. Only Kenlahar was not surprised. The dagger had once nearly killed Lahar himself! Suddenly, the tide of morale seemed to shift. The rebels no longer seemed so confident, the Guard no longer forlorn.

With Toraq's Bane in one hand, and his sword in the other, Molnar prepared to attack one last time, confident now that Kenlahar would not strike back. When his flurry of blows came, everyone saw that despite the speed of his attack, Molnar had no defense at all. Even Kenlahar saw that he only needed to strike once and the King would be forced to fall back, even if not wounded. Kenlahar defended himself, and told himself that he was only waiting for the right moment. Perhaps his lack of plans for an attack saved his life for he was able to concentrate on defense. He felt his shield arm pierced. It grew numb and the shield dropped from his hands. His arms fell limply to his side. Part of the audience erupted into cheers at this sight, and the other half groaned at the desperation of Kenlahar's plight.

Kenlahar knew that he could not heft the battleaxe with full force in his weakened and injured condition. He stood and waited for the final assault. With a roar of triumph Molnar stepped forward, swinging Toraq's Bane downward in a fatal blow. Awkwardly, Kenlahar swung the Star Axe up to meet the descent of the dagger. It moved swiftly and firmly, almost of its own accord. Kenlahar felt that he was doing no more than holding it when it shattered the sword and knocked Toraq's Bane out of Molnar's hand.

Molnar fell back with a surprised scream. Then, without pause, the Star Axe struck deep through the King's chest. Kenlahar stared down at the slain King in shock. He could not stop Alcress from dealing the fatal blow! He had commanded it to stop, and had pulled back with all his might—but it had swung down to strike the King. He felt sick.

The King's Guard was enraged. Kenlahar had played with their King, and then had struck without mercy. Several of them began to fight the rebels at their side. Only the Axe-bearer could have stopped the battle from starting again, but he was in a daze, hardly recognizing Whistler who came to lead him from the dead body of the King. So the battle began again, and would have ended only with the destruction of the entire Guard, if someone on the walls had not seen the approach of a vast army on the horizon.

Kenlahar seemed to revive at the sighting. He knew instantly who it was—it all fitted the pattern. He would not have to return to the House of Lahar or march to the Warlord's Havens to confront Toraq after all. "Qreq!" he shouted. Others took up the cry. Though few knew what the Qreq were, all could sense that they were the common enemy. "The Sorcerer King has come to enslave us!" he cried and all recognized this ancient name. The fighting was stopped and the two armies merged, drawn up before the gates of the city. There was no time for more than a portion of the host to enter the city, though men marched up the crude ramps until the last moment, and even during the battle.

The King's Guard chose to remain outside the walls and to meet the brunt of the assault. Behind them, the Seven Tribes remained with Kenlahar, who also refused to enter the safety of the city. So they stood solidly, as the disordered charge of the Qreq neared. To the people of Kernback, who had never seen the Qreq before, the warriors must have seemed frightening. The horde extended as far as the eye could see, until all of the Chalk Plain was crawling with their columns. But the army of the Star Axe stood its ground before the wave of Qreq.

Though it was outnumbered a hundred to one, the King's Guard refused to retreat. Whole lines of the soldiers would disappear at a time, swept away by the thousands of Qreq. The Seven Tribes waited their turn to confront the Qreq with pale faces, but they too stood their ground. Kenlahar's eyes were drawn to a small knoll a short distance away. *There* he sensed the evil presence of the Warlord. But at this distance he could not distinguish the form of Toraq. It did not look to Kenlahar as if he would have a chance to test the power of Alcress against the Sorcerer King. Suddenly, it seemed that there was fighting on the knoll as well.

Then the last of the Guard was down and the Qreq was before him. The Star Axe gleamed, seeming eager to fight the evil it felt around it. Then it was moving, of its own volition, protecting its master and laying a swath through the horde of Qreq. Yet Kenlahar soon saw that even the Star Axe could not hold back this army much longer. With his back to the cliff, he prepared for the end with the small number of men still standing.

Sanra could see quick blinding flashes from the middle of the vast Chalk Plains. The Qreq horde had come at last to a wide field that stretched endlessly before them. It was as if a thousand mirrors were catching the reflection of the sun's light. As they drew nearer, the Qreq began to mutter excitedly among themselves, and from beside her, Sanra heard Jonla gasp, "The White Walls of Kernback! So they exist after all..." his voice trailed off wonderingly. A huge cloud of white dust seemed to be hovering just below the high glittering walls, and she wondered what could have caused such a commotion of the earth.

They saw two hills rising out of the flat plain, and a moving and faltering flow of bright reflections, surging back and forth across the land between the twin knolls. Even as she watched the flow it stopped, and she realized that it was two giant hosts of men. As the Qreq advanced, the two separate armies joined together to face the approaching horde. The Warlord's resounding voice reached most of the warriors of his excitedly clustered army. "*There!*" he shouted. "There, behind those walls are the waters of Shallowspill!"

The giant mass of Qreq were released, and with a surge, and cries of "Qreq!" rolled across the Chalk Plains. The horde of Qreq were disordered, an unruly mob, but as the two opposing hosts converged with a roaring tumble, Sanra saw their relative sizes. Her heart sank — no wonder the Warlord had been so confident! For year, upon festering year, the Sorcerer King had been breeding his Qreq in the warrens beneath the Havens. Though much of this horde had been already destroyed, still they overflowed even the vast width of the Chalk Plains. Sanra saw that the Qreq would soon simply swallow the armies of Kernback in their frenzy for the water lying within the city.

The prison wagon had been drawn up beside the Sorcerer King and his guards, upon a low, sloping rise—perhaps the only elevation on all the Chalk Plains. The Warlord was standing only steps away, watching the battle with a look of delight at the slaughter. Toraq was surrounded by one those few he called his commanders. But his army did not need much direction—they simply fought whoever confronted them until they themselves were slain, and every Qreq was a strong fighter.

The dry bed of Shallowspill turned in a crooked and meandering hook a few yards behind them. As Sanra watched, she thought she could see two small figures emerging from over the bank of the empty river. Then the mysterious shapes dropped and seemed to disappear into the low grass. When she could see no more movement, she convinced herself that her despair had caused her to imagine the sight. She turned back to watch the battle.

Then she heard Jonla gasp, and he kicked her slightly with his bound legs. She looked back again and caught her breath. Kalese and Balor were running straight at them at a full run, like a vision out of one of their feverish dreams. None of the Qreq guards had noticed the two apparitions yet, and time seemed to stand still as the impossible distance was crossed. Kalese broke apart from Balor and ran toward the captives. Balor continued onward toward the back of the Sorcerer King, who stood absorbed in the battle.

The Lashitu broke the quiet of impending doom. "No!" he screamed. "Balor—don't hurt him!" The Qreq guards turned around in surprise at the yelp, and then Balor was among them, swinging his sword wildly. He killed in silence and with deadly effect against the weakened Qreq. Then Sanra saw the Warlord draw his sword with a grin, and move toward Balor.

Kalese's form blocked out the evolving duel. Sanra saw no more while Kalese sawed jaggedly first at Jonla's bonds, and then hers. When Jonla was freed, he jumped from the wagon, falling briefly, and stooped to pick up a sword from one of the fallen guards. He cried out in pain from even this small movement. He staggered toward the fight, as the blood began to slowly flow back into his arms and legs. Then Sanra felt her hands become free as well, and both women turned to watch the duel.

Balor was being driven backward by the surprising speed and strength of the Warlord's thrusts. The few surviving Qreq guards were merely watching the duel and made no effort to help their master. Toraq wanted to kill, and it was soon obvious that he did not need help in defeating Balor—or any mortal man. The Warlord seemed to be enjoying his battle, toying with Balor. Yet he tired with the play and sent Balor reeling backward over the body of a slain guard. Helpless, and without hope, Balor threw his sword up. Jonla's shout brought Toraq around in surprise. But the Sorcerer King did not bother to play with the Captain of the Watch. The sword moved with supernatural speed, and Jonla's limp form was sent flying sideways.

But now Balor was once more on his feet and hefting his sword. He watched Toraq warily. He knew he was about to die. This opponent was faster and stronger than any he had met before, and possessed of an evil cleverness. That these attributes were supernatural would make no difference in the outcome.

Kalese shouted for Sanra to follow and rushed toward the two circling figures. Sanra stood faltering, wondering how she could help. She had never held a weapon before; had never struck out in violence! Without drawing attention to herself, she slipped a small dagger from out of a Qreq hand and concealed it behind her palm and forearm. Moving slowly, ever so slowly, to the fight, she posed with a shocked and dazed look on her face. Over and over again she wailed, "Jonla!" as if she meant only to approach his lifeless body, and keen her grief. First Balor, and then Kalese were about to be easily overcome by the laughing Sorcerer King. Sanra saw Balor fall, with a blow to his head. He did not move again. Kalese moved without fear to take his place. For a moment it appeared that the enraged girl would penetrate Toraq's defense, but she too was driven backwards.

Sanra did not change her distracted expression, or her cries of grief. Then, only a few yards from the body of Jonla, she whirled and sank the blade of her dagger into the Warlord's back. As the Warlord stiffened, Kalese also struck, and sliced across the exposed neck of the Sorcerer King. He fell headless into the white dust. The lifeless head freed a howl that reached the White Walls of Kernback. Then the beautiful, piercing eyes in the head glazed over.

Before the gates, the defenders fought with a desperate denial of the inevitable. The eerie wail reached them, and the attacking Qreq hesitated momentarily, looking back uncertainly. Kenlahar held the Star Axe ready as the Qreq looked at each other in dread. The Qreq were backing away, not out of fear of the outnumbered defenders, but as a panicked and frightened response to some news. The army at the gates stood their ground suspiciously. But as the horde turned and ran, the combined armies of Kernback and the Star Axe roared in victory and pursued them.

"Let them be," Kenlahar said quietly to Whistler, who still stood protectively at his side. When the mountain man began to protest vehemently, Kenlahar repeated his request. "They will never threaten us again. They were the Warlord's tool, and Toraq is gone." And so the Qreq were let go, though only a few were to survive the thirsty landscape, the hungry scavengers on the route to the Havens.

Kenlahar walked from the cliffs, toward the small knoll on the outskirts of the huge battlefield. He picked his way through the tangled, tortured bodies. He already knew in his heart who had saved him again; but his hopes and fears continued to rage in his mind.

He had merely needed the *will* to use the Star Axe. The secret of the Star Axe had been to simply to use the weapon in anger. All this time he had been running! If he had turned to confront his enemies at any point along the way, it would have all ended sooner.

And yet, he had gained the good will of four of the five Peoples through his healing—not through Alcress. His Atima had proved to be a stronger force than the deadly Star Axe—though he had also possessed both powers all along. At the Island Laharhann the Kith and the Elders had accepted him only because of his Atima. In the Tream he had assumed the title of Cormatine, though he was still not sure what the duties of the Cormatine were. He had won the friendship of the Bordermen through the use of his herbs. And it had been his miraculous display of power in bringing back Whistler from the dead that had united the Seven Tribes.

As he neared the hill with a retinue of worried followers, he heard the hysterical voice of the Lashitu. "Why! Why did you have to kill him!

There was no need—we had an agreement!" The shaman was flailing, with little real force, upon the shoulders of a stunned Sanra.

Kenlahar called out her name. She turned uncertainly, and then her eyes widened in surprise. She ran to him and fell thankfully into his arms. While she sobbed, Kenlahar surveyed the bloody scene. The Lashitu, he saw, was hopelessly mad. The shaman did not even seem to recognize the man he had once zealously followed. Balor lay with a gash on his forehead, his head thrown back—unmoving. Kalese lay beside him, with her eyes closed tightly, moaning and quivering in the grip of feverish dreams. Jonla lay off to one side, barely recognizable to Kenlahar, dead.

In the center of the battlefield was a dismembered body that Kenlahar recoiled from instinctively. He was suddenly certain that *this* was the fearsome Toraq—the Warlord, the Sorcerer King. Evil still emanated from the corpse, an evil no longer concealed beneath his beautiful exterior.

Kenlahar motioned for Whistler to take the still crazed and shouting Lashitu away. As if the shaman could sense Kenlahar's grief through his madness, he fell quiet at last. Kenlahar gently handed Sanra to Sar Devern, and she seemed to trust the lieutenant as Kenlahar's man. He knelt beside Balor and placed his friend's bloodied head in his lap. Balor was dying, and there was no way that Kenlahar could recall him. He moved onto Jonla, who was cold—long dead. There was no spirit here to recall even if he somehow still had his Atima.

Kenlahar was sure that he had lost his Atima—irrevocably lost. He had compounded the death of Molnar with the killing of numberless Qreq. Bitterly, he reflected on the many months, the many, many miles he had sought to keep his healing powers, only to lose it on that day he needed it most, needed it to save the life of his friends.

Kalese moaned, and Kenlahar turned to her guiltily, recognizing her as the girl from the Tream with surprise. Somehow he sensed the link between the two Companions. Her wounds were also serious, he saw, perhaps fatal. If a healer did not soon stop their bleeding, Balor and the swampgirl would die! A healer--which he no longer was.

"Whistler!" he shouted, and the little man approached with respect. All his followers, he now saw, had kept reverent distances from the Companions, for they could sense the magnitude of their efforts. "Save them!" he pleaded to Whistler.

Whistler looked back at him in surprise and puzzlement. "But my lord, you are more accomplished in healing than I!"

"Do as I tell you!" Kenlahar shouted.

"Your friend is right, Kenlahar..." a new voice ventured. "You are the only one who can save them." Kenlahar turned angrily on the speaker and saw the tall form of the Queen's physician standing at the edge of the watchers, and a head over them. "You do not know what you ask!" he said. "I have *killed*, not once but many times. I cannot heal!"

"You are the bearer of the Star Axe," the tall man replied. "You are the rightful heir to all the powers of Lahar. Use them before it is too late!"

Kenlahar turned back to the bodies of Balor and Kalese uncertainly. Kalese's eyes opened and she looked uncomprehendingly up at him. Then she smiled. "Cormatine! We have been searching for you. All we have done has not been for nothing!" She tried to turn her head in a frantic search. "Where is Balor? He will be so happy to see you."

Kenlahar did not answer but tears filled his eyes. She looked down on the body she had flung herself upon, and saw the still disarrayed figure of Balor. Her face drained of color, and despite her wounds, she turned and covered him with her own body. Then she too became still. Kenlahar quickly called for medicines from the doctor, Karrack.

Within a few minutes, he knew that he had saved the swampgirl—though he doubted she would thank him for it unless he could save Balor as well. He turned Balor over and gently straightened his limbs. Balor was still breathing, a very shallow and ragged motion. Kenlahar bent over and breathed his own life into that of his friend. He was amazed when the action seemed to briefly revive the warrior. Balor opened his eyes just long enough to smile weakly, and Kenlahar knew that he too would survive. He had not lost his Atima! Once more he hovered over Jonla and searched in vain for a way to call him back, but it was beyond him.

At his instructions the wounded and dead were carried with much honor to the gates of Kernback. There, at the base of the cliffs he spent many days saving the thousands of wounded, with Sanra and Karrack at his side. Again and again came the call from within the White Walls, from the grateful people of Kernback. "Come!" they would plead. "Enter our gates and take your rightful place on the throne of our city. Such menial work is not for our King. Leave it to the doctors."

But Kenlahar refused to enter until his work was done, and that would not happen until the House of Lahar had been saved. In his place he sent Balor and Kalese to preside as his regents. The girl had recovered from her wounds quickly, though Balor was slower in regaining his strength. "People of Kernback," he shouted to the White Walls. "I must leave you, for a while. When I return I will enter the gates and take my place as your ruler. But, while I am gone, I ask you to follow the orders of my friends, Balor and Kalese."

Kenlahar asked Whistler to muster a small army, one that was no more than a small portion of the total might that had taken part in the battle of the Chalk Plains. Sanra asked to stay with Kalese—she had still not recovered from her grief for Jonla—and had no wish to see the House of Lahar. The feeling between Sanra and Kenlahar had changed, for they both had gone through much. Kenlahar felt it was best not to argue with her. She had shared a long journey, and suffering, with Captain Jonla.

So Kenlahar set off alone, without the Companions, for the House of Lahar. At last, after unforeseen adventure and triumph, he would fulfill his promise to the Elders. With him went the Lashitu, whose madness he had not been able to cure. Sar Devern also came along to command the army, and the Whistler and Karrack came without being ordered to.

The awesome host stopped first at Herald's Manor, and Sar Devern entertained Kenlahar as he had before. This time, as a tribute to his new ruler, Sar Devern freed the slaves of his estates. In return, Kenlahar named him once again Herald of Kernback, a hereditary title. The army continued on to the Pass of Lava. Again they stopped and Kenlahar proclaimed the Sanctuary Mountains to be free forever from the threat of the King's soldiers. The mountains would now truly be sanctuary for all people. The Seven Tribes of the mountains were recognized as one of the Five Peoples, the term "outlaw" banished.

At the Borderlands, Kenlahar stopped once more at Swamp's End. There he buried Toraq's Bane, and to it he added the unadorned blade Sanra had plucked from the Chalk Plains. The barrow was to be guarded forever—forever watched with vigilance, that another Warlord may not arise. Kenlahar bowed before the shattered shall of the Hermit's cabin. Then the host entered the boundaries of the Tream, and was met by representatives of the Swamp People. They were guided safely and uneventfully through the swamp. At the village of the Cormat, Kenlahar beckoned the Cormatine to follow, and to bring with him as much of the blood of the sacred Cormat as his people could gather.

And so at last, the army approached the barren territories Kenlahar recognized as those surrounding the Island Laharhann. He wondered why he felt so anxious and scared—he was returning as a victor, yet he felt strangely unsure of himself. His heart began to beat faster as they drew close to the ancient home of Lahar's descendants. Then the army was at the banks of the River Danjar, and a view of the huge structure was granted by a clear dawn.

Qreq ships were moored on the island, but the House of Lahar stood intact. There was no sign of life on its many docks and balconies. It was one sight Kenlahar had not expected. If the House of Lahar had been charred, burnt hulk he would have been downcast, but not surprised. What he had hoped to see was a battle, still raging; the House of Lahar miraculously holding back the furious attacks of the invaders. But the thought that the House of Lahar would surrender had never entered his mind. Yet that is what appeared to have happened.

The huge building no longer looked spectacular to Kenlahar, not after his long journey Outside. The army he had brought with him, which he knew to be small by all standards of Kernback, lined the banks of the river on both sides of him, as far as the eye could see.

Even as Kenlahar watched the House of Lahar uncertainly, several men jumped into the river and began swimming toward the island. They scrambled onto the far shore of the island and disappeared into the edifice. A few, harrowing minutes passed as nothing moved on the island. Then one of the men emerged and clumsily sailed back one of the small fishing boats. "There are no Qreq on the island," the scout reported, obviously mystified. "I could find no one at all."

This made no sense to Kenlahar, and he tried to understand what could have happened. Surely the family would neither desert nor surrender the House of Lahar! They would have died first. The Qreq did not capture their targets, but burned them to the ground! "I will explore the House of Lahar myself," he said. "None of you know its hallways the way I do. An Army could hide among its many rooms, and you would never find them. Perhaps they are simply startled by our appearance and are hiding. Once they see me, they will come out."

Sar Devern objected. Once inside, he explained, there would be no way to protect him completely from attack. The old soldier begged to be allowed to lead the search party. "Just tell me where to look!"

Though he did not feel as confident as he sounded, Kenlahar turned him down. "No. This is something that only I can do. Do not worry, Sar Devern. I will have Alcress with me." His reassurance did not keep Sar Devern from almost overloading their one boat with guards. Whistler insisted on coming along as well. After a moment's thought, Kenlahar decided to bring along the Lashitu also. The deranged shaman had ceased his endless, stricken babble at the sight of the House of Lahar. Perhaps once he was inside its walls, or so Kenlahar hoped, the Lashitu would come to his senses.

The little boat moved sluggishly toward the House of Lahar, and Kenlahar examined its shape warily. It appeared abandoned, yet Kenlahar had a sense of being watched by many eyes, unfriendly as well as friendly. They landed at last on the rain-slicked docks. With a shudder at the eerie silence, Kenlahar entered the familiar hallways.

As soon as he had passed into the inner passages, Kenlahar knew that the House of Lahar could not have been empty for long. The sisters had swept the many hallways free of dust until just recently. Reluctantly, Sar Devern allowed Kenlahar to lead the way, but only because there seemed no way of anticipating his path. Kenlahar walked steadily toward the Great Hall, in as straight a line as the winding corridors would allow.

Finally, he entered the Chambre, sure that here, if nowhere else, there would be a sign of where the family had gone. He stopped short, shocked by the sight of a slimmer, but still nastily grinning Jakkem. The big man stood before the dais, where the Elders sat with bowed heads. The Healer Coron, though, looked back at him from one side calmly, and nodded in greeting. Too late, Kenlahar saw that the walls were lined with Qreq warriors. It was a trap, and he had walked right into it. The Elders looked at him unhappily, but Kenlahar noticed a glint of hope in the High Elder's eyes.

"At last," Jakkem said mockingly. "I thought you would never arrive, Kenlahar! I was even able to prepare this little surprise welcome for you. I must admit that I did not think the Warlord would allow you to escape. Still, now I will be able to present you to him myself! I would not look for any help here, Kenlahar. Toraq owns the House of Lahar now. I have captured it for him without even harming it. I think he will be pleased."

The Healer Coron interrupted Jakkem's boast. "You captured the House of Lahar only through the treachery to your own people. I would not be so proud."

"Silence, Coron!" Jakkem said, and the healer was reminded of his place by a blow from the Qreq.

"You should listen to the Healer Coron," Kenlahar said at last. "He is a wise man. You should brag, for the evil you have done has been for nothing, Jakkem. Toraq has been destroyed and his armies have fled. You are alone!"

Jakkem believed him, but did not want to, Kenlahar saw. Addressing the Qreq more than the others in the room, the traitor said, "I do not believe that a coward such as you could kill the Warlord!"

"I did not kill the Sorcerer King," Kenlahar said with a vindictiveness he did not like in himself. "Remember Sanra, Jakkem? *She* destroyed the Warlord!"

Now the Qreq were glancing at each other uneasily. Kenlahar turned to speak to them. "I have set your people free. After Toraq was slain, I allowed the others to return to the Havens, which is now yours to live unmolested. No one will bother you again."

Kenlahar lifted the jug of Cormat's blood from where it hung by a cord to his belt. "I know the Qreq have suffered. I know how you suffer even now. And I know why! The disease with which the Warlord had infected your people, and has made you his slaves, causes you great pain. I can cure you of this pain if you will let me."

One of the Qreq stepped forward to look at him closer, searchingly. The Qreq seemed to sense that he was speaking the truth. In his hands he held the Star Axe, which all Qreq had feared and respected. "You know of the Curse?"

In answer Kenlahar drank of the blood of the Cormat and then handed the jug to the Qreq. He stepped backward warily, then hesitantly reached for and sniffed the jug. Then he drank from it. Minutes passed in an ominous silence, while Kenlahar clasped the Qreq hand, and the two figures remained frozen. Finally they broke apart.

"He speaks the truth," the Qreq announced to the others. "I am free of the Curse!" The other Qreq began to approach Kenlahar eagerly, but Sar Devern and his guards flourished their swords menacingly. Kenlahar motioned for them to be let through. One by one the Qreq moved forward and underwent the transformation.

No one noticed Jakkem moving away from the dais and approached Kenlahar from behind. Then the traitor leapt at Kenlahar — and his sword would have pierced Kenlahar's exposed back if it had not been for the Lashitu. With a screech, the shaman threw himself between Kenlahar and the long blade. The assassin's sword struck and the shaman, clinging still to Kenlahar, slowly slid to the floor.

Before Kenlahar could forbid it, a Qreq had cut down Jakkem with a savage blow. Kenlahar hung his head at the murders. The Lashitu had begun by hating him, Kenlahar thought, he had ended by dying for him. Many others had died in his name. Killing seemed to follow him wherever he went. It seemed that he was helpless to avoid it. But perhaps now the killing was over. The Healer Coron grasped Kenlahar around the shoulders. "You have fulfilled the prophecies, Kenlahar. You are truly the Son of Lahar."

The Healer Coron sat behind his desk in the corner of the library and watched Kenlahar pace unhappily. In the chair by the window sat

Whistler, while Karrack stooped at one end of the room glancing at the rows of books. They all avoided each other's eyes. At last the door opened, and dust spread through the cavernous room. The Cormatine entered and stopped, surprised at who else was within the Archives.

"Come in, Cormatine!" Kenlahar said. "Now…how do you usually convene a session of the Raggorak? I regret that the Hermit could not be here as well." The Healer Coron only smiled at this statement, proud and not at all surprised. The Cormatine though, scowled, while Karrack looked at the Axe-bearer sharply. It was the Whistler who calmly asked, "How do you know who we are?"

"It was the Cormatine who first told me," Kenlahar held up his hand at the man's protest. "Oh, at first, I did not remember what happened when I drank of the Cormat's blood and was questioned. But when I drank it again, the entire, illuminating conversation came back. I had to guess who some of you were, but when I thought it over it was simple. At every stage of my quest it seemed I was saved and helped by one man. When I remembered how there was supposed to be one Raggorak among each of the Five Peoples, and that all the Starborn were healers, it was easy to identify you.

"Only one thing bothered me. Why would the Raggorak help a descendent of Lahar? Once the Sorcerer King was destroyed would you try to manipulate me? I told the Cormatine that I would destroy you, but I have changed my mind. I will accept your advice, as my father once did, but that is all. I will no longer be pushed from one action to the next. I have only brought you together to warn you that I know of you.

"I know that you want me to take the throne of Kernback immediately, but first I will be going to the Havens. I cannot let the Qreq suffer their disease any longer. Before I leave I wish to know — will you follow me, or not?"

The Healer Coron spoke for the Raggorak. Bowing respectfully, he said, "We will do as you ask." Kenlahar smiled, for he had known the answer. From the moment the stranger had first come to the House of Lahar, the Raggorak had been helpless to change the fate of the world. Somewhere, they were all aware, the God Lahar was still alive and free.

To be concluded in:
SNOWCASTLES & ICETOWERS

About the Author

Duncan grew up and spent most of his life in Central Oregon, the dry side of the Cascades, and whose terrain is featured in many of his books. He wrote several books out of college, including the heroic fantasy novels *Star Axe*, *Snowcastles*, and *Icetowers*. In 1984, he and his wife Linda bought Pegasus Books in downtown Bend, Oregon, which they still own and operate. They also ran a used bookstore, the Bookmark, for 15 years.

In the last five years, he's been able to get back to writing again, and found that he has a lot of pent-up creative energy. He's written numerous books for several different publishers, mostly in the horror or dark fantasy genres, though recently has been branching out into fantasy again, as well as thrillers.

BIBLIOGRAPHY

The Tuskers Series
Tuskers I: Wild Pig Apocalypse
Tuskers II: Day of the Long Pig
Tuskers III: Omnivore Wars
Tuskers IV: Rise of the Cloven

The Vampire Evolution Trilogy
Book I: Death of an Immortal
Book II: Rule of Vampire
Book III: Blood of Gold

The Virginia Reed Adventures
Led to the Slaughter
The Dead Spend No Gold
The Darkness You Fear

Other books
Star Axe
Snowcastles & Icetowers

Blood of the Succubus
Castle La Magie
Deadfall Ridge
Eden's Return
Faerie Punk
Freedy Filkins
Gargoyle Dreams
I Live Among You
Shadows over Summer House
Snaked
Takeover

Curious about other Crossroad Press books? Stop by our website:
http://crossroadpress.com
We offer quality writing
in digital, audio, and print formats.

Subscribe to our newsletter on the website homepage and receive a
free eBook.